## PASSIONATE ENCOUNTERS

Her breath caught in her throat as he kissed her ear while with his thumbs slowly massaged the tops of her breasts spilling over the lacy cups of her bra.

"No, I'm not deliberately making you wait," was her breathy answer. With the hands of a magician, Ras released the honey-colored mounds that he craved from their restraints, and with his lips, she was showered with a downpour of fiery sensations.

"Oh, Ras" poured from her mouth repeatedly as her center became liquid fire. Her hands became Ras' undoing as she stroked and caressed every inch of his face and his muscular chest. As he suckled her breasts, her hands moved lower. She pushed down his silken pajamas and moved her hands until they rested at the seat of his manhood. He threw his head back, and as an electricity from the universe sent a current through his body, he held her tightly and nestled his head between her breasts.

# Passionate Encounters

## Chilufiya Safaa

**Kensington Publishing Corp.**
http://www.kensingtonbooks.com

DAFINA BOOKS are published by

Kensington Publishing Corp.
850 Third Avenue
New York, NY 10022

All Kensington Titles, Imprints, and Distributed Lines are available at special quantity discounts for bulk purchases for sales promotions, premiums, fund-raising, and educational or institutional use. Special book excerpts or customized printings can also be created to fit specific needs. For details, write or phone the office of the Kensington special sales manager: Kensington Publishing Corp., 850 Third Avenue, New York, NY 10022, attn: Special Sales Department: Phone: 1-800-221-2647.

Dafina Books and the Dafina logo Reg. U.S. Pat. & TM Off.

First Dafina mass market printing: June 2006
10 9 8 7 6 5 4 3 2 1

Printed in the United States of America

*"One day, after we have mastered the winds and the waves, gravity and the tides, we will harness for God the energies of love. And then, for the second time in human history, mankind will have discovered fire."*

*Teilhard de Chardin*
*French Philosopher*

# Prologue

The throng of people moved shoulder to shoulder. Thousands of them, forming the shape of a long, lithesome snake, traced the route that their ancestors had walked countless times centuries before. Ras Selassie had come alone to Lalibela, Ethiopia, to celebrate the high holy day of Timkat, the Ethiopian celebration of the Epiphany. He strolled majestically through the crowd, tall and proud, with an air of regalness that clothed him like wind rustling through leaves on compliant willow trees. As he moved along the path, with only his thoughts and his observant demeanor, he was filled simultaneously with pride and sadness as he thought of his people. With a flick of his hand, he adjusted the indigo-colored silk cloak, trimmed in silver, which covered his stark white traditional jodhpur-like trousers and shirt.

He looked around; his eyes moved, photographing all that he surveyed. He saw before him men, women and children of varying hues of earth, cocoa, toffee, raisin, copper, café au lait, mahogany and ebony covered in a sea of white garments. Bold splashes of color flooded the crowd, emanating from priests wearing elaborate brocade robes, carrying ornately carved Ethiopian hand crosses, walking under brocade umbrellas in vibrant colors of gold, purple, scarlet, garnet and emerald green, trimmed in gold fringe.

There was chanting and singing to the accompaniment of ancient drums and sistrums. The smell of frankincense and myrrh filled the air as the crowd followed the *tabot*, a tablet of wood or stone representing those contained in the ancient Ark of the Covenant. As the crowd neared the first church on the path, Ras' spirit was renewed. He was once again reminded why he had come. The edifice he saw before him was monumental in scale. Some would say of superhuman proportions. The scale, the creation and the execution were all magnificent. Like his people, this complex structure was mysterious, ingenious, bewildering and clearly one of the world's great wonders. He was reminded that he, too, had structures to create and lives to mend and heal. As he heard the prayers of the priests, he said his own, silently vowing to touch the lives of children who had been devastated by the greed and shortsightedness of adult depravity.

# Chapter 1

The angry heavens filled with ominous clouds as Ras Selassie paced the floor of his mountain hideaway. A shadowy haze fell over the cavernous room, diffusing the light.

Ras felt it again, a cloying sickness in the pit of his stomach. He willed it away. The air in the room swirled with tension. The heaviness of an impending storm permeated the space and added to the agitation felt by two longtime friends in the throes of a disagreement. Bradford Donald spoke.

"Earth to Ras. Man, where are you? We've got to pull this mess together before it blows up in our faces."

Bradford Donald, Ras' sometimes business partner and longtime family friend, pulled himself up from his chair and almost hurled his athletic body inches away from Ras' face.

"Man, we are in deep crap here! You don't have time to lock yourself up in that private world in your head." Brad placed himself back in his chair, leaned forward, his eyes narrowed and his gaze lasered in on his friend.

Ras Selassie slowly looked up with hooded eyes. When the light hit them, golden flecks danced in the light brown pools. His stare was cold and had been known to send lesser men running for cover. Bradford Donald stood his ground. Brad and Ras were equal in strength, courage and passion, though they displayed these attributes very differently. Ras, the son of an Ethiopian general and a mother whose family had been Ethiopian landed gentry for generations, was brought up in the lap of luxury. An only child, he had always felt entitled. Only his eyes spoke. His body did not move from his seated position.

"Look, Brad, just back off! OK? I hear you. I've heard every word you've said since you arrived. You know damn well I'm not going to let any person, place or thing get in the way of the completion of this project." His tone was impatient and laced with barely controlled rage.

Brad leaned back in his chair, crossed his muscular legs in his favorite position, his right ankle resting on his left thigh. From where he sat, he studied his friend, a man with deep mood swings and a volatile temper. Brad had come to know Ras through his best friend, Keino Mazrui. Keino and Ras were first cousins. Their mothers were sisters. Keino and Ras were both intense, but Ras had a deeply brooding side that was nothing like Keino. The two men sat silently for a moment. Brad knew it would be up to him to lighten the mood. With a forced levity in his tone, Brad began.

"All right. That's what I needed to hear—man, sometimes you worry me. Where do you go when you space out like that?"

Ras' gaze softened this time as he heard his friend's concern. The toffee-colored skin around his jaw line relaxed into what could have been mistaken for a smile. He spoke to his friend in a voice full of weariness.

"I don't go anywhere, Brad. You need to allow people to just be. Squash your American tendency to need an answer for everything. Sometimes there are no answers, just situations, and we deal with them as they come."

Brad retorted, "Oh, oh, great philosopher. All I have to say is if we are going to get past a gang of mercenary Ethiopian warlords to complete the construction of that expansive community you've designed to house orphaned

children, we need all of your mental energy right here dealing with this situation!"

That steely gaze was back, and this time the tone rose
to a shout.

"I have never begun a project and not seen it through to
its end. That is not in my character, and I will not start now!"

Brad responded while shaking his head and staring with
squinted eyes directly at his friend. "Man, I am this
close"—he gestured with his thumb and index finger a
fraction of an inch apart—"to going all the way off. I am
not questioning your character. I'm here at your request,
remember? Man, you asked me to join you up here in this
house in the Colorado Rockies, which it would take the
FBI to find, to help you strategize about how to get the
project finished. Don't play me, Ras. I'm your boy. We've
been through a lot of bull together. Now stop looking at
me like some hired assassin, and let's get moving."

Ras snarled, and they settled back down to continue the
process of fulfilling a promise Ras had made to himself
years before. The two men waited silently for a time, until
tempers cooled and reason prevailed. They were seated in
the study of Ras' hideaway retreat. Ras' home was a massive structure of stone and timber. The nearest neighbor
was five miles away. His home had once been an old
mine. When Ras first saw it, something about its desolate-
ness and its isolation called to him. He saw the beauty in
what it could be. He bought it, and with the eye of the
master architect he was known to be, he transformed an
old mine into a showplace. It had everything that suited
Ras' sensibilities. It was cleverly designed, with soaring
ceilings and plentiful windows, some reaching the height
of the ceilings. There were decks on the three-leveled
structure. All of the decks provided unobstructed views of
the Rocky Mountains. The feature of the property Ras
clung to and needed most was the ski trail that meandered
through his remote mountain retreat. Skiing had come so
easily to him as a boarding school student in Switzerland.

He knew it was the solitude of the slopes that called to him. It was the only time he was alone but not lonely. When he skied, he was alone with the elements. He could soar or he could coast, whatever he chose; it was his decision. As a young boy, he felt that he alone controlled his adventures on the ski slopes. He answered to no one, especially not to his father, the general who controlled everyone around him. He answered only to the power of the winds and the strength of his legs and arms.

Ras was the first to break the silence. He began his apology in the smooth tones of his tenor voice.

"Brad, before we get started, the first thing I should do is at least thank you for meeting me here to help iron out the kinks in this project. You are one of the few people, other than Keino, who understands my need for solitude and my way of shutting out the world when I need to think." Ras stopped, cleared his throat and continued. "Look, Brad, I know I'm a hard man to be around sometimes, but I am who I am—the only son of Tafari and Amara Selassie. I am not perfect, but I am a man of integrity, and I will always be true to my word. Enough talk. Let's find a way to kick butt."

Brad beamed his megawatt smile and said, "Thanks for releasing the Ras I like. Man, I can't hang with your evil twin."

With that exchange, they both had to laugh. Even Ras, as unaccustomed to raucous laughter as he was, could not contain himself.

At the end of three days, Ras and Brad had strategized their way around territorial warlords and corrupt politicians, at least in theory. With only a few pieces left to put in place, they were ready to make their third of many trips to Addis Ababa, Ethiopia. They had both decided that Keino's diplomatic skills could certainly be useful. He needed to be brought up to speed, and Ras needed to make the call. He welcomed making the call to Keino. Brad had gone, and though he reveled in his solitude once again, he was always happy to connect with family. Unless it was Tafari Selassie, his father.

Ras walked from his large master bedroom out onto an adjoining deck. Clad in flannel pajama bottoms hung low on his hips, with a bare torso, he allowed the hint of a fall breeze to wash over his skin. He stood with outstretched arms; each hand rested on an expanse of perfectly hewn timber that served as deck railing. As Ras stood there, it was easy to see why women the world over had found him arrestingly handsome. He was long of limb, appearing taller than his six feet three inches. His muscular build was like that of a well-trained track star. Though he had never run track as an organized sport, he did like to run for the pleasure and the solitariness. His angular face reflected a mysteriousness, which women yearned to understand when they met him. His high cheekbones and full sensuous lips framed his intense deep-set eyes, and his hair, the color of ravens' wings, caressed his perfectly formed head.

Ras strolled back inside his master bedroom, picked up his portable telephone and began punching in the numbers to his cousin Keino's private cellular telephone, knowing that way he'd reach him wherever he might be in the world. As he listened to the ringing of the telephone, Ras smiled to himself. His cousin was now a married man and, from all indications, after half a year was still enjoying what looked to everyone like an extended honeymoon. As his thoughts ended, he heard Keino's distinctive baritone greeting.

"Keino Mazrui here. How are you, Ras?"

Ras, with as much of a chuckle as he could muster, responded, "I hate caller ID. It shoots all to hell the element of surprise."

"Yes, cousin of mine, I think that is why it was invented. It is good to hear from you. Aunt Amara was just visiting Mom the other day, and we were all inquiring about you. Ras, we haven't seen you since the wedding! It's always good to hear your voice, but seeing your face would be better."

"I know, Keino. Old habits are hard to break. Once a loner, always a loner. At least that's what they say."

"Who is this they? Whoever they are, they fail to take into account the fact that any human behavior or pattern can change. The only thing needed is a willing participant."

"Okay, Keino, I get the message." Ras rerouted the conversation. "Speaking of more pleasant subjects, how is married life? And how is your beautiful wife, Amara?"

"If anyone had told me that I'd feel this good as a married man, I would have done it long ago," responded Keino, with schoolboy charm. "The only catch is it is only this good because of the wife I've chosen. If she gets anymore beautiful or loves me with any more intensity, I think I will just give up the ghost and travel beyond heaven. Man, life is good." Reining himself in, as he often had to do when he spoke of his marriage, Keino took a deep breath, calmed himself and said, "Enough of my maniacal raving. To what ancestral spirit's favor do I owe this call?"

Ras lowered himself into the leather camel-colored wingback chair positioned in a corner of his enormous bedroom. He stretched his powerfully strong legs with ease and gentility. He placed them on the matching ottoman in front of him and crossed his bare feet at the ankles. As he continued the conversation, he began massaging his left temple.

"Keino, I think your expertise is needed on this new project. Brad agrees and thought I should bring you up to speed to get your assessment of the situation and figure out how to proceed."

"Is this the orphan project?" Keino asked, with obvious admiration in his voice. "I want you to know that only a man with a big heart would undertake such a venture. You, my cousin, under that rough, gruff, moody temperament, are a man with a generous heart. I will come on board in any way I can. Just let me know what I need to do."

"Thanks, Keino," was Ras' low response. Emotionally moved by Keino's words, Ras continued. "Hey, don't spread any rumors about me having a generous heart. We really don't need to blow my cover." The two men shared a moment of deep, warm laughter, after which Ras added, "Later this week we will get together and iron out the details."

"Hey, I have a better idea. I'll be in the States, in Virginia, later this week. Amara and I are coming to visit. Brad is meeting me at the Virginia office for golf next Friday. Join us. We can do business and pleasure."

"That's a deal. See you then."

Cassandra Terrell appeared to fly through the door as she entered her interior design studio. The renovated two-story Victorian in the heart of Georgetown served as her design house. The elegantly restored edifice was tastefully filled with showroom-quality furnishings representing a number of periods and styles, with corresponding accessories.

Today was a day like so many. Cassandra started her day and ended her day with a flurry of activity sure to tire even the most energetic soul. Not Cassandra. She was invigorated by the variety and constancy of the myriad functions she performed.

With her cellular telephone on one ear as she mouthed instructions to an assistant, she walked with grace, ease and ever so much style, like a model on a runway, down the long expanse of hallway leading to her office at the end of the building. As she walked and talked on her telephone, she waved and smiled at staff members. When she entered her office, she put down the two designer shopping bags she was carrying, sat down behind her Regency desk, and continued her conversation.

"Mrs. Inman, you do not have to worry. The painters will arrive tomorrow at 6 A.M. to begin the mural for your living room. This particular one is an eight-hour process. You may go about your day, and by the time you return, your pastoral scene will be completed. Day after tomorrow the workmen from Retro will complete the work on your eighteenth-century mantel shelf. I know you are going to be very pleased. Good then, I'll check back in two days. Give my regards to Mr. Inman."

Cassandra leaned back in her tapestry-covered chair, stretched her long dancer's legs, took a deep breath, pushed her intercom button and called for her assistant.

"Angela, if you aren't swamped, could you give me a minute?"

Angela's ready response came back. "Sure, Cassandra. I'll be right in."

Angela Kingsbury entered Cassandra's office, wearing a smile on her mocha-colored face. Her deep burgundy business suit was perfectly accessorized, and her hair was stylishly coiffed, with every strand in place. Angela took a seat in one of the two matching Louis the Fourteenth chairs placed in front of Cassandra's desk.

"Okay, Ms. Angela," Cassandra began. She had that gleam in her eye and the impish smile she always got when she knew she had to pull off an impossible feat. "Are you ready to work miracles today? You might as well say yes, because, Angela, we've got to really make it happen—"

Angela broke into a wide grin and interrupting, said, "And what is so different about this impossible situation?"

Still smiling, Cassandra, ever the optimist, spoke quickly. "I'm so glad you asked. Here's the deal. Please bear in mind that today is only Monday. On Wednesday, Arturo was supposed to get fabric swatches to Mrs. Drummer for her sofa, which must be reupholstered in three weeks. Guests are coming from out of town for her daughter's wedding. Now, Arturo called over the weekend. He was in a car accident. Nothing serious but the bump on the head has him on bed rest. Needless to say, Mrs. Drummer has no swatches. Mrs. Grimes ordered a Beidermeier chair, and I got a call this morning saying that the order was routed incorrectly and what we have in our warehouse is an Empire piece. Not even close to what we need. I need you to track down that Beidermeier. We really don't want to send Mrs. Grimes into shock by delivering an Empire period piece to her home. The art the Johnsons ordered from my sister Afiya's gallery is nowhere to be found. Check with Afiya. We need it like yesterday. Their much talked about cocktail party is Friday. They want to show off their art. And last but not least, darling, let all of our wonderful clients know, in your own sweet way, that we here at Willows Design Firm have personalized our services just for them. Allay any fears; let them know we're on top of any snags. Meantime, I've got a meeting this afternoon of Design International members, and after that a bid to prepare on the renovation of the old Wilkes Mansion, and tonight a cocktail party celebrating the retirement of Shelton Brown, one of the most important designers of the last four decades. Are we all set?"

"We're all set. By the way, be sure to check the messages on your desk. Your sisters Amara and Adana called, and also your mom and four prospective clients, all referrals from Mrs. Grimes. All the more reason to get that chair right," Angela said with a sly grin.

Angela walked out, closing the door behind her. Cassandra stood up, pressed the speaker phone button and dialed her sister Adana's law firm—a firm in which Adana was a partner. While standing and waiting for an answer, Cassandra removed the jacket to her persimmon-colored suit and draped it on the back of her chair. The formfitting dress complemented beautifully her caramel skin with its gold undertones and her shoulder-length tresses highlighted with hints of honey blonde streaks. As she finished draping the jacket, she heard, "Good morning, Willis, Burks and Terrell."

Cassandra, as perky as ever, responded, "And good morning to you. May I please speak to Attorney Terrell? Please tell her that her sister Cassandra Terrell is calling."

"One moment please," was the very practiced professional reply.

The next voice she heard was exuberant. "Cassandra.

Hi. I called you earlier to let you know that Keino and Amara are scheduled to arrive in town today. Mom told me to alert everyone. It really will be great to see those two."

All the while examining papers on her desk, Cassandra said, "I got a message from Amara. Maybe that's what she was going to tell me."

Adana asked, "What number did she leave? You know it's hard keeping up with our jet-setting sister while she's living on two continents."

Cassandra smiled, thinking of the wonderful life her sister was living.

"She left her private cell, so there is no telling where she is. Probably in the sky. I'll call her back and get all the details. We all have to get together when they get here. By the way, are those two working on a baby yet?"

With approval in her voice, Adana responded, "Honey, I think they are just enjoying the process."

Cassandra quipped, "Sounds good to me." The two sisters shared a teasing laugh, which was the signature of their relationship. "Talk to you later. Hey, wait," a breathless Cassandra asked, "where is Afiya?"

Adana replied, "I spoke to her last night. She's getting ready for another opening dealing, with a really temperamental artist this time, so she's got her hands full."

"OK. We'll talk later."

# Chapter 2

Ras Selassie rode silently in the chauffeur-driven town car through the heart of the Georgetown business district. Whenever Ras came into the Washington, D.C., area, or any major city for that matter, he could feel his mood shift. He subjected himself to the onslaught of hyperactivity in order to do business and to ensure that he could realize some of his goals, and keep promises he had made to himself and to his ancestors. He willed himself through the traffic, the close proximity of too many people, the cacophony of warring street sounds and the inevitable altercations that ensued when disgruntled human beings gathered.

He was leaving an investment meeting where he had successfully assuaged the jitters of a group of investment bankers who were being courted to come aboard one of his myriad development projects. It had been his experience that nervousness often accompanied the expenditure of large sums of money. He was extremely skilled at cajoling venture capitalists into parting with hard-earned dollars while making them feel as though they were both gaining and contributing at the same time. He had come to understand that most human beings, regardless of cultural leanings or financial status, desire in some way to leave a mark on the world. He believed he had found a way to allow many that opportunity.

Feeling a sudden pang of hunger, a reminder that he had not eaten for several hours, he spoke to his driver. "Grant, my gyrating stomach tells me I need to stop to refuel. Take me to Yabello's. The food is plentiful and nourishing, just what I need right now."

"Yes, sir," was the driver's laconic reply. Grant Salsbury was a substantial man, a retired amateur boxer in his mid-forties. He held the steering wheel masterfully in his powerful hands. He reveled in the duties of his job as Ras' driver. It gave him the pleasure of being on the periphery of the world of high finance and powerful dealings. He could often live vicariously a life he knew he would never experience. Grant stopped the car in front of a three-story building with an old world European façade. After stepping out of the late-model sedan that he had been driving, he moved more rapidly than his size would suggest. He opened Ras' door and said, "Here we are, Mr. S. What time do you need me to come back?"

Ras answered quickly as he moved from the car. His black cashmere coat fell gingerly around his ankles. "I should be no longer than an hour. I am heading to Virginia later tonight."

Ras entered Yabello's with long, purposeful strides. Years on the ski slopes and a privileged upbringing gave him an air of masculine power and regal arrogance, which caused men to fear him and women to swoon in his wake. As he walked through the tall wooden doors with brass handles and ornate beveled glass, he adjusted his eyes to the dimness of the light. As he acclimated himself to the absence of bright light in the room, he heard someone with a heavily laced, welcoming Italian accent say, "Hello, Ras Selassie. It has been a while since I've seen you. It is so good to have you here."

The voice belonged to Rudolfo Guido, Yabello's proud owner. Rudolfo stepped forward with outstretched arms and embraced Ras in the traditional European greeting, kissing alternate sides of the face, ending in a tremendous bear hug. Ras, not fond of spontaneous displays of emotion, nevertheless returned the embrace and with heartfelt sincerity said, "It is good to see you, too, Rudolfo. It has been a long time. I was here on business today, and when my agitated stomach let me know that food was in order, I thought immediately of Yabello's."

An exuberant Rudolfo offered, "Come, my friend; let me show you to your special place."

The restaurant appeared almost vacant. The traditional lunch crowd had come and gone. The dinner crowd had not yet arrived. Rudolfo led Ras up a short spiral staircase to a table that overlooked the entire restaurant but was undetectable from the lower level. Rudolfo continued speaking as he prepared Ras' table for his meal.

"Ras, seeing you, having you visit like this, always brings to mind the many years my family and I spent in Ethiopia. Such a beautiful land. I miss the beauty of the highlands, the magnificence of the Blue Nile, the sandstone cliffs, ah, and the food and the women." With a gleam in his eye, a smile on his heart-shaped face, gesturing with a pointed finger for emphasis, he added, "I would wager that the women are by far some of the most beautiful women in the world."

In his low, smooth tones, Ras concurred. "Rudolfo, you could not be more right. They are God's gifts."

As Ras removed his coat, revealing a black silk collarless shirt and black slacks exquisitely tailored for his lean, powerfully muscled physique, Rudolfo continued speaking, but now his tone was laced with melancholy. "Such a beautiful land. It was God's country. A senseless war removed us from the land and people we loved and still love." Coming out of his almost trancelike state, Rudolfo questioned Ras. "Ras, when was the last time you were home? In Ethiopia?"

"As a matter of fact, I was there last month. I am doing

some building. I'm trying to repair some of the damage of that senseless war you spoke about."

Just as Ras started to position his chair, she walked through the door. Her entrance was as much a feast for his eyes as he had hoped Rudolfo's food would be for his body. Stroking her hair almost as an afterthought while waiting for her eyes to regulate themselves to the semi-darkness, she stood as if lost in a swirl of thoughts.

Rudolfo, mid-sentence, noticed his distracted friend. He had to smile to himself as he saw his old friend transfixed by the entrance of Ms. Cassandra Terrell. During the time he had known her, he had seen many heads turn at her entrances and exits. It appeared Ras Selassie was no exception.

"Excuse me, Ras. It appears another of my favorite customers is here." Before Ras could respond, Rudolfo had slipped away to welcome Cassandra. By the time he reached her side, her eyes were adjusting to the darkness. She could not clearly see him coming toward her, but she responded viscerally to the warmth of his booming voice.

"Ms. Cassandra, what a pleasant surprise. It is good to see you."

Cassandra adored Yabello's. She had discovered it quite by accident a few years before. She found Yabello's quaint and intimate, and it was decorated with a Tuscan flair, which she found appealing. Most importantly, the Greco-Italian food, with Ethiopian touches, soothed her palate. Rudolfo was an added bonus, because as owner–maitre d', he made all of his customers feel very much at home and catered to them in a way that only small private venues can.

Cassandra greeted the diminutive Rudolfo with an effusive "Rudolfo, my friend, what wonderful specials do you have to entice me today?" Rudolfo put his hand to his chin and began to speak as though he were tasting the food as he described it.

"Today we can tantalize your taste buds with lamb prepared with garlic and rosemary, lemon saffron rice, or perhaps *doro wat.*"

"All of it sounds wonderful, but on second thought, I only need a small Greek salad and a Pelligrino with twists of lemon and lime." While placing her order, Cassandra made herself comfortable at a table for two. She set her black calfskin briefcase on the floor and retrieved from it her Day Runner.

As she prepared to write, Rudolfo stopped her, saying, "Ah, Cassandra, you work too hard, and you eat too little. When is there time for pleasure?"

"Rudolfo, you sound like my parents. I eat quite well, thank you," she said with a smile, shifting her head to one side. "And as for pleasure, my work is my pleasure. I am surrounded by beautiful things all day, and I work with exciting, sometimes eccentric, fun people. I'm in heaven, and besides, you know I have my family and a pretty active social life."

"Some social life!" Rudolfo said, gesturing with his hands lifted toward the sky. "Where is the special gentleman who should be attending to your every whim?"

"Now, Rudolfo, I know those men do exist, those special gentlemen. My sister married one. However, they don't seem to appear as if by magic. They seem to be far and few between, or as my grandmother used to say, as scarce as hen's teeth." She smiled thinking of the humor in that image.

While Rudolfo and Cassandra shared pleasantries, Ras, with an unobstructed view, unseen by Cassandra, was thankful for the emptiness of the restaurant so that he could hear bits and pieces of the conversation she shared with Rudolfo. He examined every movement of her long limbs as she sat and crossed her legs. He watched as she smiled in a way that for him rivaled the sun. He remembered now why he had been attracted to her when he first saw her months ago, at the marriage of her sister to his cousin. Something about her was as enticing now as before. Sitting there watching her, he remembered how velvety she felt while dancing in his arms. He remembered the ambrosial scent of the perfume she had worn. He had not forgotten the flawless copper-colored skin. No, he had not forgotten her. Here she was again thrown into his path. A woman who almost made him forget that he had no time for the complications that women bring to a man's life. He had no time to contemplate longings and misgivings. Relationships were just too complex. They required more than he would ever be willing to give. Yet as he sat mesmerized by the feline way in which she moved and gestured, a small part of him longed to feel once again the softness of her body, to hear her melodic tones and to be transported by her scent. He was relieved that she could not see him. He sat in shadowed privacy, contemplating whether to act on his desires or to heed the course he knew to be less dangerous. While he waited for his food, he decided he would allow her to finish her meal, and then he would leave the restaurant and get on with his life.

After leaving Yabello's, Ras prepared himself for his trip to Virginia to meet with Keino and Brad. He looked forward to his encounters with his two dearest friends. The two of them were the only men in the world who truly knew him.

Virginia welcomed Ras with a cool, sunny day. The trees were completing the shedding of their leaves, and the smell of a coming frost was in the air. As he walked into the imposing structure that was Mazrui Industries, a structure he, Ras, had designed and built, it amazed him to think of his cousin Keino handling the numbers of people, projects and continents he dealt with on a daily basis. Ras knew that he would suffocate if he had to deal with all of those elements daily. He needed his solitude and time whenever he could have it, but he admired his cousin. Ras walked up to the receptionist on duty, and with piercing eyes that seemed to probe the depths of anyone or anything in their line of vision, he studied her for a moment. He thought how young she looked and how old her youth made him feel. Then he spoke. "I am Ras Selassie. I am here to see Mr. Keino Mazrui."

The receptionist, both nervous and enthralled simultaneously, stammered, "One moment please." She made the appropriate calls and spoke hastily. "Someone will come to escort you to Mr. Mazrui, sir." Ras nodded his head and thanked her in a way that was for him perfunctory but for her dripping with a sensuality of which he was not aware.

Just as Ras turned to walk in the direction of the elevator, a lean young man dressed in a dark blue suit approached him, saying, "This way, sir. I will escort you to Mr. Mazrui."

The two men rode the private elevator in a silence that was surprisingly comfortable. Once off the elevator, Ras was led into Keino's office. When he entered the opulently decorated space, he found Keino and Brad huddled in deep conversation. Ras sauntered into the room, his flat eyes unreadable as he said, "Am I interrupting something?" Both men turned at the sound of his voice.

"Yes, you are," replied Brad in his comic-laden, flippant style. "But come on in, anyway." A smile trailed the end of his sentence.

Keino and Brad both moved toward Ras to embrace him. After their embrace, Keino held his cousin at arm's length, looked him over and said, "My cousin, it is good to see you. I can report now that you are alive and that you look well."

They all laughed while Ras asked, "Who said I was dead?"

Keino replied, "No one said you were dead, but you know you surface once in a blue moon. No one ever knows what is happening with you. We can't keep tabs on you."

Ras, with humor in his voice, had a quick comeback. "Keino, you exaggerate. You know my mother always knows where I am, and if she knows, then your mother knows, and between the two of them, they alert the fragments of the clan on at least three continents."

Keino, with both hands raised skyward, his face beaming, conceded, "All right, so I am prone to hyperbole, but you must admit, you do have a way of making yourself difficult to locate on occasion."

Continuing with the playful bantering, Ras said, "Okay, let up. I'm here now; let's get down to business."

Brad concurred. "Let's do this thing. There is a golf course waiting with my name on it. We can't let this crisp, clean air and bright sunshine go to waste. I plan to lay a whuppin' on you brothers today, yes, I do."

Keino chimed in, "In what universe? The last time you won a game was . . . let me see"—he feigned loss of memory—"when was it again?" Once more they broke into uproarious laughter—happy to be in each other's presence.

Each man took a seat in the section of Keino's office that was designed to look like a grand salon. Brad sat legs apart, elbows on his knees, with his body leaning forward. Ras sat with his legs crossed, aristocratically positioned in his chair, clenching and unclenching his fists, a nervous habit acquired years before. It was done so often now, he was unaware of it. Keino sat relaxed, each of his hands placed on the chair's armrests.

Feeling they had settled in, Keino asked, "All right, Ras, how can I help you in your latest venture?"

Ras began slowly, his voice and his eyes full of the pain he felt when speaking of the devastation in the land of his birth. "You two know the history of the ongoing civil strife and famine, two things that seem to have become synonymous with Ethiopia. Even when it is not visible for the world to see, for those who know the situation, it is always present. Any negotiation is tinged with the very people who are at each other's throats because of religious preference or geographic location. It makes me sick to my stomach. Our family alone has ties to people all over

Ethiopia. Some are Muslim, some are Orthodox Christian Coptics, some are Semites and some follow traditional African monotheism. My diplomatic skills are rusty—"

Brad interrupted. "Rusty? Let's try nonexistent."

"Okay, okay, so I have a lot to learn about diplomacy, I'm not sure I can or want to learn. That's where you come in, Keino. I need you to make a few telephone calls and smooth the way so that when I get to Addis Ababa, I will not have to start with a blank slate to get these men to move old grudges aside so that I can build some beautiful facilities to give children who have been displaced a much needed home. We have uncles in the Ministry of Land Development who have contacts in every known strata of the Ethiopian populace. I need them to use their influence for a worthwhile cause. I am afraid that on this subject my rage gets the better of me, and one harsh word and I've blown it."

Keino responded, "I understand. Listen, I think you are on the right track. I'll consult with both our mothers and your father—"

Ras didn't allow Keino to finish before he blurted out, "Leave Tafari Selassie out of this." His voice laced with bitterness, he continued. "He may be my father, but I want him to have nothing to do with my business affairs—"

Keino interrupted. "Ras, whatever your feelings about your father, this is not personal. You know in business the rules are different. Your father and your mother and my mother are our best resources when it comes to knowing where all of the bodies are buried. Many of these people are of their generation, and if not, they are the children of people they know or have known intimately. Don't tie my hands here. However we have to do it, we want homes for these children, correct?"

Ras nodded in the affirmative. He was too angry at the mention of his father to open his mouth, certain of what was to spew out. Brad and Keino gave Ras a moment of quiet sitting, waiting for him to settle himself and once again join them in conversation. After a time Ras responded, "Keino, of course, you are correct. We will do it your way."

Brad, jumping up from his seat, shouted, "All right, now off to the golf course. All this talk about war and politics makes me even more anxious to put a hurtin' on somebody. Are you brothers up to it? Did I hear you?"

Ras and Keino looked at each other, shook their heads and in unison said, "We're up to it, Brad."

Keino said in a tone of mock seriousness, "Oh, before I forget, after golf you two have been summoned to my home this evening for dinner. You know, Ras, my wife has not yet had the opportunity to engage you in conversation. She keeps talking about you like you are some family secret that we are trying to hide. I keep telling her we really like you and that you really are a lovable guy, but she keeps looking at me and saying, 'If people like him and he is so lovable, where is he and why is he never around?' So tonight you can prove that you are not a well-kept family secret." Then the laughter began.

Ras countered, "Keino, the things I do for you. I'll be there—and I'll be on my best behavior."

"That's my cousin," Keino said and slapped him on the back. They all walked out of the office, with the easy camaraderie they had developed over many years.

# Chapter 3

Ras' day had been full. The meeting with Brad and Keino had gone well, and the golf game had been pleasurable and relaxing. Except for the discussion of his father, his day had been a combination of pleasure and productivity. Ras tried very hard in his daily life to erase General Tafari Selassie, his father, from his consciousness. He took a deep breath and erased him again. He was pleased to be spending the evening with Keino and his new wife. For a fleeting moment, he wondered if her sister Cassandra could please a man as thoroughly as it appeared Amara had pleased Keino. He smiled and thought perhaps one day, if he had time, he could test her potential. It did not occur to him that she might refuse to be tested.

Riding through the neighborhood of stately, picturesque homes in which Keino and Amara lived, Ras played the analytical mind game he often played with himself when encountering an enclave of homes that were new to him. He wondered if the façades of the beautiful homes matched the lives contained inside, or if the façades were just that—gorgeous fronts hiding pain and misery. His home as a child had certainly been the latter.

As he drove through the automated gate of the Mazrui mansion, he smiled as the house he saw ahead of him emanated the light and peace he knew he would find inside. Since Ras had announced his arrival at the gate, Amara and Keino greeted him at the door together. Ras stepped from his two-seater luxury sports car, delighted to see the two of them standing arm in arm, waiting for him. "Hello, you two," he said. "It's good to see you. Amara, you are as beautiful as I remember."

"Welcome to our home, Ras," was Keino's response.

Ras embraced Amara and said, "It is a pleasure to meet again the woman who has brought joy to my cousin's world."

"Thank you. Ras, finally, we get a chance to have a real conversation. Come on in. We invited a few other friends and relatives just to share the pleasure of your visit."

The moment he was led from the foyer to the living room, he saw her. She was deeply involved in a conversation with Brad and another woman he did not know. Brad was gesturing wildly, making a point or telling a story; it was hard to tell. The unknown woman was laughing. Cassandra was standing, with the long, tapered fingers of a perfectly manicured hand on a sensuously rounded hip, clad in a knee-length, form-fitting red dress. Her legs were as long and as supple as he remembered, and the black stiletto pumps accentuated their beauty. Her head was tilted, causing her expertly coiffed hair to fall as though it had been placed there by an artist's brush. Her full lips lifted up at one corner, molding themselves into an impishly wicked smile. Her whole demeanor made it clear that she did not believe one word Brad was saying. It made Ras want to test her potential.

Keino made the announcement. "Everyone, my cousin Ras has arrived."

When all eyes turned to Ras, Cassandra turned and was stunned that she was staring into the eyes of the mysterious partner with whom she had shared an unforgettable dance at her sister's wedding. Her heart fluttered. It skipped an imperceptible beat. Butterflies were released at the base of her abdomen. The vibrating spasms moved rapidly up her throat and stopped her breath—just for a moment. As his image floated her way, it became clear that her eyes had not deceived her then nor were they deceiving her at that moment. This man was made in the image of an African god, one that civilizations the world over had worshipped. This man, Ras Selassie, was beautiful. Only the masculine set of his jaw and the power that emanated from his trim, athletic physique kept him from being prettier than some women.

As Ras entered the living room, his eyes never left Cassandra. As he walked, heat began radiating through him like a Fourth of July sparkler. He fought to hold on to his control as her scent entered his nostrils and momentarily rendered his brain a motionless mass, sending only one signal, a raw need that gripped him at the seat of his manhood.

Through the haze of sensuality that covered them both, Cassandra and Ras heard Keino say, "Introductions are in order." He began with the woman Ras had not recognized. "Veronica Strong, meet Ras Selassie. Veronica is one of my wife Amara's oldest friends."

Veronica extended her hand and said playfully, "I may be one of her dearest friends, but I am by no means the oldest." A soft ripple of laughter went around the room.

Keino's retort was, "As you can see, she is also a jokester." Keino continued. Turning to Cassandra, he said, "And this is my sister-in-law."

Before Keino could finish his sentence, Ras moved in closer to Cassandra, took both of her hands in his, and leveled his ever so powerful gaze directly at her. Cassandra froze as the sensuality of the experience washed over her. Ras spoke in tantalizing tenor tones. "I believe I have already had the pleasure of meeting this work of art posing as a human being." Leaving everyone else in the room speechless, Ras continued, with an air of intimacy framing his words with a desire that was missed by no one. "As a matter of fact, at your wedding, I had the pleasure of holding her in my arms in a dance that ended much too soon."

Cassandra felt her feelings of awe and attraction evaporate. She stood there, both angry and embarrassed, not knowing which was the overriding emotion. Rapid-fire thoughts zipped through her brain one after the other. How dare he walk into the room and act as if he possessed her? How dare he undress her with his eyes and with his touch? Did he feel one dance made him entitled? Work of art? *How far does that line usually get you, Mr. Selassie?* Cassandra was sure his approach had worked the world over, but not this time. She smiled smoothly, not revealing how annoyed she was, and withdrew her hands, leaving Ras knowing something had been lost when their palms were separated. Cassandra offered a polite, very reserved, "Hello again, Mr. Selassie." Ras, his eyes burning with some unreadable emotion, held her with his gaze.

Bradford Donald cleared his throat, breaking through the sexually charged scene. With his ever present laughter, Brad brought levity into the room, which relaxed everyone. He shook Ras' hand, saying with his usual flash of humor, "Allow me to introduce myself."

Ras countered, amused by Brad, "I think I know you."

Keino, continuing the relaxed banter, happy to diffuse his cousin's headlong plunge into disaster, interjected, "Tonight is a night for celebration. My cousin the recluse is out of seclusion."

Brad added, "Your cousin, the dead man, is alive." That comment lit up the house with laughter. Cassandra, however, was still not laughing.

Keino and Amara led their guests into their beautifully appointed dining room. The fireplace in the room was blazing, emitting an amber glow in a room dimly lit and radiant with long, tapered bronze-colored candles placed strategically along an elongated marble-topped dining table. Two clear crystal trumpet vases filled with white French tulips served as the elegant centerpiece.

Amara had given the household cook the night off and had taken delight in preparing the meal for her guests. She had prepared a meal of shrimp Chardonnay soup, endive salad with walnuts and mandarin oranges and a raspberry vinaigrette dressing, and roasted rosemary Cornish hens. Chocolate-dipped strawberries and a champagne from Keino's private cellar added a festive touch. The soft sounds of a jazz trio piped through hidden speakers provided a muted complement to the dinner conversation.

Once their guests were seated around the table, Keino spoke. "All of you know how grateful Amara and I are for your presence in our home tonight and for your friendship. My parents always drilled into my brothers and me the importance of friends and family. The older I become, the more correct I know they were."

Brad spoke, always adding a humorous note. "Listen to the old man speak. Man, I'm glad you learned something from your father. I remember a time when you would have turned in all of your father's wisdom for the love of a woman named Amara Terrell. Now known as Amara Mazrui. You know, the one sitting next to you." He gestured toward Amara. "The one you still can't keep your eyes, or your hands, off of."

With everyone looking in his direction with knowing smiles and glances, confirming Brad's characterization of Keino's love for Amara, Keino joined in the laughter, reached over, gently lifted Amara's hand to his lips, kissed it softly and said, "Once again, my friend, your powers of observation are as clear as a bell. You are so right. I do love my wife."

Veronica Strong, sitting next to Brad, playfully tapped him on the shoulder. "Brad, you always have a way of pointing out a person's Achilles' heel, but I think Keino liked your shedding light on that particularly vulnerable spot of his."

Brad's quick, flirty retort was, "I haven't found yours yet. Your Achilles' heel, that is." The room erupted in laughter. The two of them had played a verbal game of hide-and-seek from the day they first met.

Amara chimed in, "Keep looking, Brad. Veronica's quick, but she has been known to slip up on occasion."

Cassandra added jokingly, "She does try, though, not to be human like the rest of us."

Feigning indignance, Veronica replied, "Just gang up on me, okay! Is that the way friends should come to my defense?" Pretending to pout, she continued, "You should be on my side."

As laughter swirled around the room, Ras' eyes were riveted on Cassandra. Though there was a comfortable distance between their chairs, Cassandra could feel the heat that radiated between them. In what felt like a fleeting moment, she turned in his direction and was met with a glare that was a mixture of cold distance and unbridled desire. The startling yet compelling combination pulled her deeply into the pools of his eyes. They were lethal and magnetic, while maintaining a stormy serenity. As calmly as she could, she turned her attention to the sound of Keino's voice as he, while raising his glass to propose a toast, said, "Everyone, a salute to the man of the hour. My cousin, Ras Selassie, master architect, master developer and master philanthropist. At the risk of sounding like a bragging relative, this latest project is something that brings pride to the entire Selassie-Mazrui clan. My hat is off to you, Ras, for your tremendous skill and for your generous heart." A chorus of "Hear! Hear!" rang out as Ras sat once again, astounded at Keino's generosity.

Brad loudly proclaimed, "Speech, speech. Enlighten the ladies about your latest Ethiopian project."

Ras began slowly. Once again, though, when he smiled, the smile did not reach his eyes. With a hint of sarcasm, he stated very flatly, "I can think of at least one person in the Selassie family who won't feel pride in this venture, but there is always one in every family." Everyone in the room felt the pain of Ras' terse statement. Keino and Brad, well aware of Ras' dislike of his father, would have done anything humanly possible to patch the rift between the two men, but they both understood that it ran too deep and spanned too many years. Only Ras and his father could mend the broken relationship. The women in the room felt the anguish and wondered about the source. An almost imperceptible change took place in Ras as he began to describe his Ethiopian project. His eyes softened. The raw hurt was replaced with a compassionate tone, and his terse tenor became almost tender as he spoke of the children he expected to house. As he spoke, Cassandra could feel herself melting into the words he articulated and the images he painted. The fervor in his voice could not be missed when he spoke about the young children without parents for whom he hoped to design a community unlike any other in existence. He continued speaking, gesturing emphatically at points where his passion was most intense.

"Right now the plans have been completed for the housing units. This design has not been attempted before. I want these children not to be warehoused. I want them to have some semblance of home and community. Five to seven children per household with four adult caretakers. Two women, two men, to simulate parental figures. Each household will have a housekeeper, cook and laundress. There will be a community school and activities to give the children a feeling of home and family. Everyone has to feel connected in order to function as a whole human being. I want to give these children that opportunity." Unspoken was the sentiment that Ras wanted to give these children what he felt he had missed.

As she listened, Cassandra could feel the personal connection between Ras and his hopes for the children. She sensed it was much more than just a project for him. The sensitivity he expressed brought unshed tears to her eyes, in spite of her anger at what she had perceived as his rude behavior earlier. Just as Ras finished his last sentence, he looked straight into the misty, shining orbs that were Cassandra's eyes. He instinctively wanted to pull her to him, caress her and assure her that all was well. He was distracted by Amara's voice.

Amara held her husband, Keino's hand tightly and, with a voice filled with emotion, said, "Ras, that was so touching." Exploring his plans further, she asked, "Have you pulled together your team to put into place all of the aspects of the design?"

Ras' voice lowered, laced with emotional exhaustion. He was unaccustomed to sharing his personal passions in a social setting. "Almost. The one piece I am missing is an interior designer to oversee the decoration of the homes. It's very simple, straightforward design work. All I need is someone who can give me functional, durable, comfortable spaces with some elements of charm." By the time Ras completed his last word, he noticed that all of the eyes in the room were suddenly focused on Cassandra.

Amara spoke directly to Ras. Her tone was quiet, and there was a smile on her face. "Ras, evidently you are the only one in the room who doesn't know this. My sister Cassandra is one of the lead interior designers in this city, and she is a pushover for anything having to do with children."

Ras turned to Cassandra, picked up his champagne glass, sipped and swallowed slowly, never letting his eyes leave hers. He placed his glass on the table gently and said as coolly as if he had been reporting the weather, "We must talk." The invisible shield had been erected again, and the Ras who had spoken so passionately and tenderly about the children for whom he would build homes had barricaded himself behind it.

Cassandra felt a chill so deep, it ran through her body and caused a shiver that shook her core but was invisible to those looking on. She plastered on her most professional smile, and while stroking her long, slender arms in an attempt to ward off the invisible cold, she said, "I'd like to hear more about what you have in mind technically. It sounds like quite an undertaking and a very generous gesture on your part."

Ras responded, "I am pleased to hear that you are open to exploring the possibilities."

As the evening wore on, Ras and Cassandra were never far from each other's thoughts. Ras wondered why Cassandra was pulling him in like a magnet, and Cassandra wondered why Ras was such a strange mass of contradictions. What had been a mystery to both of them for nearly a year was even more so now.

As the dinner ended and dessert was enjoyed, Brad and Veronica started saying their good-byes. As Brad was entertaining the group with his pleas to Veronica to escort her home, Ras walked up behind Cassandra so softly his steps were unheard and whispered ever so gently, "Please, before you leave, see that I have a way to contact you so that we can more thoroughly discuss the project."

Feeling a swift sensual overload from his smell, his velvet tones, his warm breath and his heated body energy, Cassandra answered with a voice that was filled with a sensuousness that only Ras could hear. "If you'll hold on a moment, I'll get a business card from my bag."

"Take your time. Keino and I need to have a quick meeting. If you should leave before we are finished, please leave your card with Amara and I'll get it."

Her perfume floated like silken ribbons into his nostrils, giving him the heady warmth and dizzying effect of a fine cognac. Without warning, he felt the need to get away from her. He turned to find Keino so abruptly, Cassandra was left wondering if the encounter had actually occurred, and feeling angry with herself that he evoked in her such traitorous emotions.

# Chapter 4

Ras walked across the Mazrui's expansive living room into the open door of Keino's library. As Ras entered, Keino lifted his head from the ledger he was reading while seated behind his elaborately carved Baroque desk. Ras stilled himself and looked around the room. He mused that it was very much Keino. Books lined the walls from floor to ceiling. There were two gliding ladders in place for retrieving difficult-to-reach volumes. The windows were draped heavily and opulently in silk and damask. Their burgundy color accented perfectly the massive wooden furniture comfortably positioned throughout the room. The power and stability that marked Keino were amply displayed.

The thought of having his cousin in his home once again brought a smile to Keino's face. "Come in, come in, Ras. Make yourself comfortable. I was just reviewing figures for a contract I need to give to one of my managers tomorrow. There, it's done." Ras closed the library door behind him and moved forward into the spacious room.

Keino closed the ledger and moved it aside. Looking directly into Ras' eyes, Keino asked, "So, Ras Selassie, cousin of mine, son to my favorite aunt, Amara, for whom my wife was named, tell me how you are now that I can see you alone and not discuss business." The look of surprise on Ras' face let Keino know that he did not know the story of his wife's name.

"Ah yes, my cousin. See what you miss when you stay away too long. All the juicy tidbits that make up family life." Ras sat on a nearby club chair and listened intently. "It seems that my mother-in-law and your mother were classmates and roommates, in fact, here in the U.S., at Spelman College. Hence my lovely wife is the namesake of your mom. Both precious jewels. It is fitting that they should share the same name."

A light registered in Ras' eyes as he spoke of his mother. "My mother is indeed a jewel. She was and still is, for me, a mother in every sense of the word. There has never been a doubt in my mind as to her joy in having me as her son. My only question for my mother has always been, why did she marry the man she calls her husband?"

Keino interrupted in a quiet, even baritone cadence. "You mean the man who is your father, the man who provided you every material advantage a child could dream of? That man?"

Ras, letting loose all of his frustration at having to try and explain his feelings about his father, with every word got louder. "Keino, you were not there. You all saw the façade. You saw the trappings. You didn't live with a father who told you in word and deed that you were nothing, a father with whom you could not share one activity. Tell me, Keino, how many extracurricular activities of yours or your brothers did your father miss? One, two, maybe? Hell, your father even showed up at some of my events. How many, Keino, did my father make? Zero, Keino, not one, not one. My whole damn life. Keino, how many nights did you hear your mother cry herself to sleep over a cold, distant, angry man who wasn't worth a single tear she shed? How many nights, Keino? Don't tell me about my father, General Selassie, world-class provider. He provided, all right. He provided pain, rejection and all-around misery. That's what he provided." Slamming his hand on a nearby table, Ras ended his cathartic explosion by saying, "I will never forgive him for the pain he caused my mother."

Keino was stunned hearing his cousin. For the first time so much made sense. His cousin's reclusiveness in adulthood, his absence from family gatherings, his refusal to have any intimate dealings with his father. Keino was well aware that when they were youngsters, Ras' dad had often not been present at family gatherings, but he had been made to believe as a child that the work of a general was all encompassing. Until now he thought Ras just felt estranged from his father. Now it was clear that he hated him.

Keino walked around his desk and placed an arm around Ras' shoulders. "Ras, forgive us all for being so blind. Had we known, something could have been done."

Ras removed himself from Keino and almost fell into a nearby chair, exhausted from the expenditure of energy it had taken to recite to another human being the pain he had been carrying for a lifetime. "Keino," Ras spoke in a voice filled with weariness, "I have not expressed my feelings about Tafari Selassie to anyone else. I would appreciate it if the words I spoke do not leave this room, except if you see the need to share the exchange with Amara. Something tells me you are not big on keeping secrets from your wife."

Keino's face lit up in an upturned smile. "I appreciate your insight, Ras. What I will promise you is this: unless the need arises, and my wife truly needs to know, I will honor your confidence."

With a not-so-subtle change in topic and a more relaxed manner, Ras stated, "Now, tell me a bit about your sister-in-law, Ms. Cassandra Terrell."

With one fluid stride to place himself comfortably in the chair opposite Ras, Keino, with a wide smile of approval on his face and playfulness in his voice, quipped, "I knew you were interested. Your interest was telegraphed so loudly, you almost blew my introduction before dinner tonight." He continued, teasing Ras. "What I want to know, my cousin, is, is this interrogation of a personal or a professional nature?"

Ras, now almost laughing himself, responded, "Hey, now, you heard your wife. She said her sister was one of the hottest designers on the Eastern Seaboard."

Keino replied rapidly, "And my powers of observation told me that you had designs on more than her decorating skills."

Ras' voice lowered in volume, and as he spoke, a pensive tone shrouded his words. He spoke almost as if speaking to himself. "Beauty she has in abundance, and I am sure her mental acuity matches her physical elegance. However, an entanglement with a woman, particularly one who appears to be extremely high maintenance, is not what I need at this juncture in my life."

Keino interjected, "You're sending mixed messages, man. One minute you act like you want to eat her for dinner, now you sit here rationalizing why you can't get involved. At this phase in your life, what you need is a good woman who brings out all of the good feelings you've been burying while you've been keeping the world away. Take it from me, there is nothing like knowing that no matter where you are in the world, someone cares whether you are alive or dead. You can vacillate all you want, but if you don't make the right choice in the end, you lose. I know. I had a similar fight, if you will recall."

Ras jumped to his feet, began pacing, and responded with irritation and frustration easing through his tone. "Keino, kill the pitch, man. All I want is to know something about the woman so that I can gauge whether or not talking to her further about the project would be worth my time. I'm not trying to propose marriage to the woman."

Keino acquiesced, and with a look of mild amusement on his face, he said, "All right! All right!" Ras sat back down, crossed his legs and listened attentively.

"There are four sisters. Cassandra is the third. She is the most obviously flamboyant in her style, but I must say they all have their moments of flamboyance, however differently they may be expressed. Cassandra is a real glamour girl. You said high maintenance, but I honestly don't know. I do know that she is a pro at what she does. She is asked to travel many places in the world to design for major corporations and individual clients."

In a cool, impersonal tone, Ras asked, "Is she attached?"

Keino laughed. "Now that sounds like a personal concern to me."

Choking back his own laughter, Ras explained, "See, that's where you're wrong, my wise cousin. The concern is purely professional. If she is attached, a clinging vine of a husband or a male suitor might cause problems for my project."

Keino weighed in. "No, man, she is not attached. If she had been, you know I would have told you. What I can say is, I know she is not wanting for male attention, including yours." Keino added with a sly grin, "I must say though, I've never seen her attach herself to anyone exclusively beyond a casual date. Anything else seems to be more than she is interested in at the moment. I know this, Ras. If testing the water and moving on happens to be a part of your game plan, I think you just might be in for a rude awakening."

"Is that a warning?"

"Just an observation. Come on, give me more details about this project."

While Keino and Ras continued to share a relaxed exchange, Amara and Cassandra worked, chatting away while clearing the table from the evening's meal. Cassandra teased her sister. "Amara, you and Veronica are never going to grow up. You two haven't changed since you were ten."

"Some days it seems that way and I like it. Aside from my sisters, my parents and my husband, Veronica knows me better than anyone. That's my girl. I wish she would give Brad a chance. He is really trying hard to get her attention, but she really just thinks that he is too brash and too outspoken and too arrogant. Now who does that sound like?"

They both said in unison "her" and laughed until they both had tears streaming down their cheeks. When they had calmed themselves, they brought the dishes to the kitchen, stacked them neatly and walked into the den. Cassandra and Amara had each prepared a slice of heated walnut pecan pie à la mode. Amara sat on a chocolate-colored chenille upholstered chaise. Cassandra sat opposite her sister on a similarly upholstered love seat. Her legs were crossed at the knees, right over left. Her right foot was swinging in rhythm with her enjoyment of the walnut pecan pie.

"Amara, this is delicious. Where did you buy it?"

"I beg your pardon," replied Amara with feigned indignation. "I'll have you know this came from my own loving hands and the ingenious combination of three recipes. I call it à la B. Smith, Mom and Grams."

"I should have known. After all, you and Mom were always the best bakers in the family."

"You want my revamped recipe?"

"No, Sis, not this time. Now I'll look at a recipe book, but I am not going to cook."

"Cassandra, you're a good cook. Mom made sure we could all hold our own in a kitchen."

Cassandra smiled thinking of their mother, Ana Terrell, and her tireless efforts to teach her daughters to do everything well. She responded to Amara with an expression that was thoughtful and serious. "I know, but these days my interest in the culinary arts is nonexistent."

Amara's concerned eyes held Cassandra's as she pointedly asked her, "What are you interested in these days, Cassandra?"

"My usual! Travel, design shows, working at my craft, trying to enjoy life." Cassandra lowered her eyes and continued enjoying her pie, one perfect morsel at a time.

Amara placed her dessert plate with her slice of half-eaten pie on a nearby side table. She pulled her knees to her chest, tucked her bronze caftan under her bare feet, leveled her gaze at Cassandra and asked, "Any special prospects of the male persuasion?"

Cassandra smiled. "Nothing that I'm interested in pursuing."

Amara rested her hand on her chin, smiled at her sister and said, "Well, I hope you didn't miss Mr. Ras Selassie's not-so-subtle advances during Keino's introduction." Now some of the fury Cassandra had felt earlier returned. She put down her empty plate and began gesturing with her hands.

"Oh, no, I didn't miss a thing. That pompous, self-absorbed philanderer got off easily because we were in your home. My time will come to tell him a thing or two."

Amara interjected, "I don't think he's that bad, Cassandra. I don't think he meant any harm. You don't even know him. Don't pass judgment so quickly. Are you open to a relationship at all, Cassandra?"

Cassandra took a deep breath and calmed herself again in order to answer her sister. "Oh, thoughts of wedded bliss flash through my mind on occasion. A good relationship is very important to me, but I guess I'm still in many ways one of the walking wounded. When Christopher was killed, a piece of me died with him, and Lord knows, I've been trying to recover that piece. It is possible that it's gone forever. Perhaps if his dying had made any sense, I could make peace with it, but for someone to randomly take from me the love of my life . . . I don't know if I'll ever find peace again."

This was the first time she had spoken of Christopher Hunter in many months. He had been her college sweetheart. After graduation they had planned to be married. Christopher had been killed, an innocent bystander in a robbery gone wrong. "I have moments when something happens to make me remember the glow I once felt, but it doesn't last long. I don't know if I ever want to risk loving that deeply again."

Amara watched as her sister wiped the trace of a tear

from her eye. Cassandra continued. "Enough about me. Tell me about life in Nairobi. Are you adjusting?"

"I am adjusting well. The Mazrui family is wonderful to me. It is fun watching Keino and his brothers. Fortunately, I enjoy all of my sisters-in-law. The only thing that is taking some getting used to is all of the servants. Keino assures me that I must use them because I am contributing to the economic welfare of the country. How's that for placing a load of guilt in my lap? But, you know, I miss you and those other two sisters of mine, not to mention Mom and Dad. I am grateful that we travel back and forth. I am sorry Adana and Afiya couldn't make it tonight. We all have to get together before I go back to Nairobi again."

"Yes, we will."

"Speaking of leaving, in spite of what you think about Ras, what do you think about the project he has developed?"

"I think the project is phenomenal, but the project developer is certainly a strange character. I'm telling you, it took all I had not to really hurt his feelings when Keino made his introductions tonight."

Amara looked at her sister with a sideways glance and a smile and said, "You have no idea how hard I was praying that the powers of the Divine would intercede and still your tongue."

Cassandra asked, "What is wrong with him? He was a perfect gentleman when I danced with him at your wedding."

Amara responded, "You know I don't know him, but he has to be a good person. Number one, he is a part of Keino's family. Number two, look at the magnificent project he has created. You can't be all bad if you love children that much. Number three, look at who his mother is. The woman Mom named me after. Since I've gotten to know her, I can attest to the fact that she is a wonderful woman. Maybe he has just been in Europe too long, and his idea of how to approach a woman is a little skewed." They both shared a laugh at that thought.

Cassandra continued, "I can tell you this. When I have

the opportunity to get him alone, I will make it very clear what he can do with his African-European sensibilities."

"Don't be too hard on him, Cassandra. Please give the man the benefit of the doubt."

"Oh, I will. I'll leave enough scraps for the coroner to identify."

They both burst into uncontrollable laughter. Cassandra was the first to regain her composure. "Okay, sister of mine. Since I've eaten every crumb, I'm going home to enjoy a long hot bath and chase that thing called peaceful sleep. Before I go, as per the request of the gentleman in the study with your husband, I will leave my information with you for him to retrieve at his leisure. I'll grab my things and be out, as the youngsters say."

Cassandra left her card, kissed her sister good-bye, and asked that she say good-bye to Keino for her. Then she drove her late-model Mercedes two-seater home to her Georgetown loft.

# Chapter 5

Saturday morning Cassandra found herself with a rare day when she had no design work, and so she busied herself with chores and generally enjoyed a quiet, peaceful day. She reorganized closets and drawers, which had been irritating her for months, while some of her favorite contemporary jazz vocalists serenaded her through the morning. Cassandra's loft was not only her home but a second showplace. When the mood struck her, she used her home as she did her design studio. She experimented with color, with fabrics, with lighting, with furniture styles and with art. The building itself had once been a warehouse. It had been given a sleek, modernist façade and was divided into four separate dwellings. The owners of the other three lofts were, like Cassandra, ambitious, upwardly mobile, progressive, well-traveled people who were friendly but always on the go. The high-end structures were custom built. The only things they shared in common were completely soundproofed rooms, the highest quality materials used throughout and extremely spacious floor plans.

About midday, Cassandra decided to run some much needed errands. She showered, put her hair into a quick ponytail fastened with a tortoiseshell clip, moisturized her skin, applied a mauve-tinted lip gloss, and scented her skin with her favorite Givenchy body radiance lotion.Over her signature black undies, she slipped a pair of mauve wool slacks, then put on a matching long-sleeved cashmere sweater and mauve-colored ankle-cut leather boots. To complete her ensemble, she grabbed a matching cashmere ruana and a mauve shoulder bag. One last look in a full-length Regency mirror placed on one wall of her bedroom let her know that the monochromatic look she had chosen for the day was just what the doctor ordered. She picked up a bag of dry cleaning she had deposited at the front door, and she was on her way.

As she stepped outside her building, the air surrounding her was crisp, cool and clean. The slight chill in the air was almost sensual as the hint of a breeze caressed her face and hands. She walked along, thoroughly enjoying her neighborhood. She had chosen it because it was an upscale community infused with wonderful restaurants, pastry shops and flower shops, all within walking distance. It reminded her of some of her favorite neighborhoods in Paris, where each section of the city had its own flavor, signature stamp and area conveniences. She dropped off her dry cleaning, stopped at her most frequented dessert shop to purchase an assortment of pastries, and then dropped by the gourmet delicatessen she most enjoyed for meats, cheeses, freshly baked French bread and a bottle of their best white wine. She could not resist purchasing freshly cut gladiolas in an array of colors from a street vendor. Three hours later she was on her way home.

As she walked back into her loft, she felt exhilarated from her shopping stroll through the neighborhood. She walked from her spacious living room into an equally large and open kitchen. She placed her packages on the charcoal-colored granite-topped center island and began to put her purchases away. As she opened the stainless steel refrigerator door, her telephone rang. She hastily placed her perishable items inside the refrigerator and turned to pick up the receiver of the wall-mounted portable telephone. In her naturally silken tones, she answered, "Hello, this is Cassandra."

The mellow, composed voice on the other end of the line responded, "I am glad to hear that. Now I know I have the correct number."

She had only been in the presence of that voice on two occasions, but she knew it was her very exasperating dance partner. Her silken tones turned lukewarm and exact. "Hello, Mr. Selassie."

Continuing with the bravado that was second nature to him, Ras said, "Ah, I see I don't have to identify myself. I hope you are still interested in talking about the Addis Ababa project. This is my last night here. I hope this evening will work for you."

Cassandra stilled herself, and with an edge in her voice that Ras missed, she responded, "I am very much interested in the project. Since this is your last night here, let's make things simple. You may come here to my home. My address is 7 Honeywell Place."

"Yes, that sounds like the perfect solution. If six o'clock will work, I'll come by."

Cassandra's terse response was, "I'll be expecting you." She hung up and thought to herself, *Mr. Ras Selassie, you are in for more than just a meeting.*


Ras rang Cassandra's bell promptly at six. He was rarely late. Never was he late if left to his own devices. The times in his life when he had not been on time always centered around someone else's tardiness. Cassandra was rarely on time, not because she had no regard for western scheduling, but because she always packed more into a day than one could possibly do. It gave her a bizarre sense of pleasure to start the day with forty activities scheduled and cross them off her list one at a time. She was always in a race against herself to see how far she could push. This time she was not late. She was on time and ready for war. Cassandra opened her massive, one-of-a-kind teakwood door and welcomed Ras into her home. He was once again struck by her beauty and her poise. Her hair was pulled back smoothly in a tight bun. Her make-up was flawlessly applied, accentuating her almond-shaped eyes. She was comfortably attired in a black silk caftan and black ballet slippers. Her neck was adorned with an exquisite turquoise necklace, and she wore matching earrings.

With a deceptive calm and a latent sensuality, Ras said, "Hello, Cassandra. It is good to see you again. Thank you for allowing us this opportunity to further discuss the Ethiopian project."

Cassandra spoke in low, soft, clear tones as she stepped aside for him to enter and closed the door. "You are very welcome, Mr. Selassie."

Stunned by her use of the formal Mr. Selassie, Ras, in an almost patronizing tone, stated bluntly, "Shouldn't we be past Mr. Selassie and Ms. Terrell?"

She answered quickly, with her hands clasped in front of her, looking him directly in his eyes. "Before we begin our discussion of your project, Mr. Selassie," she said, emphasizing "Mr." again, "I want to give you a clear picture of who I am, and who I think you are."

The velvet edge and strength in her voice was captivating to Ras even while she told him off in no uncertain terms. "Last night when we were introduced, you embarrassed me with your display of familiarity. It made me angry enough to slap your face. You were saved because we were in Amara and Keino's home. I just want you to know that if you ever again publicly humiliate me with your tired lines and barely couched sexual innuendoes, I will not hesitate to slap you senseless."

With a smile on his face and feigned severity, Ras stated, "Had I known you were prone to violence, I would not have attempted to show you how much I admire your beauty."

"I am not laughing, Mr. Selassie, and I am certain that a man of your worldly experience can find appropriate ways to express appreciation." She continued, each word clipped and distinct. "See, your problem, Mr. Ras Selassie, is that you are so self-absorbed, that all you can think about is how you feel or what you think. I have a news flash for you. You exist in this world with other people who have ideas about how they want to be treated." She stopped as abruptly as she had started. Having unburdened herself sufficiently, Cassandra felt satisfied. She took a deep breath, placed a smile on her face, and with a sweeping motion of her hand, she looked directly at Ras and said, with a hint of sugar in her voice, "Now, Ras, if you would still like to discuss the project, you may have a seat."

His half-smile softened his face as he responded as apologetically as he knew how. "I don't believe I've ever been reprimanded so thoroughly and so directly by anyone as beautiful as you, and for the record, you are even more beautiful when that glint of fire hits your eyes. I now know my place. You have made it abundantly clear."

Cassandra smiled cautiously, thinking to herself, *I have a feeling this war is not over, and that was just the first of many battles*. With all of the graciousness she could muster, she said, "If you like, you may hang your coat in the closet you passed in the entryway. And while you are doing that, I'll get the refreshments I prepared for us."

"Thank you, I will," was Ras' formal response. He walked over to the closet, with his trademark aristocratic gait, and removed his camel-colored full-length cashmere coat. Underneath he wore a matching banded camel-colored silk shirt and camel-colored wool slacks. His shoes were camel-colored lizard, adding a real flare to the ensemble. After hanging his coat in the closet, Ras turned to walk back into the room, taking in its lines and overall design. It was clear to him that this was a woman with immense interior design talent and sensibilities about space not unlike his own. He was enjoying the openness and light, the masterful groupings of art and family photographs, and the strategically placed gladiolas when Cassandra entered, carrying an elegantly etched glass tray laden with an assortment of delicious appetizers beautifully arranged. As Ras surveyed the crab cakes with chili mayonnaise, the ginger chicken kabobs, the raw vegetables and the fresh fruit on skewers, he was once again impressed by Cassandra's ability to bring grace and beauty to something as simple as preparing and serving a light meal.

As Cassandra placed the tray down on the large ebony-colored lacquered coffee table that sat in front of her sofa, Ras took a seat. Cassandra glanced up at him and noted how handsome he looked in his camel-colored clothing as he sat on her bronze-colored sofa. He looked as though he belonged there. She quickly erased that thought from her head, looked directly into eyes that were filled with admiration of her and said, "Ras, would you like a glass of wine?"

"Yes, I would. If you'll tell me where you keep it and your glasses, I will pour for both of us."

"Thank you. Try the refrigerator for the wine if you'd like white and the wine rack next to the island if you'd like red. The glasses are in the cabinet above the stove."

Ras turned to Cassandra before walking to the kitchen and said, "Which would you prefer, red or white?"

"White, please."

"Then white it is," he said matter-of-factly and walked into the kitchen. Cassandra sat on the sofa and began placing dishes, cutlery and napkins on the coffee table so that they could enjoy their meal of appetizers and white wine. While Ras was uncorking the wine and getting two long-stemmed glasses from the cabinet, he spoke in deep, rich tones laced with the hint of an accent Cassandra heard for the first time. It reminded her that he was indeed a man with a global worldview.

"Cassandra, your loft design is quite spectacular. Who was your architect?"

The question startled her. The answer to that question was known only by her family. Only they knew that her fiancé, Christopher Hunter, had been an architect and that their plan before he was killed was that after they were married, they would work as a team designing and decorating homes all over the world. A single bullet had killed that dream along with Christopher. Her answer was, "A very dear friend."

Ras heard the melancholy in her voice. He let it pass and continued to pour the wine, wondering what had caused the sound of despair in one so lovely. When Cassandra had finished arranging her coffee table for a casual meal, she turned on the soft sounds of a jazz quartet and lit a fire in the fireplace. When Ras reentered the room and once again sat on the sofa, they were both warmed by the glow emitted from the growing blaze.

Ras raised his glass, took a sip, and in a voice that was low and smooth, began speaking to Cassandra. "It is very disturbing to me that we went from sharing a wonderful, enchanting dance to having you feel the need to physically harm me. Since you have consented to offer me sustenance, I will make the assumption that all is now well."

"Ras," Cassandra began in a tone that was as patronizing as she could make it, "I was taught to always be gracious, even to people who aren't. Please do not assume that all is well because I am feeding you. The only conclusions you can draw are one, that I was reared properly and two, that I am willing to listen."

"I see!" Now smiling, Ras continued. "Ms. Cassandra, I've met mob bosses and investment bankers who were not as exacting as you are."

Now Cassandra was smiling as she said, "I would say that was their loss." Now they both laughed.

Ras' gaze fell on Cassandra's lips as he uttered, "You should laugh more frequently. It is very becoming."

Cassandra responded quickly while still smiling. "You, sir, are not the one to talk to anyone about laughing more."

Ras threw his hands in the air in feigned exasperation. With a tilted smile, he said, "All right, I give up. I think we'd better discuss the Ethiopian project before I put my foot in my mouth again. Perhaps Brad was correct. My social skills leave something to be desired."

Cassandra, with an air of calm self-confidence and a knowing smile lighting up her face, said, "You're learning and now I'm listening. Tell me what you see as my part in this project."

Ras and Cassandra ate and talked. Ras explained in detail the design part of the project, and Cassandra asked a multitude of questions. By the end of the conversation, she was almost convinced she would enjoy being a part of the team.

She had one last set of questions.

"Ras, tell me about the other members of the team. Are they people you've known for a long time? Are they a part of your regular staff?"

Ras stretched his long, muscular legs and crossed his feet at the ankles. The movement was so devastatingly virile that it left Cassandra feeling as though the heat radiating from his body traveled the length of hers. As Ras began speaking, the smoothness of his tenor intonation caressed her while his golden brown eyes studied her with a curious intensity. The probing stare left her feeling a strange sensation, which she tried desperately to mask. It was becoming more and more clear to Cassandra that interaction with Ras often left her off balance. In those rare moments when he was civil, she found him intriguing and very attractive, but the part of him that went to cold, dark places left her never wanting to see him again. Confusion and conflict were the words that came to mind when she thought of Ras, but in spite of that, something about him pulled her in.

The dreamlike state that clouded her mind as she sorted through thoughts of Ras lifted as she tuned into him saying, "The members of my team are good people. I have worked with them for many years. They are men and women from various parts of the world who are extremely proficient at what they do, and they all seem to find working with me, though perhaps not always easy, a very lucrative way to be employed. Five of these people you will see daily." The look in his eyes was laced with humor and a flicker of tenderness as he added, "That is, if you should decide to join the team. Rafael Navarro from Colombia heads the electrical crew. Kunle Odumakinde from Nigeria is project manager. Anthony Robinson from Philadelphia heads the plumbing crew. Gevre Hiwot from Ethiopia is in charge of heating and air conditioning, and Gisela Graff from Germany is my administrative assistant. They are all regular staff members who travel with me around the world, completing projects as they need to be constructed. We are together approximately six months a year. The other six months I take for myself to complete architectural plans and to consult on commissioned projects—"

Before she could catch herself, Cassandra asked abruptly, "Ras, do you exist outside of your work?"

Before she could add words to soften the blow of her statement, he matched her. "Do you, Cassandra Terrell, exist outside your work?"

The tension that had moments ago left the room was back. Cassandra threw her hands in the air in sheer exasperation. "Here we go again. I really only meant that your schedule sounds grueling, and it made me wonder about the pace."

Ras pounced. "Oh, I see. You were wondering if the frantic pace I set for myself spills over into my expectations of my employees. Don't concern yourself, Cassandra. Given what I know of your schedule, you will have no problems."

Cassandra, now thoroughly annoyed, responded, "Thank you for that quick evaluation of my work ethic, but that was not my concern."

"What was your concern?"

"Never mind! At the moment my only concerns are how long would I physically need to be in Addis Ababa and when would I need to leave?"

Ras' stern reply was, "I need a decision in three days. We leave in two weeks. You need to commit one month in

Addis. I need your answer in three days because if you refuse the offer, I need time to recruit another designer."

"That's fair. I can let you know in three days."

Ras, agitated by another heated exchange between the two of them, was as anxious to leave as Cassandra was to have him leave. He stood, bringing to mind a king rising to take leave of his subjects. He placed his business card on the coffee table. Cassandra sat, equally in charge of herself and her surroundings, thinking, *if this work didn't involve making children's lives better, I would tell you exactly where to go, Mr. Ras Selassie.* Instead she erected her own emotional barrier and politely walked Ras to the door. Knowing clearly that he was being dismissed, he made a mental note never to have a conversation again with Cassandra Terrell that was not strictly business. Little did he know Cassandra was making the same mental note.

Ras took his coat from the entry closet where he had put it upon his arrival. Cassandra opened her front door. Ras stepped into the hallway, turned and said, "In three days."

She answered matter-of-factly, "In three days," and with more force than usual, closed her door. Cassandra walked back into her living room, talking to herself while clearing away the dishes from the meal she had shared with a man who was, to her, as irritating as he was intriguing.

"What on earth is wrong with him?" she muttered to herself. "One minute he is gracious and sane, and the next minute he is an erratic egomaniac. Should I really subject myself to his madness? I really need to give this job offer more consideration. There may be some benefits I don't want, like the benefit of working with Mr. Ras Selassie."

# Chapter 6

Two days later Cassandra sat at home in her study, drawing plans and matching swatches for a remodeled living room that she had been hired to design. She had left her office early to get home before a rainstorm, which was now dropping fierce sheets of water on standing structures and people in the streets.

Cassandra watched the rain and the people, contemplating the advantages of accepting the Addis Ababa assignment. She had a great love for the history of Ethiopia, and she knew from conversations and from research that the terrain was as beautiful as the people, but it was her love for children that really drew her to the project. She never saw a child that she didn't find beautiful. She had looked forward to marrying Christopher and having his children. The thought of that no longer being a possibility still made her misty-eyed.

She placed her sketch pad on a nearby table and walked into the kitchen to fix a cup of her favorite tea, a chai latte blend that was so spicy and sweet that it warmed her very soul. The day was perfect for chai tea. Just as she touched an elegant ceramic mug to bring it down from a shelf, the telephone rang. Cassandra picked up the phone and answered with a distracted "Hello." The always upbeat Afiya answered.

"Hi, Sis. I wasn't sure I'd catch you at home. This rain is a mess, isn't it?"

Happy to hear her sister's voice, Cassandra responded, "Hi, Afiya. You made it back. I thought you were still in New York. I'm glad you're home. How was the trip?"

"It was good! You know I'm always the optimist, thinking I can bring together a group of egocentric artists and get them to forego their egos and focus on one project as a unit." She laughed at the thought. "We are trying to create an ancestral tribute that is a multimedia event."

Cassandra pressed the speakerphone button, placed the telephone back in the cradle and continued fixing her tea. Speaking hurriedly, Afiya continued, "Maybe one day I'll learn that I am not the United Nations peacekeepers." With a sudden burst of laughter, she blurted out, "Maybe I am. Considering the UN success rate, I might not be doing so badly." Afiya's way of looking at the world always brought a smile to Cassandra's face.

Afiya was unaware of how her positive outlook soothed many a ruffled feather. Rushing on as though she had forgotten to say something extremely important, Afiya inquired, "Speaking of peacekeeping missions, have you decided about Ethiopia?"

Cassandra had finished stirring her tea and was sitting at the kitchen island, sipping it. "I pretty much know that I should go. You know how I feel about children, wherever they are in the world. Once I hear about a need, I feel like they are my babies, and I have to do something. And designing is my passion, so I could be in seventh heaven. The only downside is working with Ras Selassie. Talk about Jekyll and Hyde. He is at least one of the most irritating men I have ever met. We really rub each other the wrong way. We can't seem to have a civil conversation that's longer than two sentences without winding up wanting to shoot each other."

"Is he really that awful?"

With mild irritation in her voice, Cassandra answered,

"People keep asking me that. Amara asked the same thing. The answer is yes, he can be a royal pain." She took a deep breath and added, "Maybe we bring out the worst in each other."

Afiya listened quietly as her sister continued to vent. "At any rate, this would be an opportunity to make an excellent career move, doing work that I love for little people that I love. Yes, I'm going for it. I'll call that scrooge of a man this evening and leave him a message. Thanks, Afiya. You helped me make a decision."

Afiya laughed while saying, "I am always happy to be of assistance even when I don't know that I'm helping. When do you leave?"

"In two weeks. I just need to put a couple of things in order."

"How long are you going to be there?"

"I've been asked to commit to one month."

"That's great. It will give me time to visit you while you're there. We'll talk later, and I'll carve out some time to make the trip."

"Hey, that's a great idea. I'd really like that. You can fly over and make sure I don't cause Mr. Selassie any bodily harm."

"Hey, I'm going to let you and Ras work out your own stuff. I'm coming to enjoy your company and to scope out some of the hot new artists living in and around Addis Ababa."

"OK, I got the message."

"See ya, love. Talk to you soon."

"Bye, Afiya. Love you, too."

Cassandra placed her cup and spoon in the kitchen sink. Absentmindedly listening to the clinking sound of stainless steel on porcelain, she picked up the portable telephone, walked into the living room, sat down and stretched out on her soft, comfortable sofa. The down-filled pillows provided a much-needed respite given the call she was about to make. She reached from her relaxed position to the coffee table to retrieve the business card Ras had left there during his one and only visit to her home. She noted that the card resembled the man: straightforward, classy and classic. She rubbed the fine linen stock between her fingers as she memorized the numbers she needed to dial. As she punched in the numbers, she kept repeating to herself, "This is the right thing to do. I'm doing this for the children." It was her intention to leave a message on what she was certain would be an automated answering service. True to form, however, Ras did not do what was expected. He answered, "Ras Selassie here."

Cassandra was taken momentarily by surprise. He didn't notice the tremor in her voice as she said, "Ras, this is Cassandra. I called to give you my answer."

There was silence on the other end of the phone. A deep silence like the quiet before a storm. Cassandra moved through the stony reception, remembering that she was doing it for the children. "I have decided that I would very much like to design beautiful spaces for the babies you want to house. I can be ready in two weeks, and I can commit one month on the ground in Addis."

A distant, cool tone, which she knew to be Ras', responded. "An itinerary will be forwarded to you within forty-eight hours. It will include flight information, accommodation arrangements and expense account provisions. If there are questions, a contact person will be listed. Goodbye, Cassandra."

Before she could respond in a way that was customary, she heard a dial tone. Cassandra looked in amazement at the telephone, placed it on the table and shouted out loud, "Ras Selassie, you are a pompous twit, but I am not going to let you spoil this project for me!" She stood up, shook her head in disbelief and went back to her study to finish her designs.

Ras turned in his chair to face the mountain range, which graced windows in every room of his house. He almost sneered as he said aloud, "I promise you, Ms. Cassandra Terrell, I will never again put myself in a position where I need to monitor every word that I say to you. I left my game playing in the school yard. I guessed you were high maintenance. I was more than right. Ms. Terrell, you keep your distance, and I'll keep mine. I may need your design talents, but I don't need you!"

His words said one thing, his body quite another. His anger turned to pure lust whenever he thought of her flashing eyes, her wickedly long legs and her sharp tongue, which he wanted to reserve for duels of love. Just as he was about to storm off into his den, his telephone rang again. As he snatched up the receiver from its stand, still fuming from his encounter with Cassandra, he forced himself to take a calming breath when he saw that the person calling was his assistant, Gisela Graff. He failed to wipe away all of the anger from his voice, and his greeting was tinged with the mixture of exasperation and longing he still felt.

"Ras here."

"Well, hello to you, too, boss. Did I call at a bad time?" Gisela made it her business to tiptoe around Ras. She intended to ingratiate herself with him in any way she could. They had worked together for five years, and during that time, she had fallen madly in love with him, though he did not appear to know that she was alive outside of work.

"No, this is not a bad time. What can I do for you?"

Gisela closed her blue eyes and swallowed the pain she always felt whenever Ras spoke to her as though she were an incidental, as though she were invisible. She knew she needed to accept the fact that outside of work, to him, she was nonexistent. She brushed her platinum bangs from her forehead and began biting her bottom lip in between sentences, a nervous habit she had acquired long ago.

"I thought you might need to know that the crew is on the ground in Addis Ababa. They arrived this morning. We were able to change the charter company quickly enough so that we had no delays. The equipment was shipped as scheduled. It should arrive approximately three days before we break ground. We are still lining up some of the permits needed. Your cousin Keino has been extremely helpful. He really found out where the shortcuts are. Our only holdup now is the interior designer."

Ras interrupted and stated matter-of-factly, "That is no longer a problem. She signed on today."

Gisela was cold and exact as she said, "She? Is this someone we know?"

Totally oblivious to the change in her tone, Ras' voice hardened as he thought once again of the Terrell sister who made him want to love her into submission.

"Her name is Cassandra Terrell. She is my cousin's sister-in-law, but apart from that, I am told that she is an extraordinary designer. Her recommendations come from people I trust without question. I will e-mail you her particulars so that you can make arrangements for her. She will fly in to Addis with us."

The emotional pain Gisela felt now was almost unbearable. She had been looking forward to this trip to be alone with Ras. She felt they needed the time. She needed the time. She heard her own voice but did not recognize it. It was stifled and unnatural as she continued to recite her litany of assignments.

"Ras, I need to remind you that a Ms. Miriam Zenawi has left several messages. I have given them all to you. She called today saying that you have returned none of her calls and that she needs urgently to speak to you. I explained that I was your assistant and that I would gladly take a message for you. She said, and I repeat, 'The only thing you can do for me is to tell Ras Selassie that he had better get in touch with me or he will live to regret it.' What on earth did she mean? Is this someone whose threats should concern us? Should I call the police? Who is this woman?"

Without changing his tone, Ras said, "I'll handle it. Is there anything else I should know?"

Gisela, again with a sadness she could not mask, said, "That's it for now. I'll call again tomorrow."

Ras hung up, not giving Gisela the pleasure of a parting good-bye.

He had not heard the name Miriam Zenawi in a number of years. He wondered why she was calling now, and what could possibly be so urgent? He searched his memory—calling upon his uncanny ability to recall any number or set of numbers that had ever been of importance in his life. Her number had once been important.

He dialed the number. Sitting and listening to the ringing telephone, waiting for an answer, brought back a flood of memories, mostly unpleasant. A strong, velvet-edged voice answered his call. "Good afternoon."

Without formality, Ras began, "Miriam, I understand you have an urgent message for me."

She wasted no time. "You understand correctly, Ras. It should not require an avalanche of calls to get to one man. Even a head of state is more accessible. What I need to say to you, however, requires a face-to-face discussion." With a hint of sarcasm, Miriam asked, "When will Addis Ababa once again be graced by your presence?"

"As a matter of fact, in less than two weeks. Will this urgent matter wait for a few days?"

"It will have to, because when I relay this message, I need to see your face."

"What message, Miriam? Why must some women play so many games?"

"This is not a game, Ras. When we speak, it will be a life-altering conversation, and it won't be pleasant for either of us."

"All right, Miriam. Have it your way. I'll contact you when I am back in Addis Ababa."

"Good-bye, Ras." She hung up. Ras wondered if he would ever be free of women who wanted to complicate his life. Once again he headed for his den. There he knew he could find peace and quiet.

# Chapter 7

"Hi, Daddy." Cassandra was calling her parents. She enjoyed their chats. Something about them made her feel secure and safe even though she was an adult, well-established woman; her parents were her emotional safety net when the rest of the world was too complex to fathom.

"Well, hello there, my pet. How's my Cassandra?"

"I'm fine, Daddy. I'm pulling pieces together to make the Ethiopia trip."

"Good, baby. I know you are going to do a job, but I hope you have some fun, too. Your mother and I had a great time last month when we went. Your mother was really happy because she had a chance to spend time with Amara Selassie, Keino's aunt. Those women talked and shopped every day until the sun went down." James Terrell laughed heartily at the thought of his wife enjoying herself. It always pleased him.

"What did you do, Daddy, while Mom was shopping?"

"Oh, I had a great time. Amara's husband, Tafari, and I talked politics, righted all of the wrongs in the world and indulged our wives."

As Cassandra listened, she wondered if Ras' father was anything like his son. For the sake of world peace, she hoped that the powers that be had not created two of Ras.

"I am on the way to a meeting, sweetheart. Would you like to speak to your mother before I go?"

Slightly distracted with the picture of the inscrutable Mr. Selassie still in her head, she responded, "Yes, please, Dad. Is she busy?"

"No, sweetness, you know your mother is never too busy to talk to her girls."

James held the telephone away from his mouth and called to his wife. "Ana, Cassandra's on the phone. Pick up." As he heard his wife come on the line he said, "Cassandra, take care darling. I'll see you on Sunday. Love you."

"Bye, Dad. I love you, too."

"Hi, baby," was Ana Terrell's soft greeting.

"Hi, Mama. What are you up to this morning?"

"Actually, sweetheart, I was sitting here sipping some of the new tea you sent me. And reading my notes from my last session with a very disturbed client."

"Mom, I don't know how you do it. I have trouble dealing with the so-called normal people who have momentary disturbed behavior. I know I couldn't deal with people who are always disturbed."

Ana laughed, "Sweetheart, from where I sit, some days it looks like most of the population of this country is permanently mentally deranged. I suppose my joy comes from providing momentary flashes of insight."

"Well, that's why you're Dr. Ana Chatfield Terrell, well-respected psychologist, and I get my pleasure by decorating interiors."

"Well, Cassandra, when you consider it, we are both performing a therapeutic service."

"Mom, you know you're right as usual."

"How are plans for the Ethiopia trip coming?"

"Good, I guess. I've got a few pieces to finish at the studio; then I'll be ready."

"Your dad and I had a great time."

Cassandra jokingly replied, "I know, Dad mentioned

again a few minutes ago how much of a hurtin' you put on his wallet."

"Your dad always could exaggerate a point. Amara Selassie and I did have a ball though. Every day we went to one of her favorite shops, and we did a lot of sightseeing. It is such a beautiful country. She and Tafari were wonderful hosts. They are coming to visit us soon, and we can return the favor. Thank God, Keino and Amara got married. Otherwise his Aunt Amara and I might have lost touch forever. Fate has a strange way of working sometimes."

"That it does, mom, that it does. Well, I just called to check on you two. I'm going to get back to putting my life in order so that I can leave in a few days—"

Ana interrupted. "When you get to Addis Ababa, make sure you call Keino's Aunt Amara and go by and see her. She would love to see you."

Cassandra's only response was, "Oh, Mom, I will. I'll see you Sunday."

After hanging up, Cassandra thought, *Amara Selassie may be Keino's aunt, but she is also Ras' mother, and Lord knows, I don't need another attachment that puts me anywhere near Ras Selassie unless it is absolutely necessary.*

When she finished speaking with her parents, Cassandra busied herself getting ready for her day at the design studio. She wanted to arrive ready to take on the day and clear up last minute details before leaving for Ethiopia. When she reached the design studio, she found everything humming along as it should have been. She went to her office and began her work. She had been in her office for a few hours when her assistant knocked on her door. "Come in."

Cassandra looked up from her desk and stared at Angela while Angela gleefully recited, "There is the finest man in the showroom, and he says he needs to see you now!"

Though Cassandra smiled at Angela, she could not control the sudden pounding of blood in her temples. Her body told her who was waiting in her showroom. Hoping against hope, she asked, "And does this fine man have a name?"

"Ras Selassie, and now I see why you're going to Ethiopia. Cassandra, that man is so pretty, he'll make you wanna cry."

Cassandra's flip response was, "He makes you want to cry all right, but not because he's so pretty!"

Still smiling, Angela said, "Either way, I'll show him in."

To calm the pounding in her head and to give herself the appearance of control, Cassandra readjusted her body in her chair, took a deep breath, opened one of her favorite design books, pretended to read and waited, wondering what on earth Ras Selassie wanted. Just as she started to speculate, he walked through the door. When she looked up, their eyes met. Each read an undefinable emotion in the eyes of the other. Ras, ever the epitome of self-confidence, walked farther into the room. Cassandra leaned back in her chair as the fragrant air that surrounded Ras caressed her nostrils.

"Cassandra, please excuse this unannounced appearance on your doorstep. I had to fly back into Washington, D.C., this morning, and because of a conversation I had with my mother last night, I needed to speak with you."

Intrigued by the mention of his mother, Cassandra responded, "Your timing seems to be perfect. I have a few moments between projects. Have a seat."

Ras sat and crossed his long legs in one smooth, fluid motion. As he spoke, a quiet invitation smoldered in the depths of his eyes. An invisible, passion-laced thread linked them as Cassandra drank in his every word. "It should come as no surprise to you when I say we have gotten off to a rocky start."

Cassandra tilted her head, registered a half-smile and said, "Rocky does not begin to describe it."

"I agree. My mother tells me that your parents visited her last month. She was more than pleased that she and her old school chum could catch up on years of family gossip.

She was excited to learn that you and I will be working together. She, of course, insists that I bring you home so that she can spend time with another daughter of her dear friend Ana."

Cassandra started to laugh as she said, "I was just given orders by my mother to make sure that I go to see your mother when I reach Addis."

"You see, then, Cassandra, we must get along or there will be an international incident."

This time they both laughed. It seemed odd, yet strangely comforting, to both of them that they could share laughter over the idea that their moms had given them orders they did not dare disobey.

A probing query came into his eyes as Ras asked, "So then can we bury the hatchet, at least until the project is finished? I didn't have the heart to tell my mother that together we are like oil and water."

"Ras, I don't want to be disagreeable. I can't for the life of me figure out why we always wind up arguing."

"Cassandra"—her name on his lips was like music— "perhaps our only job is to agree that for the sake of our mothers and for the project, we will get along. Human behaviors are much too complex to fathom. We can only face what happens, when it happens."

"Agreed."

"Well then," he said, rising from his chair, "thank you for your time and for being a good sport. My mother is the one woman in the world I would make these kinds of concessions for. I will see you next week."

Ras reached across Cassandra's desk, took her hand, lifted it to his warm sensuous lips, kissed it, turned, and walked through her door. She was left speechless. She thought to herself as she sat riveted to her chair, *Just when you think you've figured him out, he becomes someone else. At least I know now there is one person in the world who can make him behave, his mother.* She smiled and shook her head in disbelief.

Ras left quite pleased that he would be able to bring a smile to his mother's face. He felt that a woman who asked for so little deserved much. He did wonder, though, how much he was doing for his mother and how much for himself. Some part of him could not stay away from Ms. Cassandra Terrell. He immediately called his personal florist and had an extravagant bouquet of stargazer lilies and birds-of-paradise sent to Cassandra, with a note that read, *Here's to a new partnership and a truce, however long it may last. . . . Ras S.*

# Chapter 8

Cassandra, Ras and Gisela were flown into Addis Ababa by Ras' cousin Kaleb, Keino's younger brother. Kaleb was not only the family pilot but also the family comedian. He brought joy and laughter wherever he went. During the last leg of the flight, when Kaleb could take a break and leave his copilot in charge of the cockpit, he entertained his passengers with his comedic wit and had them doubled over with laughter at his antics. Through gales of laughter, Cassandra saw a new Ras emerge. He was more relaxed than she had ever seen him. For a flash, all of his defensiveness was gone. Cassandra joined Kaleb, egging him on to tell more stories about the childhood antics of Ras and his Mazrui cousins. Gisela withdrew, unnoticed amid the jokes and the laughter. As she sat back, her gaze rested on Cassandra, and she wondered what it was she had that compelled Ras to show this side of himself to a woman he hardly knew. Gisela had not seen this side of him in the five years she had known him.

When Kaleb returned to the cockpit, Ras and Cassandra, for the first time, had the opportunity to share their individual visions for the housing venture. Ras was pleasantly surprised that Cassandra's sketches looked amazingly as though she had read his mind. Ras was pleased. Gisela was annoyed. After Kaleb expertly landed the plane on Ethiopian soil and maneuvered the aircraft through the bustling Addis Ababa Bole International Airport, his passengers took a collective breath and waited to deplane. Ras' company limo arrived to transport Ras and Gisela to the Addis Ababa office and Cassandra to her suite at the luxurious Sheraton Addis. After dropping Ras and Gisela at the Ras Selassie Architectural Development firm, known colloquially as RS Development, the driver continued speeding through the wide, tree-lined streets of Addis Ababa. The temperature was a beautiful sixty-eight degrees. As the chauffeur whizzed along the streets, Cassandra marveled at the marked contrast between picturesque, eucalyptus-lined boulevards and meandering donkey trails. She saw beautiful Ethiopian people in a range of hues, from bittersweet chocolate to creamy butterscotch, walking in and out of shops and getting in and out of cars. The city architecture she found amazing. It was an eclectic mixture of tall office buildings, bungalows, modern conference centers, hotels and theaters, with every imaginable façade, from anodized aluminum to marble. It was indeed a lovely city. As she rode comfortably in the back of the limousine, it occurred to her that the city was much like Ras, a mass of contradictory elements wrapped in an elegant package. It was clear that whatever demons he was fighting, he would, like the land of his birth, withstand the ravages of time and move forward with even more strength and grace.

She slipped out of her daydream to hear the driver say, "We are here, Miss," as he simultaneously got out of the car and came around to open her door. She placed her hand in the driver's extended one, lifted her body out of the car and turned her eyes to the building she was about to enter. It was clear why the Sheraton Addis was purported to be the most luxurious hotel in all of East Africa. The flavor of the exterior was that of a Tuscan villa, complete with six spewing fountains executing a coordinated dance on a lake of glass. The interior was even more spectacular, with touches of marble, leaded glass and meticulous decorative ironwork throughout. It was a mixture of African and European opulence at its best.

As Cassandra walked into the foyer, her spirits were high and her runway stride was intact. She followed the driver to the reception area, where he placed her flawless set of Louis Vuitton luggage at the desk, turned, tipped his hat and walked away. Cassandra thanked him and turned to face a very handsome young man smiling back at her, saying "Welcome to the Sheraton Addis. My name is Dag, and it will be my pleasure to serve you."

Cassandra's pleasant reply was, "Hello, Dag. My name is Cassandra Terrell. I am registered with RS Development."

"Ah yes," the young man replied while gazing at his nearby computer screen. "Here you are, Ms. Cassandra Terrell. Suite 772. Though it appears you are here on business, I hope that you will find the time to enjoy the city. There is much to see and do. If you need assistance, our concierge will be at your service."

"Thank you so much. I do plan to enjoy the city while I am here."

"Good, if the truth be told, you really could have quite an enjoyable time without ever leaving the premises of this hotel. We are a Luxury Sheraton Series Hotel. Some say the most luxurious in the whole of Africa." Then he smiled. "We say at least in East Africa. We have French, Indian and Italian dining in addition to our Ethiopian cuisine. We have the lobby bar, the pool bar and the office bar. Our well attended nightclub is called the Gaslight. It has two floors and three bars, and our largest ballroom can accommodate twelve hundred people. We also have boutiques for shopping. So you see, we are well equipped to handle all of your needs."

"That's great to know. I'm sure I'll enjoy it all at least once before I leave."

"Here you are, Ms. Terrell, your key. I will have your things brought up to you."

"Thank you, Dag. You have been very helpful."

"If you need anything, Ms. Terrell, do not hesitate to call."

Cassandra took the elevator up to her suite. She was ready to unwind with good food and maybe a swim. They only had one day before work was to begin on the project. She stepped off of the elevator and walked a few feet down a lushly carpeted hallway to a door marked with a gold plaque inscribed 772. She opened the door and was not at all disappointed. Dag's description of the hotel had been accurate. She was sure the three-bedroom suite rivaled any suite anywhere in the world. The interior design was masterful, with an eclectic collection of fabrics and furnishings from around the world positioned to make one statement—elegance. As she moved through the suite, determining which bedroom she would choose, she noticed that the coffee table in the living room contained a beautifully decorated basket wrapped in delicately shimmering cellophane flamboyantly tied with a lavender organza bow. She said aloud, "What a beautiful hotel welcoming gift." As she turned the basket to enjoy the workmanship, she saw an ecru-colored card trimmed in gold with embossed initials in gold that read *RS*. She opened the card. There, in the precise lettering of an architect, she read, *Cassandra, may your stay be pleasant, and your work productive. Ras.*

She smiled and very carefully began opening the basket. She found a bottle of Dom Perignon, Swiss chocolates, an assortment of French cheeses, a bottle of the finest Ethiopian honey wine and a journal covered in red silk with her initials written in jewels on the cover. He had also enclosed a Mont Blanc with which to write. Cassandra laughed out loud. This man was full of surprises. She picked up the basket and walked into the kitchen to put away the perishable items and to chill the wines. Still smiling, she decided a swim would be perfect. She changed into a white two-piece bathing suit and sectioned her hair into Bantu knots, creating a beautifully patterned style that was perfect for swimming. She called the concierge and found the private pool on her floor. She put sandals on her feet and a white lace caftan cover-up over her suit, and she was on her way. As she entered the pool area, she found it deserted. *How nice,* she thought, *now I can really relax.* She loved to swim. She loved the feel of the water, the smell of it. She took off her cover-up and her sandals, laid them on a nearby lounge chair and dove in. She swam until time was a blur.

He watched her glide through the water as easily and as expertly as an Olympian. Stroke after stroke after perfect stroke, her arms caressed the translucent blue green water of the pool. After what she vaguely remembered as her tenth lap, she swam to one side of the pool and pulled herself up on the side ladder. She wiped the excess water from her eyes with one hand while continuing to make her way out of the pool. Still moving up the ladder, she shook the remaining water from her Bantu-knotted hair.

Her eyes focused, and there, leaning on a side wall, arms folded and ankles crossed, was the only man in the world who could take her breath away no matter how angry he made her. He wore his signature monochromatic color scheme, this time in stark white. The banded collarless shirt hung over linen trousers that lay on his perfectly built limbs as though they were a caress. He raised one hand in the gesture of a wave and spoke a low, deep "Hi." He stood there entranced by her beauty. The water clung to her skin like clear diamond strands on copper. He was enthralled by the slow rise and fall of two of the most perfectly formed breasts he had ever seen. His urge was to become the thin sliver of material that covered them, and just as he thought he could take no more, he almost lost his precious control when she walked toward him, and the slow undulation of her hips accentuated each step taken with her treacherously long legs. He was rendered momentarily speechless, and his eyes moved from her beautifully formed legs to her silky smooth flat abdomen. She smiled, returned his "Hi," and walked over to pick up a towel, her cover-up and her sandals. As she leaned over to use the towel to wipe off lingering drops of water, she provided Ras a perfect view of a profile of one side of her luscious form. He was unable to keep his thoughts to himself.

"Cassandra, do you have any earthly idea how beautiful you are?"

Cassandra looked up, smiled, slipped her caftan over her head, eased feet with toenails painted fiery red into her sandals, and said, "Thank you, but my sisters and I were always taught that for beauty one can be grateful, but it is your legacy that lasts. Beauty is transitory. Exterior beauty doesn't last forever, but internal beauty does."

"All well said, but it still does not negate the fact that you are physically astonishing. If you didn't have such a foul temper and razor sharp tongue, you would be a perfect woman." Cassandra, trying to feign anger but unable to stop laughing, jumped up, grabbed her wet towel and threw it at Ras. He caught the towel in midair.

"See what I mean? So prone to violence."

Cassandra, shaking her finger at him while still laughing, kept repeating. "You are just impossible. You are impossible." She knew she was in trouble when Ras walked closer to her and stopped an inch away. Her laughter stopped, and they stood there looking deeply into each other's souls and feeling the heat that was radiating between them. Cassandra spoke.

"I want to thank you for the welcoming basket. It was very beautiful."

"Not as beautiful as you are. I hope you liked the things I selected."

"I liked them very much. The journal is exquisite. How did you know I like to journal?"

"I think I have been feeling parts of you since the day we met. Perhaps instinctively, I just knew that you would be drawn to anything beautiful."

"Ras, sometimes you are so kind, and other times talking to you is like wrangling with a hungry bear."

"When I am home, it settles my spirit. Maybe that is what you hear. Perhaps when I am at home, the bear goes into hibernation."

"Then you should never leave home."

"I will consider that if you will consider letting me kiss you."

"If I have to consider it, I won't do it. What benefit would it be to me to kiss you?"

"The benefit is in the process. We will never know until the end."

Ras took one finger of his hand and traced the length of her face, beginning at her forehead and ending at her chin. He then lifted her chin and touched it ever so gently with a most sensuous kiss.

The radiating heat from his body floated over her as she felt the electricity in his touch. Her instinctive response to him was so powerful that imperceptible tremors began in her torso and left her pulse quickening, her heart beating erratically and a shiver of wanting burning at her center. As though on automatic pilot, her passion propelled her closer to him. He read the gesture and took a possessive step forward, which placed them face-to-face, heart to heart, center to center. His head lowered, her head lifted, and they both found what they had been seeking. In one kiss, the anger expressed so often between them became a raging, thirsty desire begging to be quenched. He felt her wrap her soft, pliable arms around his neck. He held her closer. With both of his hands, he cupped her small waist and positioned her perfectly so that they fit as if they were one. He stroked her back, breathing in her aroma, a mixture of clear water and floral magic. She could feel his strength and the warmth of his flesh. The air around them hung heavily with the fragrance of passion. When the kiss was finished, they hung on to one another, each trying to catch the breath the other had taken. Ras whispered Cassandra's name over and over again while gently placing kiss after passionate kiss on her throat, earlobes, eyes, cheeks and forehead until he took her lips in one last effort to satiate the hunger that he felt was consuming him. This time when the kiss ended, he swept her up effortlessly into his arms and carried her to the private elevator that would deliver them to her suite. Cassandra nestled her head on Ras' shoulder, thinking how perfectly at ease she felt, as though she belonged in his arms.

When they arrived at her door, he put her down, sliding her gently down the length of his lean, muscular body, and reached out his hand in a gesture that she instinctively understood as a request for her door key. She handed it to him, and he expertly opened the door and led her in. Once inside he pulled her to him with an urgency that was now familiar to her. Their kisses took on a life of their own. His maleness left her feeling drugged with unbridled passion. Her knees were weakened by the touch of his hands moving with silky strokes across the tops of her scantily covered breasts.

The gentle massage transported her to another dimension. She threw her head back and released a soft moan while breathing through parted lips. He kissed the top of each erect nipple through the strip of material that served as her bikini top, and then ever so gently, he put space between them, looked deeply into her eyes and with a tilted smile said, "Cassandra, you are enough to cause a man to lose all sense of reason and control. Before you take my mind, and leave me babbling like an idiot, I must go." In a tone that revealed his deep arousal, he continued, "I will see you in the morning. Sleep well and have pleasant dreams." He placed a kiss on her forehead and walked out the door. Cassandra stood in the middle of the floor, burning and aching with torturous desire, wondering what she would have done had Ras not put an end to their heated exchange. One thing was certain. They would never again view one another the same way.

# Chapter 9

The following morning, a car arrived to take Cassandra to RS Development for a meeting of Ras' management team. As the driver approached the headquarters, it was clear from the style of the building, which Ras had constructed and designed, that he had a deep love and respect for the design elements used by America's premier African American architect, Paul R. Williams. His signature futuristic lines and planes were all over the structure. It was a sprawling three-story edifice designed around an inner courtyard with a rock garden, which produced a Zen-like feeling. Nearby water features added to the meditative atmosphere. It shouted Ras Selassie everywhere one looked, from the bold futuristic lines to the calm courtyard, which pulled its visitors in with a strength and power that were deceptively hidden upon first glance.

Cassandra stepped from the late-model sedan and stood for a moment to take a closer look at the beautiful masterpiece Ras had created. At the moment she turned her head to look at another angle of the building, she looked directly into the eyes of the man who had just the day before set her very soul on fire. He had been standing in the window of his corner office, calming himself with the courtyard view, when much to his delight, Cassandra appeared. His pleasure could not be measured as he watched a slight breeze lift her shoulder-length tresses still crinkled from the Bantu knots. She wore a strapless sand-colored ankle-length dress covered by a short-cropped bolero jacket. Maddeningly red toenails peeked through a pair of open-toed three-inch chocolate brown barebacked sandals. He stared at the multistranded amber necklace she wore and envied the fact that it touched the tops of breasts he had kissed again and again the night before in his dreams as he endured a restless night. He waved and mouthed a "hello." She waved and walked into the building, taking calming breaths as she walked, attempting to douse the flames of the fire Ras had ignited with merely a wave and a silent hello. She entered the lobby, announced herself and was directed to the third floor, where she found the team seated in a conference room, in muted conversation around an oblong glass-topped table. She entered the room and with a smile said, "Hello, I'm Cassandra Terrell of Willows Designs here for the management team meeting."

The men in the room, Rafael, Kunle, Anthony, and Gevre, all greeted her with wide grins and admiring looks of appreciation. Just as Cassandra noticed that Gisela's reception was less than warm, she heard Ras' smooth, penetrating tones behind her say, "Cassandra is the newest member of our team. She has signed on just for this project. She will design our interiors." Cassandra had not heard him enter the room, but now as he stepped behind her and placed his hand on her shoulder, she could feel his presence slide over her like a cool waterfall on a scorching day.

They moved forward into the room to take their seats. Ras sat at the head of the table, as was his custom, and Cassandra took the empty seat to his immediate right, which placed her opposite Gisela, whose gaze was now riveted on Ras, seemingly blocking out everyone else in the room. Ras began the meeting by going around the table, formally introducing Cassandra to everyone except Gisela, whom she already knew. As Ras conducted the meeting, thoughts of Cassandra continued to ease through his mind. Though they both appeared focused on the meeting, they desired to be elsewhere, wrapped in each other's arms, exploring things more pleasurable than building and decorating. They hoped no one noticed the intensity in the looks they exchanged. No one did, except Gisela.

The group completed the strategic planning it had set out to do just before lunch, when Ras dismissed the group so that each member could move ahead with their individual agendas. As the group prepared to leave, Ras touched Cassandra's hand, leaned over and whispered softly to her, "Please wait. I'd like you to accompany me to lunch." His searing touch brought back memories of their hungry kisses the day before and left her with only the ability to nod a yes as spasmlike, ecstatic waves permeated her center.

Ras called to Gisela as she headed toward the door to leave. "Gisela, please call the Hotel D'Afrique restaurant and reserve a table for two. I'd like to take Cassandra to lunch." The pain that registered in Gisela's eyes was so stark that it caused Cassandra to wonder why.

At that moment, Ras was oblivious to anything that did not concern Cassandra Terrell. After everyone had left the room, Ras turned to the woman who was beginning to possess his soul and in a low voice taut with need said, "I am sure that it comes as no surprise that even though I left you yesterday, thoughts of you have been constantly with me. I have thought of you walking, driving, sleeping, and here you are even more beautiful than when I last saw you. You have a way of assaulting all of my senses in a manner that, I must admit, I've never experienced but am learning to thoroughly enjoy."

"Ras, you often leave me without words to say, and you've done it again."

Just as Ras was about to respond to Cassandra, the conference room door opened and Gisela entered. Her voice barely disguising the humiliation she felt watching Ras and Cassandra, she announced, "Ras, the reservation for lunch has been made, and you have a call waiting from Ms. Miriam Zenawi. Will you take the call in here?"

With a flash of annoyance on his face, he answered, "No. I'll take it in my office." He rose, turned to Cassandra and directed, "Stay here. I'll come back for you." He left the room; Gisela followed.

Cassandra took a deep breath and said quietly to herself, "What have I gotten into?"

Ras walked into his office and sat in his chair behind the antique drafting table that served as his desk, picked up the telephone receiver, pressed the button for the appropriate line and barked, "Ras here."

The sarcastic reply on the other end was, "Well, well, Mr. big shot world traveler, just when did you plan to call me back? My sources tell me that you have been in Addis long enough to ring my telephone. You are not making this any easier, Ras. Get over here soon to see me, or you will regret the day you ever met me."

"I already regret the day I ever met you, Miriam. You and I were never bosom buddies, and for the life of me, I cannot understand why you are harassing me now. I will ask you again, what is so important?"

"I will tell you when we are face-to-face. Just because it is your nature to run roughshod over everyone and act as if you are the only player in your life's drama, you are not going to bully me. You will hear me on my terms because, trust me, Ras Selassie, your life depends on it."

In an attempt to calm her down and not make matters worse, Ras established another tempo to the conversation. "All right, Miriam," he spoke slowly, "please give me the opportunity to put a few things in place, and I will see you in four days."

"I will not wait a minute after day four."

The slam of the telephone into its cradle was her parting good-bye. Ras slammed his fist on his desk and cursed under his breath. He could not begin to imagine why this woman insisted on trying to cause him such grief. Any connection he had to her or her family was severed long ago. He vowed he would put an end to her madness once and for all, but now the only person on his mind was the lovely lady sitting in his conference room, waiting to be taken to lunch.

When Ras returned to the conference room, he found Cassandra making notes on a spiral pad. He watched her, marveling at the effect she was having on him. He wanted to possess her in ways he had never desired anyone. Just as he started to call her name, she felt his presence and looked up at him with a light in her eyes that added fuel to flames already raging at his core. With a deceptive coolness, he walked over, took her hand and helped her from her seat. He pulled her to him. They were so close, they could feel their hearts hammering. Ras' fingertips became his artist's brush as he outlined every inch of Cassandra's face with strokes that were simultaneously erotic and pristine. Cassandra's eyes closed and her lips parted as she softly murmured his name. Her body shuddered when he stopped, took her hand, kissed each fingertip and led her to the car that was waiting to take them to lunch.

As they drove along the Addis Ababa boulevards on the way to Hotel D'Afrique, the day was glorious. The tree-lined streets and the crisp, clear mountain air served as perfect backdrops for Ras and Cassandra as they rode in the chauffeur-driven automobile. They chatted away about the plans for the housing units. Their conversation was interrupted with looks and caresses as they held hands and as Ras stroked the length of Cassandra's arm and kissed her palms one after the other. When they arrived at the restaurant, Cassandra found it very lovely. It was a very intimate traditional Ethiopian restaurant. It was divided by draperies into rooms suitable for intimate couples or groups. They were escorted to an area reserved for two. When the curtains were drawn, they sat across from one another, staring deeply into each other's eyes, amazed that their tumultuous relationship had turned to a passion of another kind.

Still touching and stroking Cassandra's hands and arms, Ras spoke first. "I know that you like Ethiopian food, so I am pretty sure you will enjoy the delicacies served here."

With a puzzled look on her face, Cassandra asked, "How do you know I like Ethiopian food? I don't remember mentioning that to you."

Ras continued placing feathery strokes along Cassandra's arms as he said in low, smooth tones, "Some weeks ago I stopped into Yabello's. I saw you arrive, and from your interaction with Rudolfo, I knew his Ethiopian fare was not new to you."

Cassandra froze. "You mean you saw me come into the restaurant, and you didn't even speak? You just watched me?"

"Yes." He reached for hands she had now taken off the table.

"Ras, sometimes I think you must be the most self-absorbed person I have ever known. Don't you ever think about how things affect anyone else but you?"

With disbelief in his voice Ras said, "Cassandra! Wait. Don't tell me you're going to be angry about something I did weeks ago. I made a decision based upon what I thought was right at the time. Give me a break here. You always make me out to be an ogre. I'm not that. I'm just trying to live my life with as few entanglements as possible."

Her eyes flashed as she said, "Oh, so speaking to me would have caused you to be entangled?"

Ras' voice rose. "Well, look what happened when I finally did speak to you." His smooth tone lowered again. "Here I sit totally taken by a woman who, with a look, sets me on fire. My soul knew what I was headed for. At that time, I couldn't speak to you, Cassandra. Let's just chalk it up to my idiosyncratic nature and call it a day."

Cassandra took a deep, slow, long breath, then smiled as she said, "You're not eccentric, Ras. You are just crazy.

You should be one of my mother's patients, and I have no idea why I am so attracted to you."

Ras mirrored her smile as he said, "They say like attracts like."

Cassandra's quick retort was, "No, in this case it's more like opposites attract."

"Cassandra, please don't allow my moment of cowardice to deprive me of the pleasure of your company." His golden brown stare met her questioning gaze as he added, "Yes, I said cowardice. Instinctively, I knew that if I ever made a connection with you, I would never be able to release myself from your spell. This is proof. Here I am explaining myself to you. Trust me, Cassandra, I have never explained my thoughts or my motives to any woman."

Her eyes narrowed as she smiled. "Something tells me you think I should be flattered by that. Well, let me assure you, I am not flattered." With more seriousness this time, she said, "It speaks volumes, Ras, that you've never shared your heartfelt thoughts with a woman."

"No, it doesn't," he protested. "All it says is that culturally I'm programmed differently than you are. Your African ancestors were very clear that some things just are, and they don't need explanation or analysis." He took a breath and asked, "Are we going to squabble the time away, or are we going to eat?"

This time Cassandra laughed out loud as she said, "Ras Selassie, you are one of a kind. Let's eat."

Ras signaled for food to be brought, and they spent the next hour intermittently hand-feeding each other, in the traditional way, servings of *injera*, a kind of crepe, and spicy *doro wat*, chicken with an assortment of vegetables. They cleansed their palates with *tej*, an Ethiopian honey wine. When they had finished and the table had been cleared, Ras said, "There are times when life can be good, and this, my sweet Cassandra, is a good time."

"Yes, it is. You, Ras Selassie, are full of surprises."

"Not really. Once you really get to know me, you may find that I am a pretty dull fellow."

"I find that hard to believe, but I must say, I could use more calm and less excitement when I'm around you."

"I didn't say less excitement." As if on cue, they both fell into uncontrollable laughter. Ras regained his composure first and said, with a new seriousness in his tone, "You know we must spend more time together."

"I know. I would enjoy that, as long as you quell your eccentric tendencies."

"I can only promise you that I will always be who I am."

"I didn't ask you to change yourself, Ras. Just show a little more consideration."

"I will always attempt to show you consideration, Cassandra. That is all I can promise."

"Then we'll see."

Ras repeated, "Yes, we shall see."

# Chapter 10

Over the subsequent days Ras and Cassandra collaborated and enjoyed each other's company, finding it difficult to part on each occasion when they had to do so. Though they were carefully and gingerly pacing their time, each kiss brought them closer to being consumed by the flames they ignited when they were together. One afternoon, as Cassandra and Ras were poring over drawings and calculations, the door to his office swung open, and there appeared Gisela, walking rapidly behind a very attractive, tall, imposing woman. Gisela was yelling, "I tried to stop her, but she wouldn't listen." Miriam Zenawi barely allowed her to finish her sentence.

"I think you've had more than four days, Ras. I know you don't think what I have to say is important, but you had better see me now, or else I will scream what I know to the rooftops, do you hear me?"

Ras was deadly still. His eyes did not blink; his body did not move. It felt as though hours had passed, though it had only been seconds when he spoke. Never taking his eyes off Miriam, he said, "Thank you, Gisela. Cassandra would you excuse me for a moment? We can finish later." His tone was so cold, an invisible frost hung over the room.

Gisela and Cassandra exited, and Gisela closed the door

behind them. At that moment Ras rose and, with lethal strides, stood in front of Miriam Zenawi and stated in murderous tones, "Miriam, if you ever force your way into my place of business again, you will be sorry that you did. I am not a man who plays, Miriam. You know that, and you are testing my patience."

"You are the one who promised you would see me in four days. I waited and I waited and I waited. Did you ever call, Ras? Did you ever call? I am not one of the many conquests that you can discard as readily as used-up trash. You treated my sister like your discarded trash. You used her, didn't you, Ras? Well, I am here to let you know that not all discarded material can be swept under a rug!"

"Miriam, you know nothing about my personal business, and I won't have you discuss things that have nothing to do with you. If your sister has something to say to me, she can speak for herself. I have not seen her for well over a year."

At this point Miriam dissolved into tears as she said, "And you won't see her ever again. She's dead, Ras. She was killed two months ago in a car crash."

Ras leaned toward Miriam as she dropped into a nearby chair. His anger and annoyance vanished, and his mind was flooded with memories of Zala, a lovely woman with whom he had shared time but no commitment. He had met her one evening in the hospital emergency room. He had injured his leg on a construction site, and she was the attending physician. They had dated off and on for months, with Ras ending the affair abruptly. He had said it was because of their grueling work schedules and his constant travel, but the truth was his heart wasn't in the relationship. He found her sweet and kind, but he felt no passion. He had not seen her after breaking off the affair, and now here was her sister saying that she was dead—what a loss.

As the undeniable reality of her death struck him, he put his hand on Miriam's shoulder and said, "Miriam, I am so sorry. I wish you had told me sooner. I would have assisted in any way I could. Even now if there is anything that I can do, please do not hesitate to ask."

Miriam looked up at him with tear-stained eyes haunted with pain and asked, "You really don't know, do you?"

"Really don't know what, Miriam? I have been traveling out of the country for months, and I had not seen Zala for well over a year. What should I know?"

"You should know that my sister had a son, and when her son was born, she made me promise that if anything happened to her, I must find her son's father and give him the option of raising him."

Now Ras was completely stunned. "What does all of this have to do with me?" he asked, even though his soul knew the answer.

"You are his father, Ras. You are his father."

The room was silent. The silence was deafening. All Ras could hear was his thundering pulse beating at his temples. Finally, he asked, almost pleading, "Why did she keep this from me?"

"She said she knew you didn't want her and you didn't want commitment, and she didn't want you to feel trapped. If the crash had not happened, you would have never been told."

Ras could feel unshed tears stinging the backs of his eyes, and an anger he could not describe threatened to consume him. He swallowed hard and spoke in biting clipped speech. "She really didn't know me. How could she think that I would have not taken responsibility for my child? How could she think that I would not have respect for my ancestors? She didn't know me, and neither do you, Miriam. Your sister was never discarded. We had a mutual agreement. She was a self-sufficient woman of means. She wasn't some innocent little waif who was deceived. You need to rethink your idea of what our relationship was about. You really don't know me." His voice softened and his tone mellowed as he asked, "Where is my son? How old is he? What name did his mother choose?"

Miriam spoke while brushing tears from her slightly swollen eyes with a well-worn tissue. "He has been at my home since Zala's death. He is six months old, and his name is Ras Kebran. We call him Kebran. He is an adorable, healthy little boy. We love him very much, but my husband and I know that he should not be deprived of his father."

The emotions Ras felt were beyond his comprehension. He wanted to scream and curse out loud. Instead he withdrew and went to a place only he could find. The cloying feeling in the pit of his stomach that on occasions of high stress gripped him and held on was back with a vengeance. A shadow fell over his face as he looked at Miriam and said, "I want my son." His voice rose. "At this moment I am more angry than I've ever been in my life, but no matter what, I will always take responsibility for what is mine."

His tone was bitter and cold as he said, "You will hear from me. Make no mistake, I am coming to get my son." He walked to the door and opened it for Miriam to leave. She walked quietly through the door and down the hall in the direction of the bank of elevators, which were waiting to take her away from the heart-wrenching situation she had just faced. As she continued to think of her sister's death, the tears once again flowed uncontrollably down her face. As she made her way down the hall, she passed the opened door of the office Cassandra was temporarily using. On cue their eyes met. Cassandra, almost as a reflex, offered a faint smile. Miriam, still with tears in her eyes, could only respond by nodding her head. Cassandra wondered what there was about Ras that seemed to cause so much pain and dissension. For days she had been watching Gisela try to hide her anguish every time she was near Ras. Only another woman could read those familiar longing looks and perpetually sad eyes begging for a sign of recognition. All the while Ras seemed totally unaware. She felt sad for Gisela and sad for the woman who had just passed her office. She knew that there was a part of Ras that was only concerned about himself, and in any entanglement with him, be it business or pleasure, only the strong survived. At that moment a small voice inside her head whispered, *how strong are you?* Her mental answer was, *as strong as I need to be.*

After Ras closed the door behind Miriam as she left his office, he collapsed into a nearby chair. Heat rose in his chest. His throat threatened to close as raw pain and hurt raged through him. Those golden brown eyes of his, which showed the world, at different times and on different occasions, brilliance, stony reserve, unreadable distance, lethal calm and engaging attention, now released one solitary tear, which slowly eased its way down a perfectly sculpted cheek to end at a defiant chin. Ras wiped his face with long, tapered fingers and willed himself not to give in to the overwhelming sadness he felt at the reality of having his son come into the world in the way he had at the time he had. It was not at all what he had planned. His son, he always thought, would have two parents who cared deeply for each other, who were married and living in the same household, rearing him with love and attention. He did not want his son to face any of the distance and isolation he had felt from his father. Now here he was engulfed by a pain that radiated from the center of his being, touching every part of him, but he knew he would find a way to re-solve this particular dilemma.

Cassandra finished up her drawings, outlining furniture placements for each of the housing units. She had designed interiors that were very beautiful but durable and child friendly. She had taken great care to handpick every piece of fabric and every piece of furniture. While working, she had intermittently listened for sounds of Ras' footsteps or his voice, but she had heard nothing. She glanced at her watch and realized that much of the day had passed while she was engrossed in her work. She decided to check in with Afiya to see how her travel plans were coming along. She punched in the international code along with her sister's number and listened. On the second ring, Afiya picked up and answered in her usual chipper "Hello!"

"Hi, Afiya. Where do you get your energy?"

Afiya responded with a smile, "Well, it is late morning. Shouldn't I be up and running?"

"Yes, you should, Sis. Don't let me throw a wet towel on your 'top of the morning' attitude. I'm calling to check on your travel plans. According to my calculations, you should be here in two days."

"Yes, ma'am, I'll be there day after tomorrow. I can't wait. I've scoped out some hot new artists, and I intend to see a few exhibitions while I'm there. I hope you can attend a few with me."

"Oh, I can. It's easy to schedule things around my work here."

"Sounds like you're enjoying what you're doing."

"I am! Afiya, I can't describe it. Just knowing that I am helping to create beautiful, warm, inviting spaces for precious little people makes me feel so good. I have the opportunity to enjoy two of my passions, children and design."

"How's the working relationship going with your Dr. Jekyll and Mr. Hyde?"

"Well, he still has his moments, but being in Ethiopia seems to have a calming effect on him, so I've been able to see another side of him."

"Oh, really? How much of the other side have you seen? I know that tone, Cassandra. What have you two been up to?"

"Not much, a few kisses, a meal or two, and a lot of work."

With a dramatic flourish, Afiya joked, "Oh, back up! A few kisses? Since there have been a few kisses, I'm assuming there is chemistry?"

"Chemistry like I didn't know existed. Do you remember when we first heard Amara talk about how Keino affected her when he kissed her? Well it must run in the family, because the man's touch is magic. Whenever he kisses me, I lose myself and I don't seem to care."

Afiya laughingly responded, "Girl, I'd better hurry up and get on that plane before you lose what seems to be left of your mind."

"No, he may be good at igniting fires, but Mr. Ras Selassie has more baggage than the law allows. His assistant is about to kill herself she is so in love with him, and a few hours ago a woman who came storming into his office left with tears in her eyes. I don't know what that is about, but I assure you, I'm going to find out before I lose myself in his powerful arms again."

"Oh, really? If they are that powerful, missy, you won't know what hit you."

"Well, I just want to be sure that Ras' debris isn't flying around hitting me in the face."

"I hear ya, Sis."

"Well, I'm going to pick up and go have a massage. Since I've been here, I've found this masseuse who is to die for. You would love her technique. I'll make sure I schedule you a few appointments while you're here."

"Sounds good."

"Give my love to Mom, Dad and Adana when you see them."

"I will. You know Adana is involved in a high-profile murder case, so telephone conversations are about all she has time for these days."

"That's what she told me the last time I spoke to her. I told her to be careful. There are so many nut cases around these days."

"You know I meditate on that girl's safety every day."

"Love you, Afiya. See you soon."

"Cassandra, stay out of Ras' arms until I get there. Bye."

Cassandra hung up the telephone while still laughing at

Afiya's parting quip. She packed up her things and headed to her hotel for a much needed massage and a delicious meal.


Ras had been sitting for what seemed like hours. He had asked that all of his calls be held, that meetings be canceled and that he be left alone for the remainder of the day. He had to think his way through his next moves. He now had a son. He was a father. His entire life had changed in a moment. He picked up his telephone and dialed the number of the one person in the world he knew could talk him through this situation, his cousin Keino. Through the years Keino had served him as cousin, brother, father figure, friend, business partner and confidant. There was no one he trusted more. The telephone rang and rang. On the fourth ring, just as Ras had decided to hang up, Keino's voice came on the line.

"This is Keino."

"Hey, man, this is Ras. I was just about to hang up. Were you in the middle of something?"

"My beautiful wife and I were just in the middle of a rather heated exchange when the telephone rang."

"Why did you answer? I think the call could have waited."

"Well, only family has this private line, so when I hear that distinctive ring, I tear myself away from whatever has my attention at the moment, even if it is my most desirable wife."

"I am sorry for the interruption, but this time, Keino, we really need to talk. Something has come up of a personal nature that I cannot handle alone."

"You know I'll help. How do you want to handle it?"

"I need to meet you, Aman, Kaleb, and Kamau in Nairobi in the morning. This situation requires a family council."

"I see. Should I call Dad as well?"

"Let's see what we come up with first. I think we can

handle it. Keino, by the way, let's meet at the law firm. Tell Kamau."

"See you in the morning. Let us say 10 A.M. I will make all of the calls now."

"Thanks, Keino. I am sorry for the interruption."

"No worries, my man. It was just a pause. I assure you, I have not lost my place. Ciao."

They hung up with smiles on their faces. Ras' smile evaporated quickly as he reviewed in his head his conversation with Miriam Zenawi. He picked himself up and headed home to prepare for the trip to Nairobi, Kenya.

# Chapter 11

As Ras flew over the bustling modern Nairobi skyline, his thoughts alternated between the reality that he was now a father and what this newfound information would do to his budding relationship with Cassandra. Somehow telling Cassandra seemed a tougher hurdle to navigate than the prospect of raising his son. For the first time in his life, he had found a woman whose thoughts mattered to him. He wondered what she would think or believe about him once he told her he had a son. His experience with Cassandra had been that she was not long on patience and already saw him as a bit of a rogue. This new development in his life might just send her over the edge, just when they were getting comfortable with one another. He closed his eyes, and with his left hand stretched across his forehead, he began massaging his temples with his thumb and index finger. He needed to see his family, his council of cousins. They would help him sort through the most difficult dilemma he had ever faced.

When the Mazrui company plane landed, Ras stepped from the airplane to a waiting car and was hurriedly driven from the wide expanse of Jomo Kenyatta International Airport to the center of Nairobi. The city center, approximately one square mile, was busy with people going about their business in varying modes of transportation. His car headed down the Uhuru Highway onto Haile Selassie Avenue. On his left he noted the impressive marble facing of the Central Bank Co-operative Society. While Ras was lost in thought, the driver took the first left onto Parliament Way and headed toward the Professional Centre in the direction of the Mazrui law offices. The driver parked the car in front of an imposing ten-story structure composed of glass angles and a quarried stone that produced the color of coral sea shells when the sun's rays burrowed into the façade. This building housed not just the Mazrui law firm but a testament to the strength, unity and nobility that personified the Mazrui clan. After the driver performed his ritualistic duty of opening and closing car doors, Ras walked into the building and was ushered up to the tenth-floor conference room, where he hoped the answers to his fate awaited him.

When he entered the room, the four Mazrui brothers rose to greet him with all of the warmth and exuberance that was customary when they saw one another. Today Ras welcomed being enveloped in their circle of wisdom and understanding. They were indeed the family that he needed at that moment. Before him, he saw four men with whom he knew he could trust his life. Kaleb, with a smile on his face and a body as animated as ever, spoke first.

"Welcome, cousin! I didn't know whether you'd make it here or not. After all, I wasn't the pilot today, and everyone doesn't have my skill in the cockpit."

The others laughed at Kaleb, the brother who always brought levity to any situation. Keino stepped forward, still smiling, and gestured to the chairs around the conference table while saying, "Thanks to God and our ancestors, we have other pilots as capable as Kaleb. Let's take our seats and see how we can assist our cousin."

They sat, each in his own way, examples of the splendor and the virility that is the trademark of African manhood throughout the Diaspora. They sat in varying shades of chocolate, nut brown, cocoa and copper, with keen, intelligent eyes lasered in on Ras, awaiting his explanation for bringing them all together. Ras began slowly and painfully recounting the events of the day before. It required all of his strength and resolve to control the swirl of emotions that flooded through him.

"A few weeks ago I started receiving telephone messages from a woman named Miriam Zenawi. Given my hectic schedule, I initially forgot about her calls. I knew they were personal, and I also assumed there would be high drama connected to the conversation. I was not in the mood to deal with the complexities of the female mind. You see, Miriam and I, from the moment we met, became adversaries. I was dating her sister Zala, and Miriam did not approve. She had the idea that I would not be good for her sister."

Kaleb quipped, with an upturned smile, "I wonder where she got that idea?" The remark brought a smile to everyone's face.

Ras conceded, "OK, I know I've had my moments, but her sister was no helpless waif." Now he was serious again. "She was an emergency-room physician, a very capable one, I might add."

"Wait." This time it was Keino's brother Aman, a soft-spoken cardiac surgeon, who always read between the lines of any conversation. "Ras, you keep speaking of your physician friend in the past tense. Where is she now?"

With remorse in every word, Ras said, "That's the part I'm getting to. It seems Miriam was trying to contact me not just to harass me, but to inform me that her sister had been killed in an auto crash."

A collective sound of sorrow filled the room. Ras continued now, with mounting feelings of rage and the taste of bitterness easing up his throat. "Miriam was trying to contact me not just to tell me that Zala had been killed, but to tell me that before she died, Zala had given birth to my son."

Ras' eyes were misty as he stared at his cousins, all of

whom were frozen in shock. Kamau spoke first, strictly in attorney mode. "Do you have any legal rights to this child?"

Ras, still angry at the prospect of his child being without parents, almost screamed, "Of course, I have rights. I am his father."

Kamau came back, matching the forcefulness of Ras' tone. "These are not days of old. People have become more Western in their thinking. Just because you are the father, if you believe you are, you cannot just waltz in and take the child. If Miriam wishes to do so, she could go to court and deny that her sister ever said anything. Then where would you be? You said she never liked you. What if she changes her mind and decides that she cannot part with the only remaining tangible evidence of her deceased sister?"

Ras let out a deep breath and almost slumped in his chair. "For the first time in my life, my thinking is muddled. All I clearly know is that I want my son."

Keino, who had been silent throughout the conversation, stood up, walked behind Ras' chair, placed both hands squarely on Ras' shoulders and said, "We understand, Ras, and you know you have the backing of the family firm and all of our support in any way that you need it."

Heads around the table nodded in the affirmative. Kaleb, this time in a more serious tone, asked, "How should we begin? It sounds as if there are a few things that need to be done in a hurry."

Kamau answered Kaleb. "You are so right, my brother. The first thing we need to do is to start the proceedings to get legal custody, and we will start with proof of paternity."

Ras spoke up. "I believe that Zala told the truth."

Kamau replied, "Good. I'm glad you believe what she said, but this test is not just to determine whether or not Zala lied. This test will serve as documentation that you have rights as the child's father."

"By the way," said Keino, "what is the name of this newest member of the Selassie family?"

"Ras Kebran. My son is six months old, and he has not yet been properly welcomed into the family of his father."

"It will all be taken care of," Keino remarked.

Aman, with the precision of a surgeon's cut, stated, "While we are preparing to do battle if need be, we must make sure that all i's are dotted and t's are crossed. Ras, we must look at your life. You must present the picture of a man who has a home to bring a baby into. You are a jet-setting bachelor who appears to have no roots. We've got to do better."

"Aman, that is my life, but I will make every arrangement I have to in order to take care of my son."

Aman addressed Kamau. "Kamau, you're the attorney. What do you think?"

"As is often the case, Aman, you are probably right. If it comes to a fight, Miriam and her husband have a lot going for them. One, they have kept the baby since his mother's death. Two, and most importantly, they are a married, loving couple who could provide a stable home."

Now Ras was angry again. His voice rose to a shout. "I am capable of providing for my son. Financially, I am able to provide a life for him that Miriam and her husband cannot match."

"It's not just about the money, Ras. A child needs a loving, nurturing home. Can you provide that?"

Ras stopped and stared at Kamau. His look was unreadable. Keino interjected.

"We all need time to help Ras think this through. Let's sleep on it."

"Meantime," added Kamau, "I will start the documentation trail to prove paternity. Ras, I need Miriam Zenawi's address and telephone so that I can let her know that our firm is representing you in this matter."

Ras replied, "I'll give you everything you need. Just don't make her skittish. I want my son."

The five men spent the rest of the day preoccupied with rounds of golf, lunch, and talk of boyhood pranks and punishments endured because of lies told by one sibling or other. They laughed continually as the stories got better and better with each embellishment. Ras' son, however, was never far from anyone's mind.

# Chapter 12

Cassandra stood at Bole International Airport in Addis Ababa, waiting for Afiya's plane to land. As she stood happily anticipating her sister's arrival, thoughts of Ras eased through her mind. She had seen him the day before, and he had seemed preoccupied and distracted. Not at all the focused, one-track Ras she had come to know. He had, however, insisted that he meet her after she picked up Afiya from the airport so that he could take them dancing and to dinner. He wanted to give Afiya an exciting introduction to the city of his birth. As Afiya stepped through the exit doors of the baggage claim section of the airport, Cassandra spotted her and started waving frantically while walking and shouting loudly "Afiya, Afiya, over here." When Afiya saw her sister, her wave became equally enthusiastic. With a wide grin and peals of laughter, Afiya dropped her bags where she stood, and she and her sister embraced as though they were long-lost friends.

Cassandra stepped away from Afiya, held her at arm's length, and looked at her. "You look so pretty. Your locks have grown, and they are gorgeous. I love that upswept style. It is so elegant, but free flowing. It's you!"

With her signature radiant smile, Afiya responded, "Thanks, Sis. I think I have finally found my style. It's everything I've been longing for in a hairstyle—freedom, beauty, and glam when I want it."

"Well, you hit the jackpot. It is very beautiful on you."

"Thanks, Sis. You are looking great yourself. I'd say from the glow on your face that Addis Ababa, Ras Selassie, the project or all three really agree with you."

Cassandra, with a teasing smile, answered, "I'd say all three." Her smile faded a little as she continued, "But the Ras factor seems to get to be a bit more complex every day."

"So tell me, how are things with you two?"

Cassandra's voice contained an element of thoughtfulness as she spoke. "We feel good together. When I'm in his arms, I feel safe, I feel protected, I feel wanted."

Afiya interrupted again. "What's the 'but' at the end of this description you're giving me? I hear a 'but.'"

Cassandra quickly replied, "The 'but' is Ras' life. My instincts tell me that Ras Selassie has some stuff going on that I'm not sure I want to get wrapped up in."

"Sounds like you're already wrapped, my dear."

Cassandra made a quick retort. "No, not yet. I can always back out."

"Oh really? Doesn't sound like it to me."

Cassandra responded impatiently, hoping she wasn't fooling herself. "Oh, Afiya, let's discuss this later. We have a car waiting to take us to the hotel. Tonight we have dinner with the infamous Mr. Ras Selassie, and you can judge for yourself."

"I can't wait."

Afiya and Cassandra walked hurriedly through the bustling airport to the area where a chauffeured car was waiting. The driver took Afiya's bags and placed them in the trunk of the car. The two sisters were ushered into the luxury sedan, and the driver sped off in the direction of the Sheraton Addis.

When they entered Cassandra's suite, Afiya looked around and, with a smile and a wink at her sister, said, "I can say one thing, my dear. Mr. Ras, like his cousins the Mazruis, really knows how to live. This is beautiful."

Cassandra responded, smiling, "He does know how to live. He has no problem enjoying life's finer pleasures. There are two extra bedrooms. Take whichever one you want."

"OK, great. I'll start unpacking."

Cassandra added, "By the way, I made an appointment for massages before dinner. So get ready for a treat."

"Cassandra, you are a girl after my own heart. You know I never go anywhere in the world without finding a masseuse or a masseur."

"I know you, Afiya. Besides, you know massage is truly one of my guilty pleasures."

An hour later both Cassandra and Afiya were stretched out on massage tables, being lulled into deep states of relaxation in the competent hands of two well-trained massage therapists, who administered combinations of shiatsu, Swedish and deep-tissue massage to the quiet strains of melodic violins piped in through well-hidden speakers. When the pampering ritual was completed, the sisters went into their respective rooms with adjoining bathrooms to dress for the much anticipated evening of dinner and dancing with Ras.

Ras sent a car to take Afiya and Cassandra to a beautiful local restaurant nightclub called the Ghion. When they entered, they were shown immediately to a table and were told that Mr. Selassie had sent a message that he had been detained, but that he was on his way shortly. The maitre d' had been instructed to make them very comfortable and see that they were given whatever they desired. After the waiter left the table, Cassandra looked pointedly at Afiya and said sarcastically, "Now I wonder what dramatic event has captured Mr. Selassie's attention this time?"

"I don't know, but I am sure we will soon find out. In the meantime, let's enjoy the food and the music."

Just as Afiya finished her sentence, a minstrel playing the *massinko*, a one-stringed Ethiopian instrument, strolled up to their table and started playing a haunting melody that was filled with a combination of sadness and joy. As Cassandra was thinking of how much the tune reminded her of Ras, she looked toward the doorway at the entrance of the restaurant and saw enter the man who had on more than one occasion made her world stand still. He entered the room as royally as he always did, elegant stride intact, appearing to be the master of all that he surveyed. Beside him walked a man Cassandra had never seen before. He was tall like Ras. His skin was the color of chocolate-covered raisins and equally smooth. His locked hair was pulled back and hung in soft ringlets down his muscular back. His hairline was expertly edged, and his mustache perfectly groomed. His tailored black suit flowed over his long, exquisitely formed body. His pristine white shirt was opened at the collar, and he wore a silver filigreed Ethiopian cross. When the filtered lighting of the nightclub hit the silver, it danced across his ebony skin, causing his face to glow.

Cassandra turned to tell Afiya that she had spotted Ras, only to find her sister hypnotized by the man entering the room with Ras. Cassandra smiled, gently touched Afiya's arm and said, "I was going to tell you that Ras just came in the door, but I don't think I have to tell you."

Afiya answered in a distracted tone. "I see Ras. Who is that with him?"

"I don't know."

In what seemed like a matter of seconds, Ras and the mystery man stepped up to the table. Ras began speaking as both men stood. "Cassandra, Afiya, please excuse me. I had to make an unexpected detour. Let me introduce my friend. Cassandra Terrell, Afiya Terrell, meet Ibra Diop." Ras added, "Ibra and I were in boarding school together as young lads in Switzerland. We became fast friends on the first day of school and have remained friends throughout the years. He's here on business."

Cassandra and Afiya responded to Ibra with warm hellos as the two men joined them at the table. As Ras continued speaking, Ibra sat mute. He had been stunned by the ethereal beauty of the woman with locks that mirrored his own. He had no idea that Afiya found him equally intriguing and was lost in tantalizing thoughts of him when she heard Ras ask, "Afiya, how was your trip?"

She answered in tones that piqued Ibra's curiosity even more. "It was good. Whenever I travel in Africa, the beauty of the people always takes my breath away." She rushed on, a bit unnerved by the handsome stranger. "I remember my first trip, which was to Senegal. I was so filled with pride when I stepped on that plane, and everyone, pilots, flight attendants and passengers, everyone was an African from throughout the Diaspora. I remember thinking that it was the first time I had experienced being in the majority."

Out of the corner of her eye, Afiya could see the man with the painstakingly coifed shiny black locks, staring at her in a way that gave her the sensation of suddenly being too warm, and so she finished her sentence by saying humorously, "In answer to your question, Ras, I had a great trip, and that is the last lecture you will hear from me on my pride in being of African descent."

Ibra spoke before Ras could respond. In a voice filled with the melodic tones of a lover and the charisma of a star, he said, "Your description was captivating, and I am certain that those people whom you found so beautiful saw themselves in you."

Afiya was speechless. She felt herself melting in her chair. Ibra continued, "You see, I am Senegalese, and I know firsthand how much we appreciate beauty."

The warmth of Afiya's smile echoed in her voice as she said, "Thank you, Ibra. That was very nice of you to say."

He responded, "I thank your parents and your ancestors for blessing us all with your beauty. Now join me on the dance floor. Let's not let this joyous music be wasted. We can eat later."

He placed her hand firmly in his and led her onto the

dance floor. Ras and Cassandra looked at each other and smiled. Ras, with his smile tilting at one corner of his mouth, quipped, "Well, it appears we have been left alone, and I can't say that it bothers me." Stroking her arms with light, feathery touches, he said, "It feels as though I haven't touched you in days."

Cassandra responded, teasing him, "You are right. You haven't touched me in days, two days to be exact."

"Well, please let me rectify that oversight. Let's join Afiya and Ibra on the dance floor and let the music move us as we hold each other." He helped her from her seat, placed a light kiss on her forehead, let his hand slide to her waist and left it there as he led her to the dance floor.

When Cassandra and Ras got to the dance floor, Ibra and Afiya were engaged in a very provocative rendition of the Ethiopian dance called the *iskista*. They were both shaking their shoulders forward and backward in rhythm with the scintillating beat. Ras ignored the fact that the other couples on the floor were also moving their bodies to the *iskista* beat. He wrapped Cassandra in his arms and improvised movements that were rhythmic, sensual and intimate. Cassandra molded her body to his, with her arms around his neck and her head nestled in his shoulder. Ras placed both of his arms around her waist, and as each was engulfed by the other's intoxicating scent, their racing hearts bound them even closer together.

As the evening progressed, the four of them enjoyed a fun-filled time of good food and good music. As the dinner was ending, Ras whispered to Cassandra, "Come home with me."

Since Ibra and Afiya were engaged in a heated discussion and could not hear, Cassandra whispered back, "I can't leave my sister. She just got here."

"All right, so I'll invite them to come along as well for a nightcap. Tomorrow is Saturday."

"Oh, I like that idea."

Ras spoke up, halting the conversation Afiya and Ibra

were having. "Hey, you two, I'd like to invite you to join us at my home this evening for a nightcap."

"Sounds good, man," said Ibra, "but I was just about to convince Afiya that she should join me at a reception that I'm attending this evening for one of the local fine artists. Since I am an art broker and she is a gallery owner, we can combine business with pleasure."

Afiya added, "I'll only go if it's OK with you, Cassandra."

"No problem, Sis. Go and enjoy. Part of your reason for coming was to scope out some of the local artists."

Ibra said, "So it's settled then. I'll call a car, and we'll be on our way."

He retrieved his ever present cellular from his pocket, punched in a code and spoke. "This is Ibra. Send a car to the Ghion as soon as possible."

He flipped the top of his palm-sized cellular and slid it into his pocket. In one smooth move, he helped Afiya from her chair by her hand and bid his farewell to Cassandra and Ras.

Afiya turned to Cassandra before leaving to say, "If you need me, Sis, you have my cell number. Have fun."

"You, too."

After Ibra and Afiya were out of sight, Cassandra turned to Ras, who had wrapped his arms around her. She looked at him pointedly and said, "I hope your friend can be trusted. That is my sister he's with."

Ras shook his head, turned Cassandra's face to look him squarely in the eyes and said, "Sweetheart, you can trust me or anyone I hold dear with your life or the lives of anyone you care about. Now let's go. I need to spend some time with you."

When Ras called for the waiter to bring the check, he was told that Ibra had taken care of it before leaving the building. Ras smiled his upturned smile and said, "He got me again. I should have known. That's all right. There will be other times."

Cassandra asked, "Do you two always rush to see who can pay the bill first?"

"We have been known to do that on occasion."

"Ras, you are quite a character."

"Come home with me, and let me show you a side of me you have never seen."

"That's scary. Do I want to see this other side?"

"Yes, you want to see it, and I want to show you. Let's go."

Ras and Cassandra walked out into the balmy air, stood at the entrance in a loving embrace and waited for the valet to deliver Ras' car. When the car was brought to him, Ras tipped the valet, and after making sure Cassandra was seated, he slipped in behind the wheel of his Maserati. He loved fast cars. He relished the sense of power he felt when wheeling a well-made machine along an open stretch of road. Maneuvering an automobile also gave him time to think, to clear his head. Tonight he needed time to put his thoughts in order because he had to find a way to tell Cassandra that he was a father—that he had a son. He floored the car, reaching speeds that were a bit over the speed limit, and headed for the Addis Ababa suburb in which he lived when he was home. He and Cassandra chatted on and off while listening to the soft strains of John Coltrane as they cruised down a picturesque stretch of tree-lined highway.

When they pulled into Ras' driveway, it brought to Cassandra's mind a manicured paradise. The front lawn looked as large as an eighteen-hole golf course, and the house it surrounded was, in a word, palatial. Cassandra said jokingly, "Ras, you really didn't have to build a community for orphaned children. You really could have let them all live here."

"I'm sorry to disappoint you, but the house really isn't as big as it looks."

"Looks may be deceiving, but I think I know large, and this is over the top, sir."

"I must admit, when I built it, I experimented with a lot of different architectural styles and a way in which to bring them all together, and maybe it got a little out of hand."

"You think?" she said, smiling, with eyes glistening with admiration for the multitalented man she saw before her.

Ras looked at Cassandra with an intense intimacy, which sent a tingling sensation rippling in the pit of her stomach, and said, "Miss Cassandra, are you making fun of me?"

Cassandra opened her mouth to answer, and at that moment Ras took her mouth with his and suckled each lip in its turn. Slowly, gently, he placed kiss after sensuous kiss at the base of her neck, on the tip of her nose, behind each ear and on the inside of each wrist while, using her name as a mantra, he paid homage to her beauty. As Cassandra released a soft whimper, Ras said, "Let's go inside before we are arrested for indecent exposure."

Cassandra took a deep breath and smiled, though her body continued to ache for his touch. "Knowing your family, the police department is probably your own private security force."

Ras laughed and said, "How did you know?"

Cassandra just stared at him and shook her head and laughed. She didn't dare ask if they really owned the police department. She didn't think she really wanted to know just yet how powerful his family was. What she knew was that as they walked into his home, she could feel his power radiate through her. When they entered his front door and stepped into a majestic foyer, Cassandra spoke in soft, admiring tones. "Ras, this is very beautiful. You are away so much. Don't you miss it? Do you really get to enjoy it?"

"Well, I just built it two years ago, and I spend as much time as I can here. My mother is not far from here. I do miss her when I'm traveling. Since I built here, I can at least be a little closer to her when I'm home, and it has always been my plan to make Addis my permanent home, so in the future I will spend much more time here."

He thought, but did not say, that Addis Ababa was to be the place he would bring his wife and rear his children. When he thought of children now, it was no longer a future fantasy. There was a real little boy, his son, waiting. When he thought of his son, it made his heart hurt. Through the pain, he reached for Cassandra, enveloped her in his arms and said, "May I get you anything?"

Cassandra, feeling a shift in his mood, responded, "No, I'm fine. Why don't you take me on a tour of your beautiful home?"

Ras looked deeply into Cassandra's eyes and said, "I'd be happy to if you will promise me that you will not leave until the morning."

Cassandra returned his heated stare and said, "Ras, I can't promise that I'll stay, but I'm here now, so show me the house."

"All right. I'll take your presence in my home any way I can get it, and who's to say I can't provide a tour that lasts all night long."

They both laughed at Ras' quick humor. Hand in hand, they walked from room to room. All of the rooms were tastefully decorated, prompting Cassandra to comment on various pieces and styles. Ras explained that it was his own eclectic mix of furnishings that he had chosen from his travels simply because he liked them. He did not mention that he had left room for the future woman of the house to put her stamp on everything.

The master bedroom suite was the last room on the tour. As they entered, Cassandra said, "Ras, your taste is exquisite. You really didn't need a designer for your project. You could have done it yourself."

"No, no, my darling, filling up a house with things you like is one thing. Taking on the kind of designing required for major projects demands a kind of skill I do not possess. I am not the expert. You are."

He reached out for her, and she slid into his arms as he said, "You are also an expert at clouding my senses. You leave me wanting and wanting you. Tell me, what should I do about that?"

With longing in her voice, Cassandra said, "I don't know, Ras. What do you want to do about it?"

Cassandra knew she was playing with fire, but she was willing to be consumed by the flames. His answer was, "Let me show you."

He picked her up, cradled her in his arms, walked across his long, large bedroom and placed her in the middle of his massive Italian Renaissance four-poster bed. They floated into the silky softness of the comforter that covered the bed. As Ras placed Cassandra in the center of the bed, he eased down beside her and began stroking her hair, thinking to himself how much he wanted to share his bed with her, but knowing he needed to tell her about the new developments in his life. He was, after all, no longer the unentangled bachelor she still assumed he was. She should have the choice to decide whether or not she wanted to tie her life to a man who was now a father. He continued looking at her while gently stroking the satiny smooth softness of her face and the wisps of her hair, which brought to mind the softness of cotton. The look in her eyes spoke volumes to him of her desire. She touched his face, and her long, silky fingers mirrored his strokes. Then, with her index finger, she began to trace the outline of his full, sensual lips, and as she touched the center of his mouth, he opened his lips and captured her finger. He began kissing the finger softly, taking it into his mouth inch by inch until he reached the middle. He then removed her hand and captured her mouth, and with tantalizing strokes and numbing nibbles, he released in her an ecstatic fever, provoking a tingling sensation, which she expressed in a whimper from lips that ached with passion.

Her arms wound themselves around his neck, and his kiss became deeper. Passion streaked through them both, clouding their brains and awakening needs neither of them knew they had for each other. Cassandra's body began to move like liquid fire, setting a stage of sensuality upon which Ras danced with raw abandon. With low, guttural tones, he whispered in her ear, "You make me burn. I need you." His low tone and the desire floating on his breath caused her body to ache even more for his touch. She wanted to feel his warmth on every inch of her soul. She wanted to be seared by his heat. Slowly and seductively, she led him to roll over on his back, and she straddled him. Her knees sank down into the plush down feather bed. Her center touched his core as she slowly started to unbutton his shirt, leaving a trail of kisses on each section of his muscular chest.

She became more aroused as she heard Ras release moans of pleasure. She reached the third button, and he could take no more. He took her face gently in his hands, stopped, stared, opened his mouth to speak but instead roughly pulled her to him and whispered into her hair, "I want you, I want you, I want you." Cassandra heard him through the fog of ecstasy, and as though his words had freed her, she nuzzled against him with erotic movements, and once again their hungry mouths met, feeding flames that were roaring out of control. Her flesh quivered at his touch as he gently rolled her over and began unbuttoning the top of her strapless dress. When he had freed her from the top of her dress, he took each of her breasts in turn and worshipped them with a burning mouth. With each stroke of his tongue, he knew he should tell her about his son, but the trembling of her body thundering with pleasure struck him mute. Her whimpers became wails as Ras reached behind her, unzipped the remainder of her dress and slid it to the floor. He removed her lace underwear, and with a slow, seductive gaze, he traveled the length of her body. She felt drugged by his masculine power and his captivating stare as delicious tremors rode in waves along every inch of her body. Unwilling to contain her desire any longer, Cassandra grabbed the supple leather belt that Ras wore around his waist. As she closed her eyes, and her senses became clouded by his intoxicating male scent, the buckle slipped from her hands. Ras clasped her hands and stilled them. She opened her eyes and looked at him longingly as he kissed each hand and said softly, with need hanging on the edge of each word, "Here, let me help you."

With the ease and grace of a panther stalking his prey, he removed his clothes and wrapped Cassandra in his arms. The nearness of their bodies sent explosive currents racing through each of them. They lost themselves in the heat of the moment. Cassandra rode with the waves of desire that washed over her as she felt the length of Ras' manhood rise against her. He applied feathery strokes to every inch of her body while telling her in raw, seductive tones how he intended to bring her pleasure. She clung to him, holding his shoulders so tightly that she imprinted his flesh with her grasp. She threw her head back, and with lips slightly parted, she breathed in deeply every word he uttered. When her senses had been overloaded with his touch, with his scent and with his words of lust and seduction, she found herself beneath him, writhing in delicious agony. She cried out with gusts of pleasure as he expertly played her center with the strokes of a master pianist. As he ended his artful prelude and began applying deep kisses to the core of her being, Cassandra arched up, with soft moans of passion escaping her throat like trapped butterflies, and Ras thrust into her with a hunger wrapped in more desire than she had ever known. She enfolded him tightly, and they rode waves of ecstasy repeatedly until he spilled into her with a force that racked his body with so much torment and pleasure that he smothered her with a possessive kiss that silenced both their cries. In the aftermath of lovemaking that was as heated as their arguments had been, Ras continued holding Cassandra in his arms, with their legs intertwined. While he stroked her back, he spoke in low, mellow tones, with a smile in his voice.

"You make love with as much force and as much passion

as you fight, and I must say, it is good to know that you can use your sharp tongue for something other than lashing out at me."

Cassandra looked up at him with the eyes of a woman who had been thoroughly loved and, with low, sweet laughter, responded, "I do everything with every fiber of my being."

Ras continued to speak while his mouth went from one tender nipple of Cassandra's breasts to the other. "That's good to know because I want all of you for as long as I can have you."

As Cassandra cried out his name from the ecstasy of having her swollen breasts suckled, Ras answered by entering her once again, this time with slow, rhythmic strokes. Cassandra, throbbing wildly, cried out with pleasure as she left a trail of fingernails down his back.

# Chapter 13

Over the days that followed, Ras and Cassandra enjoyed their time together. Their lovemaking became more and more intense, bonding them in ways neither had ever experienced. They also enjoyed the time spent in the company of Ibra and Afiya, until Afiya left for home and Ibra went back to Senegal.

Ras knew clearly that he needed to confide in Cassandra, to tell her about his son, but he had not done it. He knew he was being unfair, he knew he was being selfish, but he had developed a hunger for her that he knew only time could satisfy. He wanted that time. He needed time to convince her that he wasn't the bad guy in this situation. There was one thing working in his favor. He had just learned that a part of the project was stalled because of a permit snag. He knew he needed at least another month with Cassandra in Addis Ababa, which would buy him time legitimately. He hoped he could plead the case well enough that she would consent to stay and set up a temporary Addis Ababa office at RS Development for Willows Design Firm while she continued work on his project. He knew it could easily be done; he just had to convince Cassandra.

Meantime, all systems were go at the Mazrui law offices because Miriam Zenawi's lawyer had sent the devastating word that Miriam had changed her mind, and she was not going to let go of the only living reminder she had of her sister. Ras knew he was in for the fight of his life, and he wanted Cassandra by his side.

Ras was standing in his favorite spot of his corner office, calming himself with the view of the Zen-like rock garden, when his private line rang with a shrillness that jolted him back to the reality of his life, which had recently become so complicated, it bore little resemblance to the life he had previously known. He walked over, picked up the line and answered with a distracted "Ras here."

The crisp, authoritative voice on the other end of the line responded, "Hello, my cousin. This is Kamau, your relative who is also your lawyer."

Ras responded anxiously, "Kamau, I've been waiting for your call. Where do we stand with the case? When do I bring my son home?"

"Slow down, Ras. The wheels of justice do not roll as quickly as you would like. At the moment this is where we are. I spoke with Miriam's attorney this morning, after he called you. It seems Miriam did not waste much time after my initial conversation with her. After we spoke, I was under the impression that she was ready to keep her word to her sister and give you your son without any difficulty. All of that has changed. I don't know why she changed her mind or if someone changed it for her. What I do know is that it was providential that we had already begun to strategize as though we were going to trial because if a settlement isn't reached, that is exactly where we are headed."

"Kamau, I want my son. We are not going to lose this battle. Whatever you have to do, my son will be reared by his father, and I know that I am his father."

"Fortunately for you, my cousin, the clinical tests bear witness to your assertion. According to the DNA test results, which arrived this afternoon, you are indeed the father."

"So what on earth are you waiting for, Kamau?" Ras

said even more forcefully than before. "Petition the court! Get my son!"

"I am way ahead of you, Ras. Documentation clarifying paternity was ready to be delivered to the court as soon as the test results were returned, but that does not mean that we are not in for a fight. We must still wait for a response, and my guess is Miriam and her lawyer are, as we speak, thinking of ways to nullify your paternity by vilifying your character. Speaking of which, make sure, Ras, that you have told me everything. I don't want any slipups. I am certain they will have you investigated. Are there any other children out there on any continent that I should know about?"

Ras was furious. "Who in the hell do you think I am? You know me, Kamau, and you also know that just as I came to my family when I was told of this son, you would know if there had been another. And for your information and peace of mind, that was the only time until a few nights ago that I have ever been that careless."

Kamau pounced. "A few nights ago? Damn you, Ras. Are you deliberately throwing your life down the toilet?"

"Calm down. What I just said has nothing to do with this case."

Almost screaming, Kamau said, "It has everything to do with this case. Until this madness is over, keep your pants zipped."

In a tone that was lethal in its delivery, Ras responded, "Kamau, all I need from you is for you to get my son. I will take care of my pants, my zipper and my personal life."

"Ras, it is clear that if you took care of your personal life, we would not be engaged in this conversation."

"Kamau, I think I've heard enough, and we have both said enough. Call me when I can bring my son home."

Ras ended the conversation by releasing the phone into its cradle. His conversation with Kamau had brought Cassandra vividly to mind. He had been careless with her. It occurred to him that in the times they had made love, not

once did either of them mention pregnancy, wanted or unwanted. Since Zala had been a physician, he had been
led to believe that there was no danger of an unwanted
pregnancy. He had no idea that Zala very much wanted his
child. His mind started doing somersaults. What was Cassandra thinking? Why had she not mentioned making sure
she did not become pregnant? More importantly, he
thought to himself, why didn't he protect them both? He
had to concede that Cassandra Terrell had him acting in
ways that were definitely out of character. In the silence
of the office where he sat, he had to admit to himself that
he wanted Cassandra more than he had ever wanted any
woman. He knew the moment she walked into his home
that she belonged there. He knew that those spaces that he
had left for his wife-to-be were for Cassandra, and he
knew that he had not protected himself because she was
the woman he wanted to bear his children. There, he had
admitted it to himself. He was in love with Cassandra Terrell. Perhaps he had been from the moment they first
danced, all those months ago. Now he had to convince her,
and he needed to start by getting her to stay in Addis
Ababa longer, for him and for the project.

He picked up the telephone and dialed Cassandra's
office line. She answered "Hello" in a voice that made
Ras want to repeatedly smother her with deep, penetrating kisses. Instead, he said, in an aroused baritone, "Hello
to you, too."

With a faint hint of longing in her voice, Cassandra responded, "Is this *the* Mr. Ras Selassie calling me in the
middle of the workday, using his I wanna play voice?"

With every syllable reeking with seduction, Ras responded, "Oh, do I sound as though I want to play?"

Continuing the suggestive game of words, Cassandra
replied as a shiver of excitement fluttered through her
core, "I think I've heard that tone once or twice, but never
when you were working."

With desire seeping through every word, Ras countered,

"But you see, my beautiful one, that is where you are mistaken. All of this time I have been working to make you mine."

Her voice lowered, and the softness of it dripped slowly over him like honey as she asked, "Is that what you've been doing?"

"Haven't you felt it, Cassandra? There have been times when our spirits have become one. I know that I have flown to unknown places, and you were on the journey with me. We have been locked together in a dance of destiny, my sweet."

"Ras Selassie, your lines are so good, they really should be outlawed."

"I don't use lines, beautiful. I only speak the truth as I know it. We have something very magical, Cassandra. Let us enjoy it. Now I will ask, would you like to come out to play?"

Cassandra hesitated for a moment and answered, "I would love to play, Mr. Selassie, but I have a very demanding boss, and you see, I am working on this very important project. I have to meet Kunle, the project manager, in ten minutes. So you see, I think I'll just have to put my playtime on hold."

"Such dedication, but then I was once told that you do everything with every fiber of your being, and so it is. But tonight you are all mine. I am taking you to my mother's for dinner."

"That's great. You know I was given strict orders to see your parents before I left home."

"I didn't say my parents. I said my mother."

"OK, when should I be ready?"

"About five. See you then, and be careful out at that site."

Smiling and teasing, Cassandra answered, "OK, Mr. Boss Man. See you tonight."

With a husky whisper, Ras ended the call, "Good-bye, Cassandra."

* * *

RS Development's company driver picked Cassandra up and drove her to the outskirts of the city, where the community to house orphans was under construction. As her chauffeured car made its way down a graveled path, she spotted Kunle, the project manager, waving to her. She instructed the driver to pull up to the front of the structure, where Kunle stood. When the car stopped, Kunle rushed over to open the door for Cassandra to exit. As he opened the door, she smiled and said, "Hi, Kunle. Sorry I'm a little late. The boss called."

"No worry, Cassandra. When Ras calls, we must all stop," he said jokingly.

"I'm here now. Let's get this show on the road. Show me the structures that are nearest to completion. We've got to select materials for flooring and fixtures."

"All right." He looked at her feet and said, "Let me transport you in our little golf cart. I'm not sure your shoes can take the graveled paths."

"I'm sorry. I was in such a hurry, I forgot about changing shoes."

They got into the cart, with Kunle in the driver's seat. He was a long, lean man with ebony-colored skin and a quick smile. He had worked with Ras on numerous projects over a number of years. He knew Ras well and considered him a friend. Watching him with Cassandra, he sensed that this was a different attachment for Ras Selassie. He had never seen him as attentive or as concerned. This was new, indeed. He turned his head slightly while driving and asked, "Well, Cassandra, how have you found your stay in Addis so far?"

"Oh, I love the city. The people are warm and friendly. I've been having a really good time. One of my sisters came to visit since I've been here, and we had a ball. This particular sister owns an art gallery, and she found a thriving community of contemporary artists here."

"Well, good. I hope that means you will visit again. I am Nigerian myself, but I always enjoy coming here. We are here so often, many times I bring my wife and children. They love the country as well."

"You have children? How many?"

"My wife and I have six. Four sons and two daughters."

"Oh my, you two certainly have your hands full."

"Yes, we do, but we both believe that family is everything. In our culture one does not exist without family. I hope that some day my friend Ras is able to find a mate and create a family."

Cassandra asked, "Are you sure that is something Ras really wants to do?"

"Yes, I know that he is a man whose heart is bigger than he will ever let anyone see."

As Kunle and Cassandra walked through the half-finished structures, thoughts of Ras floated in and out of her mind. Scenes of their passionate encounters washed over her in waves. She had flashes of the sound of his erotic whispers and of the air around her becoming permeated with his scent. It took all of her effort to focus on scale and dimensions, colors and textures. Her body craved the scale, dimensions, colors and textures that were Ras. She wanted never to be released from the long, lean, muscular legs that enveloped her after the raging power of his love-making. She ached for the touch of his copper skin, which was both hard and soft as it blanketed her trembling body. She wanted over and over again the taste of full, sensuous lips that belonged to a mouth that nipped and bit and kissed and caressed all at once, commanding and demanding cries of pleasure shrouded in the pain of deep longing. She wanted Ras. She had experienced with him a dimension of love and loving she never knew existed. She had never thought she would ever find someone to love again after Christopher, and yet here she was, continents away, yearning for every touch of Ras Selassie's hand.

After the project inspection, Kunle and Cassandra said their good-byes, and Cassandra was driven back to her hotel by a waiting driver. On the drive back, she continued

her thoughts of Ras, thinking about how troubled he sometimes seemed. In the throes of lovemaking, the Ras who
loved long and hard, who cared deeply and who was
fiercely loyal and possessive, came to the surface, shedding all of the bravado and the short-tempered antics of a
taskmaster. Even now, though, there were parts of him
clearly hidden and off limits. One of those areas was a
father he never mentioned and who caused him to become
agitated if anyone else did. Maybe the visit to his mom's
home for dinner would shed some light on a very touchy
subject.

Just as Cassandra entered her hotel room, her telephone
rang. She spoke into the receiver, "Hello."

The familiar, sultry voice on the other end of the line
responded, "I am coming to play."

As easily as it had spoken, the voice was gone, leaving
only a dial tone. Cassandra looked at the telephone,
placed it in its cradle, smiled and said, "So you want to
play, do you, Mr. Selassie? Let the games begin."


One hour later, Ras knocked on Cassandra's door. When
she opened the door, he entered and was enveloped in
burning oils emitting the scents of jasmine and lavender.
They were Cassandra's favorites. The scents relaxed her
and left her feeling a welcomed euphoria. The music being
played was a haunting Ethiopian instrumental melody, a
song about the agony and the ecstasy of unfulfilled love.
Cassandra's feet were bare, and she wore a red caftan made
from a vaguely transparent silk. She wore nothing underneath, and therefore, when near any illumination, her
silhouette left much to the imagination. That was her intention, to tantalize Ras to the point of absolute and total
distraction. As he entered the room, he embraced her, gathering her into his arms like lost treasure, softly kissing
her eyes, cheeks, forehead, nose, chin and the base of her
neck while telling her how much he needed to hold her, to

touch her and to be inside of her. Then he took her mouth, and the kiss released a fire that seared them both. When the kiss ended, Ras lifted Cassandra into his arms and started walking toward her bedroom. He whispered in her ear, "What game are we playing now?"

Cassandra answered through a fog of sexual heat, "I don't know. It's your call."

In a voice so filled with need, she felt it at her core, he said, "Oh no, my beautiful one, I came to play. You name the game." He placed her on the bed and began to kiss and suckle one red toenail after the other while using one hand to lace his way up the length of her smooth, silky thighs. As Cassandra repeated his name over and over again, he continued to ask her, while teasing her and bringing her to maddening heights of ecstasy with each kiss, stroke, nibble and bite, "What game are we playing?"

Cassandra in a tortured whisper answered, "Surrender."

Ras, with finesse and speed, removed his clothing while he watched Cassandra as she moved on the bed with a sensuality that set his soul on fire. He continued making love to her verbally by painting vivid pictures for her of what surrender meant to him. When he had freed himself of his garments, he gathered Cassandra's caftan and removed it with one hand, and with the power and force of a man possessed, he entered her as she released cries of sweet surrender. They made love until all they could do was hold on to one another for fear of floating away. They both marveled at the fact that they had found so much pleasure in another human being. Ras silently traced the outline of Cassandra's body with his hands while thinking about how he should tell her about his son. He knew he had to, but he couldn't bring himself to do it, and so he talked about other things. He spoke with a voice still coated with the remnants of a passionate encounter.

"My sweet, I really don't believe I will ever have enough of you. Each time we come together is better than the last. I never know what to expect. You give yourself to me in ways that leave me mad with desire. I never want another man to touch you. You should always be mine, as I will be yours."

Cassandra became so still, Ras could not hear her breathe. He whispered, "Cassandra, did you hear me?"

She heard him, and his words touched her heart, but she also knew that before she committed anything to Ras, she needed to be very clear about what he meant in terms of their exclusivity. What was the purpose, the point, the reason? What was he asking?

She answered quietly. "I heard you, Ras, but what are you asking? Are you asking that I only make love to you for the rest of our lives? Just hang around being available for your pleasure? Are you asking me to be your long-distance lover? Do you want us to grow old together, making love in bedrooms around the globe? What are you asking?"

With exasperation in his voice, Ras answered, "I am asking that you let us be so that time will tell what we become."

Looking into his eyes and finding love so deep it almost frightened her, she asked, "Is time all that we need, Ras?"

"I do need time, my darling." He hesitated, then said, "There are some affairs I would like to settle. One of them is this. A project snafu has occurred with a permit, and I need you to please extend your stay for another month. Everything you need will be at your disposal. And, my lovely Cassandra, before I put any more pressure on you to give me your heart, please know this, my sweet, I will always give me your heart, please know this, my sweet, I will

"I'm not sure I know that, Ras. I know that you will always give me the physical part of you any time you or I desire that, but even now, there are parts of you that you do not allow me to share. You go somewhere deep inside yourself, and when you do that, no one can reach you, no one."

Ras thought quickly and rapidly weighed the pros and cons of taking the moment to share with the woman he loved his deepest secret, that he had a son. He decided in a flash that the time was not right. He enfolded Cassandra in his arms and stroked the length of her body with long, feathery strokes while he kissed the nape of her neck with adoring, sensuous kisses. When he had aroused them both again, he looked at her and said, "Cassandra, I want you to know that whatever happens as our lives unfold, I will always want you. I will always want you. Do not forget that. And now, my sweet, I would suggest that we prepare to go to my mother's for dinner." With a loving tap on Cassandra's bottom and a kiss on her cheek, he left the bed and moved with the sensuality of their lovemaking still dripping from his limbs as Cassandra watched. The rhythm of his movements left her longing for more and wondering what was missing.

Some time later the two of them were once again riding on the outskirts of Addis Ababa, headed toward the home of Ras' mother and father, Mr. and Mrs. Tafari and Amara Selassie. The early evening air was pleasantly warm, and so Ras had the top down on his Bentley coupe. The car was one of Ras' favorites because it combined luxury and high performance. As he drove, he thought how seamlessly Cassandra moved in his life, whether it was in his office, in his home, riding in his collection of cars or in any social setting. He was clear he did not want her to evaporate from his life.

Cassandra sat beside him, resting comfortably on caramel-colored leather seats, head back, eyes closed, feeling the sensation of gentle breezes tiptoeing across her slightly moist skin. Her mind was filled with thoughts of Ras as he skillfully maneuvered the high-performance automobile to the strains of an Ethiopian instrumentalist being piped in through surround-sound speakers. She wondered where he went when he closed off that part of himself that no one could reach. It was such a contrast to the open, giving, thoroughly present man she experienced when the two of them made love. She wondered what that said about any future they could have together, and she wondered if the closed part of him had anything at all to do with the pained looks on Gisela's face and the tall, attractive woman she saw crying in the office.

Just as she took a deep breath and resolved that she would put her thoughts aside for the time being, she heard Ras say, "My beautiful one, here we are." He touched her thigh, and the heat of his hand seared her through the fabric of her linen dress. She opened her eyes and slowly sat up in the seat as Ras drove the car down a driveway that resembled a long road. Each side of the road was lined with lush trees. They looked as though they had provided years of shade, comfort and beauty for all who traveled the road. The home, which she could see at a distance, was stately and old-world. It looked as though it might have been set in one of the old kingdoms in Gonder or Auxum in ancient Ethiopia.

As Ras pulled his car up to the front door, a gentleman appeared and said, "Hello, Mr. Ras. I will park your car in the garage for you."

Ras and Cassandra turned to walk to the front door to enter Ras' parents' home. When they reached the door, he looked at Cassandra and, with an upturned grin, whispered while ringing the doorbell, "I was so busy trying to get to you to see which game we would play that I left my key. Now you can see clearly how much I am yours for the taking."

Her senses whirled with his closeness and with the wisps of his breath, which carried the aroma of freshly scented air. Her center melted as she remembered the game they had played, and as she was regaining her composure enough to respond to him, the massive door opened. A stoic woman with graying temples and a frown on her pinched face announced as though she were declaring an edict, "Mr. Ras, you do not have your key."

Ras, keeping a straight face though he felt like laughing, said, "Mama Fana, you are correct. I have left my key, but may I still enter my childhood home?"

Fana Berhane smiled a reluctant smile and said, "Yes, come in even without a key."

Once again Ras turned to Cassandra and said, "Mama Fana, I'd like you to meet a very special friend, Cassandra Terrell. Cassandra, this curmudgeon of a woman is Mrs. Fana Berhane, my Mama Fana. She has known me since I was two years old, and she still treats me as though I'm two, don't you, Mama Fana?"

Now they were both smiling as Mrs. Berhane said, "Only when I need to."

Cassandra and Mrs. Berhane exchanged greetings while Cassandra laughed to herself at visions of Ras as a two-year-old. She knew he had to have been a holy terror. She was sure he had put a new twist on the phrase terrible twos. She looked up to see Ras' mother standing in the archway of a room at the end of an elongated hallway. She stood erect, smiling and beautiful. Ras took Cassandra's hand, and they walked toward his mother. Her smile got brighter the closer they got to her. She reached out first to Ras, wrapped him in her arms and said, "My one and only son, it is so good to have you home, and I am doubly pleased that you have brought such a lovely guest. When you told me you were bringing Ana's daughter for a visit, I was so excited." She was addressing them both but spoke directly to Cassandra as she said, "Welcome to our home, Cassandra. I almost feel as though I know you. When your mother was here, she shared many stories about her lovely daughters. She is so proud of all of you, and rightfully so. Come, you two. Let's sit before dinner and visit a while."

Cassandra and Ras followed Amara Selassie through two heavily carved doors into a room that was as exquisitely adorned as its owner. The walls were washed in ivory, with a gold-leaf trim accentuating archways and the pillars that were their foundation. The unusually high ceilings were ringed with molding reminiscent of the eighteenth-century rococo period. Crystal sconces hung on walls that were covered in a textured bronze silk. Chandeliers and tall bronze lamp stands were anchored in place, waiting to flood the room with light when needed. Overstuffed sofas and chairs covered in lush fabrics invited one to sit amid tapestried pillows adorned with strategically placed tassels.

One corner of the room held a grand piano, and over the mantle of an elaborately carved fireplace hung a family portrait in a gilded frame. In the portrait Ras sat between his parents. He appeared to be no more than ten years old. The portrait captured a sadness in his eyes that still remained. The only smiling face in it was that of Ras' mother. Ras and his father sat, two stoic figures appearing to be there out of obligation and duty. Tall leafy plants, beautifully green and obviously well cared for, stood in designated spots around the room, giving it an added warmth.

Ras and Cassandra sat on a sofa facing the one on which Amara Selassie sat. Watching them as they sat, Ras' mother noticed an air about her son and the lovely young woman beside him. A certain electricity radiated in the room when they exchanged a glance. And she noticed that the discreet way her son found to touch their beautiful guest was protective, territorial and filled with a need that only an observant mother would recognize. Cassandra was the first to speak.

"Mrs. Selassie, your home is very beautiful and very warm. I'm happy I had a chance to visit with you while I'm here in Addis."

Amara Selassie, still smiling, feeling the joy of seeing her son happy, responded, "I am happy that my son brought you to visit. May I have some refreshments brought out before our meal?"

Cassandra, still feeling the remnants of Ras' devastatingly powerful lovemaking, answered in a quiet relaxed tone. "No, thank you. I am fine. I'd rather not take the risk of spoiling my dinner."

Taking advantage of an opportunity she did not often

have, Amara Selassie responded, "Then while we wait, Ras should play for us. I haven't heard him bring his magic to the piano for a very long time."

Cassandra turned to Ras with a look of complete surprise on her face as she said, "You never told me you could play."

With sparkling eyes and a tilted smile, Ras answered, "You never asked."

Cassandra laughed out loud. "Ras, the mysteries surrounding you just keep unfolding."

His mother added, "Ras doesn't just play. He could have been a professional musician." Now it was her turn to laugh aloud. "But he just couldn't bear to bring the world that much pleasure."

Ras rose fluidly and moved toward the piano while saying, with a lightheartedness that was rare for him, "I hope you two are enjoying all of this laughter at my expense."

He slid onto the leather tufted piano bench and automatically took the position of a master pianist. With hands skillfully poised over the keys, he began the most beautiful rendition of *Moonlight Sonata* that Cassandra was sure she had ever heard. As she watched him play, the passion that seemed to drip from every inch of his body was mesmerizing. He moved effortlessly into a jazz piece and then a traditional Ethiopian song, which his mother sang in a voice that was lilting, haunting and beautiful. Cassandra was amazed at the talent of both Ras and his mother. Just as she was applauding the last song, the houseman entered and said with quiet authority, "Dinner is served."

Cassandra was so moved by Ras' playing that she walked over to the piano as he stood and took both of his hands in hers and said, "You are full of surprises, Mr. Selassie. That was more beautiful than I can say. Your mother was right. You could be a professional musician."

Stroking the backs of her hands while holding them, he responded, "It is not the life I chose, but I am grateful for the gift."

Ras' mother, noting the exchange, smiled and said, "Dinner awaits us."

As she moved toward the door to enter a magnificently appointed dining room, Cassandra thanked Amara Selassie for being such a gracious hostess, and for her beautiful solo, and followed her into the dining room, feeling very much at peace.

Through dinner it was evident to Cassandra that Ras and his mother cared deeply for one another. Ras was very solicitous of his mother and once again showed Cassandra a side of himself that was open and warm and loving. She felt safe whenever he exhibited the kind of compassion he showed toward his mother. The doubt came when the warmth disappeared, and his countenance took on the grave severity of a polished steel blade. His mother was a very kind woman. Tall, stately and extremely beautiful, she was physically a female Ras. She enjoyed laughter and really enjoyed telling Cassandra stories of Ras' escapades as a child and as a teenager. She also regaled Ras and Cassandra with stories of her college days with Cassandra's mother, Ana. Cassandra came away from the conversation with the idea that Ras was indeed a handful, and that she admired his mother's wit, charm and exquisite beauty.

The lavish meal of fresh tomatoes and green peppers; mixed vegetables with blended spices; okra *bamya alich'a*; lentil soup; a mild potato stew; *yedoro t'ibs*, or fried chicken; *injera*; fresh juices and honey wine was followed by an elaborate coffee ceremony. The coffee ceremony, a tradition in Ethiopian households, was the part of the meal that Amara Selassie enjoyed most. Coffee's origination in Ethiopia gave it a place of respect and appreciation in homes across the country. The ceremony itself gave Mrs. Selassie a sense of calm and tranquility, not to mention immense pleasure to her senses of taste and smell.

Two housemen entered the room, carrying a four-legged altarlike table, and gingerly placed it in a corner. They then left the room, and a woman entered carrying a silver tray laden with objects to be used for the ceremony. Cassandra watched the ritual with keen interest, and Ras watched her with deep love and affection showing on his face. Amara Selassie watched them both, extremely pleased with what she saw. The woman preparing the utensils for the ceremony started spreading fragrant grasses on the floor in one corner and on the table itself, symbolic of bringing some of the freshness from outside indoors. She then sat on a low stool in the corner where the grasses were scattered, beside a charcoal brazier. She then lit incense to further heighten the senses. Over the charcoal brazier, she began roasting green coffee beans, shaking them and turning them to roast them evenly.

The aroma was pungent and powerful. The scent rode pleasantly through pleased nostrils as the preparer of the coffee walked easily around the room with the pan of evenly roasted coffee beans, shaking them to enhance the aroma for each person present at the table. She then heated water in a traditional clay coffeepot, added the coffee, let it boil and poured it with grace and finesse into tiny cups without handles. She added sugar to each cup and served Ras, Mrs. Selassie and Cassandra. The tradition normally required the drinking of three rounds, with each round getting weaker with the addition of more water. Thoroughly satisfied, they stopped at two.

The evening had been a treat for all. Cassandra had been given a further glimpse into the life of Ras Selassie. Amara Selassie had experienced for the first time her son bringing a woman to her home. Though he had done so under the guise of bringing a friend's daughter to visit, she knew as his mother that there was more to Cassandra's appearance at her dinner table with Ras then just his willingness to do a good deed.

Ras was conflicted. Though he was thrilled to have spent time with Cassandra and his mother, he also knew that he had to end the evening knowing that there were two women whom he loved but with whom he could not share the most important happening in his life. The existence of his son. He needed the whole dreadful custody business finished so that he could place his son rightfully within his circle of family and friends. He hoped the time would be soon. While he and Cassandra sat enjoying his mother's hospitality, the sun had disappeared in the heavens. He hoped that the sun's disappearance was not a cosmic statement about the light in his life.

# Chapter 14

After Ras and Cassandra said their good-byes to Mrs. Amara Selassie and were on their way back to the hotel, Cassandra realized that she had not seen Ras' father. Still in a lighthearted mood from dinner, she asked, "Ras, where was your dad? It just occurred to me that he didn't join us for dinner."

Ras' very curt, clipped answer cut her like a knife. "I do not know. My father is not attached to my hip."

The silence following his statement was deafening. Cassandra turned in her seat to face him more squarely. She wanted to check to see if the Ras she had come with had been replaced by a double. He looked the same, but the mention of his father had changed the vibration of their universe. Cassandra spoke in a tone that was as deliberate and as icy as she could make it.

"Ras Selassie, I have no intention of turning flips every time your mood changes. I merely asked about your father, and you responded to me as though I had committed a crime." She almost screamed, "What is wrong with you?"

Her flaring temper shook him to his core. He had had no intention of hurting Cassandra; he was simply protecting himself. Cassandra threw up her hands in exasperation and turned her body so that she was facing straight ahead once again. Ras reached over to touch her, and she recoiled from his touch. "Don't you dare touch me after treating me like a pariah. This is it, Mr. Selassie. You don't ever have to speak to me again, and then neither of us will have to be concerned about offending anyone. I am beyond tired of your mood swings, Ras."

He swiftly pulled the car over to the side of the road, turned off the motor and slumped in the seat. He lifted his head slowly, and with hooded eyes lasered in on Cassandra with an intensity that was dark and powerful, he began to speak slowly and quietly. "Cassandra, you have no idea about my relationship with my father," he added sarcastically, "or should I say the lack of a relationship. I did not intend to hurt you or to make you angry. I am not accustomed to engaging in conversation about General Tafari Selassie."

Cassandra took a deep breath and began speaking calmly, with a tinge of despair hanging on the edge of each word. "Ras Selassie, we have shared the most important parts of ourselves with one another, our hearts and our bodies, and here you sit telling me that you can be excused even though you attempted to bite my head off because I asked about your father's absence at dinner. There is something horribly wrong with that picture."

Ras sat up straighter and continued looking deeply into Cassandra's eyes while hers stared back with equal intensity. He answered her in words that were slowly measured, wrapped in a defensiveness that Cassandra could feel as well as hear.

"Are you telling me that you have told me every feeling and thought you've had about everyone in your life, past and present?"

"No," she began patiently, as though explaining something rudimentary to a child. "What I am saying, Ras, is that I would not cut off your head if you asked me a simple question. I would not treat you like an enemy for an expression of curiosity. I don't like being treated badly and neither do you, and I am not going to allow you to dismiss my feelings about anything, no matter how small. Do we have an understanding?" She didn't wait for an answer before saying, "Now take me to the hotel. I no longer care where your father was."

With that parting shot, she turned away. Unable to handle the reality of Cassandra shutting him out, Ras turned in the seat and, with two strong hands, grabbed her shoulders and turned her to face him. The emotion in his eyes riveted her to the seat. The underlying sensuality in the words that followed broke her fragile resistance. "Cassandra, I have never shared my heart with a woman in the way that a man does when he loves completely and wholly. You have made me understand what has been missing in my life. I can't lose you now. I can't." He brought her close to him slowly. He could feel her body release the momentary anger it had stored in her shoulders and back, and so he ravished her mouth, pulling from her a depth of feeling reserved only for him. When the kiss faded in its intensity but lingered in its essence, Ras whispered while touching Cassandra's lips with his, "Please, my sweet, don't shut me out. Please don't shut me out. I need you, I need you."

Cassandra responded in ragged breaths, caused by her response to his touch and his impassioned pleas. "And I need you, Ras, to let me in. I need you to share more with me than just your body. I need that. I can't exist in a relationship where the man who says he wants me hides from me important pieces of who he is."

She took a deep breath and continued. "Your relationship with your father is an example of that. For the last few minutes, we have been in the throes of an argument because of your father, and I don't even know why. Is that really fair?"

Stroking her arms as he spoke, Ras said, "No, my sweet, it is not fair, and most importantly, I want us to be able when necessary to tell each other everything that is important to our well-being. And so I will say this." In a voice filled with sadness and remorse, he spoke of his father. "My father is a hard man. He is, after all, career military. My grandparents on both sides were landed gentry, educated business people. My father decided to blaze another trail and broke with family tradition. I have heard stories that he was always combative, and so the choice of a military career should not have surprised anyone. Maybe it didn't surprise them, but it certainly angered my paternal grandfather, and so the kind of estrangement that has become the mark of the Selassie family began with my father and his father and continues with my father and me.

"Between the estrangement from his own father, his natural combativeness and the military training, being my father's son was no easy task. He was uninvolved and he was uncaring. I never remember my father touching me out of love, or offering a word of encouragement, and most importantly, memories of my mother's tears will always haunt me. Wasted tears over a man who knew nothing about love. To this day he is roaming the world in search of something it is doubtful that he will ever find. And so you see, my sweet, conversations about my father usually leave me angry and bitter. When you questioned me, I wasn't prepared, and so I just reacted. I behaved badly, and I promise that with you it will never happen again."

"Ras, that behavior really shouldn't be directed toward anyone, should it?"

"I can't even begin to analyze how I should behave with other people as it relates to my personal life. I can only say definitely that I promise you that with you it will not happen again. I also need you to trust me, Cassandra. Trust that whatever it appears that I am doing, I will never hurt you or put you in a situation that is detrimental to you."

"I do trust that, Ras. I do know in my heart that you don't intend to hurt me."

Looking longingly at the woman he adored, Ras asked, "And so, my sweet, have you forgiven me enough to share your bed with me tonight? I need to fly to Kenya in the morning, and the person I must wake up to is you."

Cassandra paused and with a half-smile answered, "After your behavior tonight, ruining a perfectly good evening, do you think that you deserve my presence?"

"Love of my life, if the truth be known, I have probably never deserved your presence, but tonight I'll do whatever you require to have it."

Cassandra shook her head, lowered her eyes and asked, "Ras, what am I going to do with you?"

He simultaneously started up the car and said, "Let me show you."

Cassandra and Ras rode in silence under a starlit sky, lost in thoughts of each other. Ras kept his free hand on the part of Cassandra's dress that covered her left thigh, touching gently, not wanting to disturb their tenuous truce, anticipating what was to come.

Cassandra was filled with emotion as they cruised along the suburban roads leading away from Ras' parent's home, heading in the direction of the Sheraton Addis. Her heart was his, yet she had her doubts about the potential of any longevity. Ras was Ras in all of his glory, prone to mood swings, arrogance, and an erratic temper. At the same time he could be vulnerable, compassionate, and had a way of setting her body on fire that was beyond anything she had ever imagined.

When they arrived at Cassandra's hotel, they made their way to her suite and made love with an urgency neither of them understood.

When the early morning sunlight caressed her closed eyelids and gently shook Cassandra awake, she stretched her long limbs with feline sensuality. As she moved her slender, shapely legs across the softness of the bed's Egyptian cotton sheets, she was fully awakened by the absence of Ras in her bed. She quickly opened her eyes, looked at the pillow where he had slept and smiled when she saw a note. It read: *My sleeping angel, you made my night blissful, and your sweet love will keep me smiling as I fly to Kenya this morning. I will call you when I return.*

With thoughts of a night of pleasure tiptoeing through her mind, she eased out of bed, took a leisurely bath, had a continental breakfast and was chauffeured in to her temporary offices at RS Development. She needed to organize her work schedule since she had consented to move a number of Willows Design projects to Addis Ababa due to her extended one-month stay. The new arrangement was a mixed blessing personally and professionally.

Cassandra strolled into RS Development, still basking in the glow of a night of lovemaking that had been shrouded in smoldering heat and raw possession, and a morning graced by delicious food and a loving note. The Ras she knew and loved was back, as attentive and as loving as ever.

She passed Gisela in the hallway on the way to her office. The two greeted one another. Cassandra's greeting was more enthusiastic than Gisela's, but she took it in stride and moved on to begin her day. Cassandra's temporary office was comfortable and very sleek and modern. She placed her handbag on a glass-topped writing table, and when she sat down in a high-backed leather desk chair, she felt herself release a breath she didn't realize she was holding. She smiled a contented smile as a picture of Ras floated before her mind's eye.

She reached for the telephone near her and decided to call her sister Amara, who was now at home in Nairobi, Kenya, with her husband, Keino Mazrui, Ras' cousin. She punched in the numbers and waited for the foreign ring tone to begin. After a few seconds she heard a cultivated East African female voice say, "Hello, this is the Mazrui residence."

Cassandra responded, "Hello, my name is Cassandra Terrell. May I please speak with my sister, Mrs. Amara Mazrui?"

"One moment please, ma'am."

Shortly she heard an exuberant, "Cassandra, how are you? It is so good to hear your voice."

"Hi, Sis. I finally got a minute to just breathe, and so I thought I'd give you a call. So how is life in the grand city of Nairobi?"

"Good, good, really good. I've even been doing some consulting and expanding my Virginia business. My staff in Virginia has really been great. Everyone has settled in to make this transition work, and the travel back and forth has been easy."

"It is great when it happens easily. I'm experiencing a taste of that myself. We ran into a few snags here, so Ras has asked me to extend my contract for a month, which means a little shuffling to keep Willows Design moving smoothly while I'm in Ethiopia. Thank God for a great staff."

"By the way, Miss Cassandra," Amara interjected, "Afiya tells me that when she was in Addis, things were really heating up between you and Mr. Ras. I told her she had to be lying, because I remember how you were going to kill him and only leave enough pieces for the coroner to identify, remember?"

They both keeled over with laughter. Cassandra, with humor in her voice, feigning amnesia, asked, "Did I say that?"

"Yes, you said it, and at the time you meant it."

The laughter faded. Amara asked, "What has changed?"

"Now *that*, my sister, is a million-dollar question, and my answer is so trite. How about he made me love him. Or he grew on me, or the man is so fine, he makes me weak, or sometimes I want him so badly, I can taste him in my sleep, or—"

"Sis, you can stop now," Amara interrupted, laughing again. "I think I get the picture. We were always told by our parents that Africa was a magical continent. Sounds like you found the same magic that I discovered."

"Funny you should mention that. I just told Afiya when she was here that whenever I talk about Ras, I sound like you talking about Keino."

Amara added to Cassandra's assessment of Ras and Keino. "Honey, those Mazrui Selassie men ought to be recorded as the Eighth and Ninth Wonders of the World." They again fell into easy laughter.

"Hey, I just thought about something. While Ms. Afiya was tellin' all of my business, did she tell you that she was here running around with Mr. Ibra Diop?" Cassandra's speech sped up as she joked lightheartedly about Afiya's new friend. "Did she tell you that we could hardly enjoy our first night here because she had to accompany him to an art reception, and did she tell you how much chemistry was flying between those two?"

Amara, totally amused by the humorous banter, said, "I think I got the picture, and the answer to all of your questions is yes." They could not contain their laughter. As the laughter faded, Cassandra switched gears.

"Hey, Amara, have you heard how Adana's high-profile murder case is going?"

"I don't know. I haven't been able to talk to her, and all she tells Mom and Dad is that she's going to win. You know if the case can be won, she will win it!"

"I do know that. Amara, are you doing any better making the adjustment to having servants? I know it was difficult at first. Is it any easier?"

"A little. I think Mom and Dad were so busy preparing us to serve our community, I for one was not prepared to be served, but Keino insists. And it is the norm for people who can afford it here, and as my husband keeps reminding me, it is a boost to the economy. I think it helps, too, because in most households people who work in the household are treated like family, and you know the Mazruis treat everyone well. That makes it easier for me."

"Good. I am really happy for you that it's all coming together. By the way, Ras flew in to Nairobi this morning. You might see him. Take another look if you do, and tell me what you think."

"I might see him. I know Keino said this morning that they were all meeting in Kamau's office and that he would call me later about dinner plans. I've got a women's association meeting today with Keino's mom, my sisters-in-law and a number of other extended family and friends. These meetings go on all afternoon. They remind you of a sorority meeting on steroids."

They laughed at the picture Amara painted and said their good-byes.


Gisela Graff sat at her desk with the blinds closed, blocking light, thinking about how hopelessly lost she felt. She had tried for years to let Ras know how she felt, and he had missed every clue. She had tried being indispensable to him. She had learned every quirk and idiosyncrasy. She had studied him in the hope that she could find the right button to push, the right word to say, but nothing had happened. He had never looked at her the way he looked at Cassandra Terrell. He had never looked at her period in the way that a man looks at a woman. Even now she knew something was going on with the Zenawi woman, but Ras shared nothing. She was his personal assistant, after all, and a part of her job was to protect him from unwanted advances from anyone. How could she protect him if she didn't know what was going on? Well, no one could stop her from finding out. After all, she had to protect Ras. Didn't she?

# *Chapter 15*

Gisela pulled the telephone to her and reached for her well-ordered Rolodex file, scrolled to the Zs and found Miriam Zenawi's telephone number. She sat for a moment developing in her mind the ruse she would use to find out why Mrs. Zenawi was making Ras' life so difficult. She knew she had to make it good; after all, her job was on the line if she overstepped her bounds, and she would never see Ras again. With trembling hands, she dialed the number. As the telephone began ringing, a dewy film of perspiration covered her face, her stomach did a quick somersault and her immediate instinct was to hang up. But just as she held the receiver more tightly, forcing herself not to release it, a voice said, "Zenawi residence."

With as much steel in her voice as she could muster, she spoke. "Mrs. Miriam Zenawi, please. This is the office of Ras Selassie calling."

"One moment please," came the practiced reply.

For Gisela, it felt like hours had passed, but in a matter of seconds Miriam Zenawi came on the line, with venom in her voice.

"This is Miriam Zenawi. Who are you?"

With as much confidence as she could find after the icy

reception she had just received, Gisela answered, "I am the personal assistant to Mr. Ras Selassie—"

She was not allowed to finish as Miriam countered with, "Well, if you are his personal assistant, then you should know that he was told through my barrister that no one from his family or his organization is to contact me unless they are acting legally on his behalf. Until the custody battle for his son is complete, I only want to hear from his legal representation."

Miriam hung up, leaving Gisela feeling as though her life were hanging in the balance between death and destruction. What she felt was a hurt and a betrayal that were for her beyond description. She didn't know what to do next. She stood up and began pacing, with her arms wrapped around her body, saying, "Ras has a son. He has a son." She started screaming, "How could he do this? How could he do this? What am I going to do?"

The floor that Gisela occupied at RS Development contained a conference room and three offices, Gisela's office, Cassandra's temporary office and Ras' office. As Gisela ranted to herself, Cassandra was finishing up the last touches on a design she needed to have couriered to Virginia. She had also completed a prospectus Ras had asked her to leave with Gisela for perusal upon his return. Cassandra gathered up the prospectus pieces, looked them over one last time, placed them in order and headed to Gisela's office. As she neared Gisela's door, she could hear muffled sounds that seemed too loud to be normal conversation. As she got closer to the door, the sounds became clearer. What she heard sounded like a wounded animal. Thinking that Gisela might be hurt, she knocked on the door and in a voice full of concern, she almost yelled, "Gisela, are you OK? I need to come in." She opened the door and found Gisela now huddled in a corner, sitting on the floor, with her knees drawn to her chest, rocking back and forth, crying, "How could he do this?"

Cassandra placed the papers on the desk and kneeled

down in front of Gisela. "Gisela, tell me what's wrong. How can I help you?"

Gisela answered with a vacancy in her blue eyes that Cassandra found very unsettling. "How could he do it, Cassandra? How could he?" Gisela continued to speak while tears ran down her face like drops of rain. "I've loved him for so long. How could he do it? I would have done anything for him. Why didn't I know? Why did he do it?"

Cassandra was starting to feel an uneasiness she couldn't name. Instinctively, she knew that Gisela was talking about Ras. From the looks she had seen in Gisela's eyes when she was in his presence, Cassandra knew that it was unlikely that any other man would cause Gisela the kind of anguish she saw on her face and heard in her voice. With a sick feeling in the pit of her stomach, Cassandra pressed for answers.

"Gisela, calm down and tell me what has you so upset."

"I loved him, Cassandra. For years I've watched him ignore me. I watched him with you, and I knew he would never look at me that way. But I never thought I would have to listen to a woman tell me that she has his son."

At the end of that statement, Gisela's tears began again. This time she was wailing, "Oh God, no, not a child."

Cassandra was more devastated than she had ever been in her life. Christopher's death had not shaken her in this way. She felt as if she had been beaten and left for dead. She clamped both hands to Gisela's shoulders and shook her, saying, "Gisela, pull yourself together. Your ranting doesn't make any sense, but right now my life depends on you making sense, so pick yourself up, dry your face, and tell me clearly and slowly who you are talking about and what you are talking about."

Being shaken seemed to bring Gisela back to the earthly plane. Both women stood up. Gisela walked over to an ebonized wood cabinet and took out a box of tissues. She wiped her face, and after throwing the tissue in a small garbage receptacle near her desk, she removed the cream-colored jacket to her pantsuit, revealing a white silk shirt. She hung the jacket over her chair in slow motion. Cassandra watched in silence, preparing herself for the worst. The only part of Gisela's ranting that haunted her was the word "child." Whoever this man was, he had a child. This story was going to be worth the wait.

Gisela sat and took a few deep breaths. Cassandra sat in a chair facing Gisela's desk, crossed her very long legs, crossed her wrists on her lap and waited for Gisela to speak. The two women looked at one another with studied anticipation, neither really knowing what to expect.

Gisela began, saying, "You saw the woman, Miriam Zenawi, who stormed in here, causing quite a scene."

Cassandra nodded a yes. Gisela continued, a sob still lingering. "Well, I knew by Ras' behavior and his frequent meetings with his cousin Kamau Mazrui, the attorney, that something was wrong. Ras also would not let me handle any of the correspondence from Kamau. That in itself was highly unusual. I just couldn't take it any longer, and so I set out this morning to find out what is going on. I called Miriam Zenawi and told her the truth, that I was calling from RS Development and that I was Ras' assistant. I really didn't know what I was going to say after that, but I didn't have to say anything. Ms. Zenawi lit into me, saying that Ras' people were only to contact her through an attorney until the custody battle for his son is complete. She hung up on me, and I went to pieces. I guess that was the final blow for me. My hopes were dashed in a moment. Although, if the truth be known, my hopes were dashed when I saw Ras look at you for the first time. I really can't stay any longer. I am handing in my resignation when Ras returns."

When Gisela finished, Cassandra couldn't move. With every word Gisela had spoken, Cassandra's worst fears had been realized. Gisela had confirmed that the infamous Mr. Ras Selassie had perpetrated the ultimate betrayal. In a voice as cold and as disconnected as Gisela had ever heard, Cassandra asked, "Who is the mother of this child?"

"Ms. Zenawi didn't say, and she didn't leave room for me to ask any questions. So I don't know."

Cassandra didn't wait for Gisela to finish her thought. She stood up in one fluid motion and left the room. She walked down the hall, enraged by the thought of Ras' betrayal. She entered her temporary headquarters and slammed the door behind her, causing an object on a shelf near the door to leave its perch and clatter to the floor, hitting the carpet with a thud that resembled the pain that was echoing in Cassandra's heart. She continued walking toward her desk. Once she was standing in front of it, she could feel hot tears behind her eyes threatening to release themselves onto cheeks that were burning with rage. She said out loud, "Oh no you don't, Cassandra Terrell. You are not going to waste one solitary tear over that lying dog Ras Selassie. Not one tear. What you are going to do is to get away from him as fast as you can. You do not need Ras and his drama. So calm down, and call Amara so that someone in the family will know where you are, and then pack and go."

She cued in the numbers for Amara's cellular telephone, insuring a greater likelihood of reaching her. Within seconds she heard, "Hello, this is Amara."

"Hi, Sis. I'm sorry to bother you, but something has come up and I'm leaving Addis."

Amara could hear Cassandra holding on by a thread, and so she asked, "Cassandra, what's wrong? Tell me. You know you're not bothering me. I'm in the car on the way to the Association. You know I'm being driven, so I don't even have to concentrate on the road. So talk to me."

"Let me get this out quickly before I lose it. I just learned a few moments ago that Ras has a child, a baby, and is evidently embroiled in a custody battle. Your brother-in-law is representing him. So I am sure that your husband knows all about it."

"What! Are you sure?"

"Yes! His assistant was doing some snooping and stumbled upon the information. I found her in her office, crying her eyes out because she thinks that the baby really kills her chances with Ras. Can you believe that?"

"What!"

"Yeah, that's a whole other story. I knew Ras had drama, but that lying creep has really done it this time. Look, I'm going somewhere to hide out for a while. I feel like my soul has been ripped away. I loved him, Amara."

"I know, honey, I know. Look, I'll get to the bottom of this. When you make up your mind where you are going, call and leave all of the info on my cell. That way I can reach you."

"I will. Thanks for listening, Sis. Love you."

"Love you, too."

# Chapter 16

*Nairobi*

Amara flipped the top of her cell phone closed and made a quick decision. She said to her driver, "Please take me back home. I'll just be late today for the meeting."

"Yes, ma'am," was the dutiful response.

She once again flipped open her telephone and keyed in Keino's private line. He answered upon seeing her number on his caller ID.

"Is this my wife?"

Not a day went by that Keino did not marvel at the depth of his feelings for the woman he had married. Amara was indeed the love of his life. He committed to memory every movement of her body, every intonation of her voice, and this time when she spoke, he knew something was amiss. There was a distance that he had only heard on rare occasions. He felt as if he were waiting for the other shoe to drop as she said, "Hi, Keino, I really need to talk to you."

Her voice was low and calm, too calm, as she continued. "I am on my way back home. Can you meet me there?"

Keino tipped in softly with his answer. "Yes, I can. May I ask what is troubling you? I can hear something in your voice that is beyond the ordinary."

"We just need to talk, Keino. I will be home in fifteen minutes. I'll see you then."

"All right, Amara, I will see you at home."

Amara closed her cellular telephone at the same time as Keino flipped his closed. She leaned back in the cocoon of the smooth leather seats of the luxury sedan in which she was being driven. She closed her eyes and thought about how she was going to approach her husband about family secrets, lies and plots to deceive.

Keino leaned back in his wingback swivel chair in his office and wondered at the mysterious nature of his wife's call. He pushed the intercom button, which gave him a direct line to his secretary, and said, "Bella, have a car brought around to drive me to my home. If there is an emergency, you know how to reach me."

"Yes, Mr. Mazrui," came the practiced response.

Keino placed a stack of papers from his desk into his black leather briefcase, locked it and stood. He moved with his usual regal strides through his office doorway and took an elevator down to where his car was waiting. An impeccably dressed chauffeur tipped his hat and opened the door for Keino to enter the backseat. Keino settled himself and unbuttoned the bottom button of his black pin-striped suit, undid the French cuffs of his gleaming white shirt, crossed his legs and rode in silence, waiting to meet his wife and have her tell him what was causing her such distress.

Amara walked into her house, and for the first time since her marriage to Keino, she felt uneasy in her own home. She walked past the expansive living room, where so many joyous family gatherings had been held. Amara could almost hear the laughter, hear the music and smell the food. She smiled at the memories, but an aura of sadness lingered in her eyes as it occurred to her that her husband, the man entrusted with her life, may have put his family secret before their marriage. Amara continued up the stairs to the bedroom she shared with her husband.

She opened the double doors and stood looking at the massive four-poster bed, where she and Keino had lain on many occasions, wrapped in each other's arms, sharing hopes, dreams and raw passion. She could only wonder if all that time he had been hiding from her a secret that affected not just them but her sister, her unsuspecting sister. Did Keino actually stand by and allow his cousin to deceive her sister? She had to hear the details of this story. She refused to believe that her Keino had been a party to such blatant deception.

Amara moved farther into the room, and as she walked, she started unraveling the elaborately wrapped cobalt-colored gélé that she wore on her head. It matched the business suit she wore, which was fashioned from elaborate African fabrics. As the gélé came off, she placed the fabric on the brocade- and silk-covered bed. Her hair fell to her shoulders in fine, wispy strands. She turned toward the doorway of the bedroom to go back downstairs. As she stepped onto the landing, Keino, who was entering the front door, instantly looked up into his wife's eyes. He could tell they were in for quite a conversation.

"Hello, my sweet. Shall I come up there, or will you come down here?"

"Why don't you come up here," was Amara's quiet response.

Keino dropped his briefcase beside the door and started for the stairs. The carved staircase was long and curved, giving Keino time to steady his thoughts as he climbed it. He reached the bedroom door as Amara turned to walk in. He followed her. Attempting to lighten the mood, Keino said to his wife, "I don't think I have seen that particular outfit. You wear it extremely well, but then you wear everything well."

"Really?" Amara asked sarcastically. "Is that the truth, or is it some lie that you are telling to lighten the mood, to make small talk to appease a wife who appears to be unhappy at the moment?"

Thoroughly confused, Keino placed both hands on Amara's shoulders and said, with his temper slightly rising, "I have never lied to you, and why on earth would I lie about something as simple as the fact that I admire your beauty or the way you adorn yourself? I have been saying those things to you almost from the day we met. What is at the bottom of this state you are in, Amara?"

Amara took a deep breath and slowly released it before asking, "Keino, since we've been married, have you ever kept something from me? Something important? Something you know I should know?"

Keino could not for the life of him figure out what Amara was talking about. All of the talk about withholding information that she should have was bewildering, baffling. He didn't understand and so asked, "Amara, what are you talking about?"

"Keino, I just asked a question. Have you been keeping things from me? I thought we shared everything, everything, and now I find out that you have been keeping family affairs from me."

Somehow when he heard the phrase "family affairs," Ras came immediately to mind. Then it hit him. He didn't know how Amara knew, but instinctively, he knew she did. And so he took her hand and led her to the love seat positioned in one corner of the bedroom. He sat down and sank into the plush fabric. He placed Amara on his lap, stared deeply into her eyes and said, "My wife, there are two things that have happened since we have been married that I have not shared with you. I did not share with you what was told either time because it did not involve me. Each time the situation was Ras'. Each time it was his private affair. Much to his credit though, I must say, the first time he asked me to maintain his confidence, he did so with one stipulation, that I be able to tell you if the need should present itself. The second situation is very recent, and Ras called upon the men of the family to help him handle it. We are having another meeting today. So you see, my wife, I am not withholding anything from you. What I am doing is performing my duty as the eldest son of Adina and Garsen Mazrui.

"As the eldest son, much responsibility falls on my shoulders. I am sometimes the caretaker not just for my immediate family but for extended family as well. You must trust, my darling, that you or anyone you love will never be irreparably damaged because I withheld information you should have. When you married me, my love, it was understood that I would always lead this family, and that I would always lead it with love and the utmost respect. You are my wife and my heart. I will never intentionally hurt you."

"I'm sorry, Keino, but when Cassandra called me today to tell me that Ras has a child, I was livid. Actually, I was more stunned than anything. I just couldn't imagine that you would allow your cousin, a man without moral integrity, to make a play for my sister and keep her in the dark about his past."

"Sweetheart, until very recently Ras was in the dark. He did not know. Had he known, he would have had the child with him. I am glad he told Cassandra."

"Oh, he didn't tell her. Gisela told her. Gisela went snooping and found out more than she bargained for."

"This certainly complicates matters. But we are dealing with very intelligent, resourceful people here. They will figure it out. I need to know if I have my wife back. Are you my wife, my woman, my love?" With both of his hands he held her shoulders tightly, looked deeply into her eyes and waited for an answer.

"I am," had barely left her lips when Keino claimed Amara's mouth as he had done countless times before. The urgency, however, was new. It spoke to the desperation a man feels when he has felt the love of his life erect a barrier between them, causing hurt that only loving can mend. While kissing Amara's throat, he unbuttoned the top of her suit, and slowly, ever so slowly, he began to massage the tops of the cinnamon-colored peaks that were her breasts. "Amara, you are more beautiful as the days go by. I will never tire of you, and my hunger for you only increases."

Amara emitted a whispery, "Keino, I love you so, but what about the meeting you were on your way to?"

"My sweet, before I go to a meeting to discuss Ras' child, I am going to lie with my wife and create one of my own."

Before Amara could respond, Keino lifted her from the love seat and walked to the bed. He placed Amara in the center of the bed and said, "Indulge me, my sweet. The future father of your children needs you right now."

Amara smiled and said, "I'm yours."


With all of the command of one who has won much and lost little, Kamau Mazrui spoke. "All right, family. We are in for a fight. It is my studied opinion that at this juncture we need to add to our arsenal Judge Garsen Mazrui and General Tafari Selassie."

Ras spoke up, with a deadly stare pointed at Kamau. "Uncle Garsen is not a problem, but everyone here knows it is not my wish to have the general involved in this."

Kamau countered, "We are not here to grant your wishes. We are here to get custody of your son. And we must not forget that those two men are the heads of our families, and in a situation of this magnitude, it would be unspeakably disrespectful not to include them at this point. Did you really believe that we were going to chance that?"

Ras sat back with legs crossed, giving an appearance of calm he did not feel. Keino spoke, attempting to placate both men, hoping to diffuse the hostility between them that was simmering in the room.

"Kamau, we know that your legal acumen is not easily surpassed. We recognize and applaud your gift. However, we understand Ras' anxiousness concerning this custody battle. Any one of us in this room, if faced with similar circumstances, would respond with our hearts."

Affirmative nods were given by Kaleb and Aman. Keino continued. "Ras, if you think about this objectively, you will probably see that Kamau is correct. Not only do those two men have great tactical minds, they are our elders. We cannot shun them, and we cannot favor one over the other. It does not matter how acclimated we become to things of the West. Some cultural tenets are ingrained forever."

Ras answered with a tinge of sadness. "And so it is. Let's just bring my son home."

Kamau answered, "Good. I sent a car for both men. Your father was flown in last night. I hoped you would come to see the importance of their being here."

With a bit of sarcasm, Ras said, "Thank you, Kamau. You've thought of everything."

Kamau countered, "For your sake, I hope I have."

The morning progressed rapidly as Kamau brought them all up to date on the case. The afternoon brought new developments with the arrival of General Tafari Selassie and Judge Garsen Mazrui. Both men, dressed in Western business suits tailored to fit them perfectly, walked in regally, as though they were commanding subjects. Ras' father's back was ramrod straight from years of military discipline. When the two men entered the room, their sons stood to welcome them. When General Selassie and Ras greeted each other, it was, "Good to see you, my son," and "Father." The coldness Ras directed toward his father was felt across the room.

Tafari Selassie resigned himself to the blinding hurt he felt whenever he and Ras were in the same room. He couldn't remember when it had started; he only knew that one day he looked up, and he had lost his only son. He had hoped against hope that things would change and he would have with his son what his brother-in-law Garsen had with his four sons. It had not happened.

Judge Mazrui spoke after everyone was seated. "Well,

my sons and my nephew, why have we been summoned here on this fine day?"

It had been determined earlier that when the elders arrived, Ras would begin by setting the stage with his story, and so he began. As he spoke, every word was laced with bitterness, anger, remorse and embarrassment. The bitterness and anger were because Zala had made a decision for him without his consent. The remorse was for the circumstances into which his son was born, and the embarrassment was because he was having to publicly dissect a piece of his life. When Ras had finished, Kamau laid out the legal ramifications of the case and the legal strategies they wished to employ. When both Kamau and Ras had finished, the judge and the general looked at one another, and the judge spoke first.

"Nephew, legally speaking, we have quite a case here. I only have one question. Do you want your son?"

"Yes, Uncle, with every fiber of my being."

"Then we shall fight to the death."

"Son, have you told your mother?" General Selassie asked in a voice that rang with a tenderness Ras did not remember ever having heard.

Ras' answer was a quiet, "No" as he thought of the fact that Cassandra also did not know.

"I'd like us to tell your mother together."

Resigned to the fact that sooner or later he was going to have to deal with his father, Ras answered, "I am flying home this evening. We can tell her then."

"I agree, son, the sooner the better."

Having settled the issue of breaking the news to his wife, Tafari Selassie turned to the group and said in a voice that was both commanding and kind, "Kamau, since you have very expertly explored all of the legal machinations, it would be wise for your father and me to explore the cultural underpinnings of this matter. Though laws exist, many times cultural mores win out. And so we must examine our options in case the courts should fail us."

"Yes, Uncle, we definitely defer to you and Father in matters of cultural civilities."

The general and the judge went off to Judge Mazrui's office to put their heads together. Kamau, Kaleb and Aman went their separate ways, and Keino stayed to console Ras and to be a sounding board.

Keino turned to Ras and said, "See, you made it through. The picture in your mind was worse than the reality, was it not?"

With deep gratitude in every syllable, Ras said, "Man, how can I ever repay you for the moral support? And for acting as a go-between when Kamau and I are ready to murder each other."

Keino smiled. "You two have been at it since we were boys in the play yard. I never understood why you two are so contentious with each other."

Now Ras was smiling. "Maybe it's because Kamau thinks he knows everything, and I know I know everything."

The two of them shared a much needed laugh, and when it faded, Ras said, with a frown etched in his brow, "I haven't told Cassandra."

Keino was silent for a moment and then said in an exasperated tone, "What do you want me to say, Ras? This one is a no-brainer. You know, Mr. Know Everything, that you should have told her a long time ago. Man, this is not good. Suppose she finds out before you tell her?"

Keino didn't have the heart to tell Ras what he knew about Gisela's revelation to Cassandra. He trusted that God and the ancestors would intervene and all would be well. He silently prayed for the best for his cousin.

With weariness and despair covering his words, Ras replied, "I have thought of every scenario, but I could not bring myself to tell her. I want her, Keino. I want her in my life. I want her. I couldn't take the chance of losing her."

"If you don't tell her, man, you might lose her, anyway. Cassandra is much more willful than my wife, but if Amara found out that I had kept a secret of that magnitude from her, I would be dropped like the proverbial hot rock. I shudder to think what you may be in for. When you go home tonight, you had better tell her. You need to talk to her."

Ras massaged his temples as he spoke. "I will. She has to be with me through this."

# *Chapter 17*

Ras and his father were flown home together by Kaleb on one of the Mazrui family jets. They were chauffeured home to find Amara Selassie waiting for them. Tafari had called his wife to alert her that their son had very important news. They found her waiting in the drawing room. When she heard them enter the house, she sent one of the housemen to the kitchen to have the cook prepare a pot of traditional Ethiopian coffee, strong, hot and aromatic. When they entered the drawing room, she rose to greet them both with kisses and embraces, saying, "Well, isn't this wonderful, my two favorite men in the same place at the same time. Have I died and gone to heaven?"

Ras' father assured his wife, "No, my pet, the two of us are really here, in this place, at this time."

Ras looked at his father and wondered if he had really heard him refer to his wife as his pet. As Ras was taking a seat, preparing himself to tell his mother the news of his son, the houseman entered with an aromatic tray of piping hot coffee. To Ras, the coffee was a welcome sight. Since he knew strong Ethiopian coffee freshly ground had enough kick to wake up a dead man, he gladly took a cup when offered. He knew that between his mother and Cassandra, he would not sleep tonight. Ras' parents sat next to each other and across from him, sipping slowly and waiting for their son to enlighten them on the new developments in his life.

Ras began, "My mother, I want to start by saying I have never done anything intentionally to hurt you or bring you shame. Father heard earlier what I am about to say now, but there are other things I need to say that neither of you have heard."

Ras told the story of his relationship with Zala, of the agreement that he thought they had, and of the baby that was the result of an agreement not being kept. His mother began to weep, and Ras thought how sad the contrast between the flowing joyfully colored traditional robes she wore and her tear-stained face. He had caused that pain, and he knew he would cause more before the night ended. He told his mother about Miriam and the possible court battle, and then he stunned both of his parents with his next statements. Ras, angry again at the thought of having his son reared without him, launched into a tirade, which brought more tears to his mother's eyes and sadness to his father's. "I will never consent to having my son grow up in an atmosphere like I did, with an absent father."

Hearing his only son hurl the ultimate insult at him, General Selassie spoke slowly, painfully. "Son, where have I been?"

With contempt marking every syllable, Ras answered, "You were chasing your next war, or your next promotion. You know, Father, I don't know what you were chasing. All I do know is that most of the time you weren't with your family. I can't tell you one school event where you were present. My son is not going to have that experience to remember as his childhood."

His mother spoke through sobs as she tried to get a handle on her mixed emotions of hurt and confusion. "Ras, what are you saying? Your father has been a good father and a good husband. We were always loved."

"Mother, how can you say the man loved you when you

cried constantly. I never knew why you were crying. I just knew that the tears seemed to be shed for no good reason."

She raised her voice, desperate to make her son understand. "Ras, Ras, oh, my son, is that what you thought?"

"Yes, Mother. What was I to think?"

"Oh my God, if only I had known. Sweetheart, I cried because I missed my husband. He was serving our country, doing his duty as he saw fit, but I wanted my husband home. I was afraid for his life. We endured death threats and many years of torturous time away from one another. One of the reasons we decided to send you abroad to school was for your own protection. Your father always loved us both." A deep sadness invaded her tone. "I suppose in trying to protect you, we sent the wrong message."

Ras felt as if someone had stuck a pin in him and released all of his air. All of these years he had been viewing his parents through a skewed prism of his own making. His father spoke again with deep pain.

"Son, every hurt I caused I would erase if I could. You spoke earlier of missed events and unexplained absences. Many times my life was literally in danger, and I was hiding out to save my life. I couldn't come near you or your mother for fear that harm would come to you. There were times when I was able, with the aid of wonderful, courageous comrades, to sneak on to your boarding school campus in the dead of night and watch you sleep. I didn't even dare touch you for fear of waking you. I couldn't let you see me, because if you were ever asked, we always wanted you to be able to tell the truth, to say no, you had not seen me."

When Ras' father finished his sentence, all three of them were crying. Ras' mother spoke haltingly through her tears.

"My poor baby, all these years you did not understand how much you were loved. Oh, my son, I am so sorry."

When she completed her sentence, she wept openly, sobbing so forcefully that both Ras and his father got up to comfort her.

"Mother, I understand now, I understand, and I am sorry that I spent all of this time warring inside my head instead of coming to you two. I have missed valuable time with my own father because I was too bullheaded to take another look. Father, I am so sorry that I have robbed myself of time with you."

"My son, if I have learned nothing else, I have learned that if the sun rises on another day, there is always a chance. We have time, my son, we have time, and if your mother and I can assist you, we will all have time with the newest addition to the Selassie clan, little master Ras Kebran."

"I will appreciate any help that you can give."

As Amara Selassie was wiping her eyes, she said, "Ras, I didn't have a chance to tell you how much I enjoyed the visit with Cassandra. She is such a special young woman. And I was especially pleased because she is the only woman you have ever brought home, and I sensed there was more to the visit than helping her keep a promise to her mother."

"You are right, Mother. She means a great deal to me."

"Son, does she know about the baby?"

"No, I am afraid I have been waiting for the right time. Keino reminded me earlier that I should have told her sooner, not later. I just did not want to lose her. I am on my way to her hotel as soon as I leave here. I have got to make this right."

"Oh, darling, I think she will understand. Just let her know that she has your heart. She does, doesn't she, son?"

"Yes, Mother, she does."

Ras picked himself up from his chair, embraced both of his parents and had his parents' driver take him to the Sheraton Addis. On the way to the hotel, he decided to call Cassandra just to hear her voice before seeing her. He dialed the number and heard the familiar, "Good evening. Welcome to the Sheraton Addis."

"Yes, good evening. Would you please ring Miss Cassandra Terrell's room."

"One moment, sir."

Ras waited, anticipating Cassandra's voice when he heard, "I am sorry, sir, but Ms. Terrell checked out this afternoon."

Ras was speechless. He closed his cellular phone and said aloud to himself, "What in hell is happening? Where did she go? She wasn't leaving. She had agreed to stay another month. What is going on?" He said to the driver, "A change of plan. Take me home."

By the time he reached his home, he knew he had to call Keino. If Cassandra was gone, Amara would know where and why. By the time he sat down to call Keino, his nerves were on edge, and he was more confused than he had ever been. He walked into his paneled study and dialed Keino's private line. He answered immediately. "Hello, this is Keino. How are you, Ras?"

"I've been better. Cassandra has checked out of her suite, and I don't have a clue where to look for her, but I knew she wouldn't leave without telling Amara, Afiya and Adana. I knew I could get to Amara through you, so here I am calling, hoping that Amara can give me some answers."

Keino's hasty response was, "I know she can, but I am not sure she will. When I got home this afternoon, I thought my wife was going to tar and feather me just because I am your cousin. Cassandra knows about the baby. I couldn't tell you earlier. I thought you would have time to talk to Cassandra."

Ras yelled, "No! How did she find out?"

"It would appear, my cousin, that Gisela was snooping around, that she called Miriam to feel her out, and Miriam gave up the whole story, unaware of what she was doing. Cassandra walked into Gisela's office, found her in a state, tried to console her, and Gisela told her Miriam's story. You have the picture now, I presume?"

"Oh my God, where is Cassandra now?"

"My wife arranged for one of the family planes to take her to Punta Cana in the Dominican Republic. She wanted to get to a place where no one would look for her. Actually, she said so that no one named Ras Selassie would look for her."

"Did Kaleb take her?"

"No, Ravi was her pilot."

"Keino, he has to take me to her as soon as we can fly out. I have got to clear up this mess that I have created. I can't lose her, Keino. I can't lose her."

"I'll get Ravi to pick you up tomorrow morning."

"Thanks, Keino. I owe you."

"Yes, you do."

*Punta Cana, Dominican Republic*

Cassandra sat on a deep purple, fluffy towel flung on a white sandy beach in Punta Cana, where she had rented a small cottage. The deep purple was a magnificent complement to her deep, rich caramel-colored skin. Her long, shapely limbs were clad in an ever so skimpy snow-white bikini. Cassandra was basking in the sun. She wanted the sun to burn away her anger, her disappointment, her sense of betrayal and her hurt. The longer she lay in the sun, the more relaxed she became. With every breath, the tension began to ooze from her fingers and toes. Her limbs became liquid, her mind eased and she drifted into a dream state.

Ras watched her as she slipped into her trancelike state of sublime relaxation. He watched her limbs soften with each deepening breath. He watched, unclear as to what he would say to her, unclear about how he would say what he had to say to her. The only thing he knew clearly was that she had to be his. Without her knowing, he stood on the balcony of her cottage, watching her on the beach below. He watched until he could no longer wait. He knew he had to speak to her immediately because she did, after all, hold the key to his future. He took long, graceful strides across the sand, feeling the hot, soothing particles sift through the toes of his beige linen sandals. The sandals were a stunning complement to his white linen pants and shirt. As he reached her side, he knelt down and extended his toffee-colored hand to gently arouse her from her angelic slumber. As his hand touched her, she jumped, startled, and with an anguished sound, yelled, "What are you doing here?"

"I came for you," he answered.

With a cold distance, she said, "I'm not going anywhere with you."

"You have to," he said softly.

"Ras Selassie, I don't have to do a damn thing you say! I hate the sight, sound and smell of you. You're like a rabid dog, infecting everything around you. I wish I had never met you. I hate you. Get out of my sight. Get out of my life."

"Cassandra, please let me explain. You don't know the whole story. Give me an opportunity to tell my side. I need you, Cassandra. I need you."

"Your only need for me is in your bed. You don't need anyone. Ras, you discard human beings like toilet paper. I won't be discarded—I take myself out of the race. Get out of my face. Go back to your women and your secretive ways and your mood swings and your power plays and your horrible temper. You can have it all, Ras. I'm finished, and don't ever follow me again. Just leave me alone."

Ras looked at Cassandra, with pain hanging in his eyes. He turned and walked away. Cassandra plopped back down on her towel, still agitated from her heated exchange with Ras, and attempted to regain the peace and tranquility she had started to experience before Ras invaded her space.

Cassandra sat on the beach until her temper cooled along with the sun. She stood up, grabbed her towel and beach bag, and headed for her rented cottage to shower and dress for dinner. When she reached her door, she dug into her bag and after a second found her key. She turned the key in the lock and pushed open the door. The sun was setting, and shadows played across the room. As she moved farther into the room to put her bag and towel down and to turn on a lamp, she heard, "Hello, Cassandra. Are you ready to talk now?" She swallowed hard, feeling a mixture of momentary fear and raging anger at the fact that Ras seemed able to get whatever he wanted whenever he wanted it. She silently vowed, *Not this time.*

With venom dripping from every word, she said, "If you do not leave this house, I will call the police and have them arrest you for breaking and entering. Now get out!"

"Cassandra, I am not leaving until you agree to listen to me."

He started walking toward her in slow, measured steps. As he approached, she screamed, "You lying dog! Why should I listen to anything you have to say?"

It was Ras' turn to be angry. "Whatever you think I've done, you have no right to call me anything other than my name, and if I remember correctly, my parents did not name me lying dog or rabid dog." By this time they were so close, each could feel the other's rage.

"Don't preach to me, Ras Selassie, and if you don't like the names I call you, you can get out now."

"I am not leaving until you hear me out, do you understand that?"

"What makes you think I care what you have to say?"

Ras reached for Cassandra, and as quickly as he could blink, she slapped him hard enough to leave the print of her hand on his beautifully chiseled cheek. Before she could think, he grabbed both of her wrists. She yelled, "Let me go, you cheating son of a cockroach."

That was more than Ras could take. He picked her up, threw her over his shoulder, kicking and screaming, walked into the bedroom, threw her on the bed, locked the door and sat on the floor, blocking the locked door. She knew she was defeated. She sat glaring at him, then picked up the clock radio on the bedside table, started to throw it at Ras, thought better of it and threw it at the wall. It cracked into pieces resembling their shattered hearts.

Ras looked at Cassandra and then looked at the wall.

Frost hung on his every word as he said, "Now, so my parents are cockroaches, and your anger has caused you to destroy property that isn't yours, all because you believe half-truths and suppositions. At least in a court of law, my side would be heard. Right now you are going to hear my side. I am not leaving until you hear me. When you have heard me out, if you still ask me to leave, I will leave, and I promise I'll never bother you again."

Cassandra's coldness was still intact as she answered, "It will be worth it to hear you out if you will truly leave me alone." Ras remained seated on the floor, his long legs stretched out before him, with his feet crossed at the ankles. With his hands resting in his lap, his head tilted to one side and his light brown eyes locked on Cassandra's sable-colored ones, he began slowly.

"I am a man, Cassandra, who has until this moment lived primarily for himself. I created a life for myself that did not make room for any inconveniences, and definitely not any deep personal commitments to a woman. I was on a fast track to either the life of a confirmed bachelor having an occasional fling or a man who would settle for a companion when I approached middle age, just because I wouldn't want to be alone. In my quiet moments, I certainly had the desire to find what I see in my cousins' lives and in the lives of many of my friends, an adoring wife and children for whom I would give my life and with whom I would live to share my life, but I didn't see it happening. I didn't see it. To tell you the truth, I had decided I was doomed to another fate, and then my cousin Keino took a bride, and at the wedding, I danced a slow, sensual dance that changed my life. I didn't realize it then, but at that moment I fell in love with the possibility of you, Cassandra, the possibility of us.

"When you consented to work with me, I had no idea that being with you, near you, making love to you, would consume me with a passion I had never experienced. My past is my past, and I had no idea it would follow me in the way that it has. When I pictured my life with my children, I pictured them all with the same mother, all under the same roof. Estrangement from my children was never in my plan. Zala Tamrat, a woman I dated briefly, decided, without consulting me, to have my child. I was under the impression that we had an agreement. Since she was a reputable physician with a thriving practice, I trusted her. She had other plans. She gave birth to my son, and had she not been killed in an auto accident, I am told by her sister Miriam Zenawi, I would never have known about my son. I didn't know how to tell you all of this. It was dropped on me like garbage from a dumpster. For days I was in a fog, adjusting to betrayal, to deceit, to being a father, to knowing that somewhere in Addis, there is a little boy who doesn't know me, his father, and his mother is dead. I thought about the homes that I am building for orphaned children, and yet I am faced with Miriam Zenawi, who is threatening to make my son an orphan because she wants to salvage some part of her sister.

"I didn't know how to tell you. I started to tell you more than once, but my desire not to lose you outweighed everything. For the first time in my life and for the last time in my life, Cassandra, I am in love, and I am in love with you. I want you in my life for the rest of my life. I want you to be my wife. I need you, Cassandra. I need you for me, and I need you for my son. He deserves a mother like you, a woman who can nurture and love any child, and I know that if you love me, you will love my son. Search your heart, Cassandra. If there is any love left for me and room for my son, you will know where to find me."

He rose slowly and looked at Cassandra. He saw tears glistening in her eyes as she dared them to fall. He smiled his crooked smile and said, "Good-bye, my love," and walked through the door. When Cassandra heard the front door close, she dissolved in a torrent of sorrowful tears, tears that she had been holding since she had first heard that Ras was a father. She cried for herself and her hurt.

She cried for Ras. She cried for a little boy who was minus both his parents. She cried because of life's pains and inconsistencies, and she cried because she knew that either in spite of or because of Ras' revelations, she loved him more than she had ever loved any man in her life, and she had no idea what to do about it.

# Chapter 18

Ras flew back into Addis Ababa prepared to do damage control in a number of areas of his life. When he walked into his office, he found a resignation letter from Gisela describing her pain and anguish after years of having to watch him look at other women with adoration but treat her as though she didn't exist. He laughed out loud and said, still laughing, "The world has gone mad, and all of the craziness has landed on my doorstep." Just as his laughter subsided, his phone rang. Happy for the distraction, he answered, "Ras here."

"Ras, this is Kamau. Just calling to tell you that you are most favored by God and the ancestors. I was just called by the Zenawis' counsel and told that your son is to be placed in your custody this afternoon at three o'clock."

"I can't believe it. What do you think happened?"

"I don't know exactly, but if I had to hazard a guess, I would say the elders intervened and brought to bear some of those cultural mores that a court of law can't touch, and I would say your father exacted a coup d'état. Never underestimate the cunning of the seasoned military mind."

"I never will again. Where at three do I pick up my son?"

"The arrangement is that your son is to be delivered to

the home of your parents, and he will be brought there by his maternal grandparents."

"I see." Ras wondered what that all meant but said, "Well, I have a great deal to prepare. Thank you, Kamau, for all of your legal maneuvers."

"I can't say it was my pleasure but I can say, my cousin, anytime that you need me, I will be there, right next to my brothers."

"Thank you, Kamau," was Ras' heartfelt reply. The two men hung up, and Ras stood paralyzed for a moment, knowing he had to prepare a home for his son. He became misty-eyed when he thought of how attached he already was to a little boy named Ras Kebran, his son, whom he had never seen. He cleared his throat and started to call his assistant to tell her he'd be out for the rest of the day. Then he remembered that he had no assistant, and so once again he laughed out loud, because though he had no assistant, he had his son, and in a few hours he would hold him for the first time.

Still smiling at life's ironies, he telephoned his lead staff members to let them know that he would be out for the rest of the day and that in an emergency he could be reached by cell. When that task was completed, he headed out to turn his house into a home where a little man, his son, could grow and thrive. He went to one of the high-end retailers in the city and told everyone who would listen that he needed everything that a six-month-old might enjoy. By the time he left the emporium, he had arranged for the delivery of everything from a crib, bedding and clothes to a hobbyhorse and an electric train set. He knew he had probably gone too far, but the only other time he had ever felt as alive was when he was with Cassandra. It pained him to think that she might never be a part of his life again. He shook off the debilitating thoughts and focused once again on the joy of newfound fatherhood. The hours went by so quickly; three o'clock was only an hour away. He called his parents and let them know that he was on his way. He wanted to be there early in order to have time to truly relax and enjoy the moment when he and his son connected for the very first time.

When he arrived at his parents', he found his father pacing and his mother busily instructing the cook about a tray of appetizers that she wanted prepared for the arriving guests. It was never permissible for Amara Selassie to have guests come to her home, no matter what the occasion, and not offer them refreshments of some sort. She intended, as always, to be prepared. Ras greeted both parents with embraces. It had made such a difference in his life psychologically and emotionally to be able to openly show love and affection to both of his parents. He knew that his son was going to be a well-loved little boy.

General Selassie, grateful to his God and his ancestors for the presence of his son, spoke. "Ah, my son, this is a great day. We will meet the newest member of our family. Your mother and I are bursting with pride."

"Thank you, Father. I only hope I can prove to be a worthy parent."

"Well, son, as you know, sometimes you can do your best, and your children will still miss it."

At that reference to Ras' past bullheadedness, they both shared a welcome bit of laughter at Ras' expense.

"Father, you will never know how grateful I am that we have a connection to one another, which will never again be broken."

"No, it won't, my son. It will never be broken, not even in death."

"Not even in death."

Amara Selassie rushed into the room in a silk caftan layered in hues of gold and purple. Her hair was pulled back in a bun, and gold jewelry graced her neck and ears. She smelled of jasmine, her favorite scent. She made Ras think of Cassandra. The first time he had visited her home, she had worn a caftan, and her hair had been pulled back in a tight bun. Like his mother, she enjoyed the scent of jasmine. He remembered that she sometimes smelled of it when they made love. He wondered if he would ever stop thinking about her. Would there ever come a time when odd places, people or things did not bring her to mind?

Ras' mother ripped him out of his reverie when she said aloud to her husband, "Husband of mine, in just a few minutes we are about to meet our grandson."

"Yes, wife, we are." He turned to Ras. "It must be said, my son, that your mother and I would have preferred, as we know you would have, to have had our first grandchild come as the result of a loving, productive marriage, but true to the traditions of our people, this baby, given life by God, will be nurtured in the bosom of his people."

"Father, before the Tamrats arrive, there is one question I must ask."

"Yes, son."

"How did you get Miriam Zenawi to relinquish my son?"

"Ras, there are some laws that are beyond the courts, and though Miriam may not have understood that fact, I was certain her parents would, and I knew they would prevail upon her to do the honorable thing. That is why her parents are delivering their grandson to his father today." Ras looked at his father with deep admiration and love. He knew that without his father's intervention, he would not have gotten his son as easily and without public humiliation.

The doorbell rang, and Ras, his mother and father waited for the houseman to usher their guests into the drawing room. Excitement and long endured anticipation filled the room. As the Tamrats walked in with the baby in the arms of his nanny, Ras saw a miniature version of himself. Ras was frozen in place. He didn't know whether to step forward and take his son, or wait for him to be handed to him. He was saved from doing anything by his father's timely interjection of "Welcome to our home. We are most grateful that you have brought to us the son of our son. May a gracious God always be with you for your kindness. My son, my wife and I will always be in your debt. We will see to it that you will always have access to the son of your daughter, and we will all make sure that the memory of this child's mother will live in his heart forever."

Ras marveled at the smoothness with which his father, the military strategist and seasoned diplomat, brought ease and comfort into the room. Tafari Selassie continued, "Please be seated. Make yourselves comfortable. My wife has requested that the cook prepare refreshments for us."

Mrs. Tamrat spoke while standing and staring tearfully at the observant little boy, who was looking around the room, fixing his gaze occasionally on the man in the room whose eyes mirrored his. "We appreciate your kindness, but I am certain you realize how difficult this must be for us. I would rather give our grandson to his father and leave quickly so that the grief of this moment is not prolonged."

Mr. Tamrat spoke. "My wife is correct. This is not an easy task for any of us. We will dine together another time."

"We understand."

Mrs. Tamrat walked over to Ras and said, "Our daughter was precious to us, and so is her son. We would be most appreciative if you would continue to allow us in his life, as your father has suggested. Any help you need with him, we will gladly give. We love him so very much. He is our pride and joy. We are sending with him, if you do not object, the governess who has been with him since birth, Mrs. Moi."

With a slightly distant formality, Ras greeted the woman with the warm face who was holding his son and accepted the Tamrats' offer of the much needed help he knew he would require.

With tears streaming down her face, Mrs. Tamrat instructed the governess to hand the baby to Ras. He slid into his arms so easily, it felt as though he had always been there. Ras spoke with calm and gratitude. "Mr. and Mrs.

Tamrat, I am so grateful to you for bringing my son. Your daughter was a wonderful, talented woman, and the memory of her talent and her love of her son will always be made known to him, and he will have the opportunity to know and love all of his grandparents."

The Tamrats thanked everyone and said their good-byes. Arrangements were made for the governess to be driven to Ras' home later in the evening.

When they left, Amara Selassie turned to Ras and said, "Son, may I hold my grandson?"

"Yes, Mother." He handed his son to his mother as his mother began to cry. "Oh, Ras, he is so beautiful. He looks like you looked as a baby. He has your eyes. His face is a miniature copy of yours."

Hearing Ras' mother's voice made the baby smile, which caused Amara to launch into a string of sentences designed for babies and grandmothers to increase their enjoyment of each other.

"Oh, you are so precious. Are you Grandma's love? Yes, you are Grandma's love. Oh, we are going to have so much fun."

Little Mr. Ras Kebran babbled away in answer to his grandmother's conversation. All of this was beyond exciting for Mrs. Selassie and a joy to watch for Ras and his father. After an hour had passed, Ras said, "Parents of mine, I must get this little man home. He and I need time together to get to know one another."

"Oh, Ras, must you go? The two of you can stay here tonight."

"No, Mother, we need to settle in as soon as possible, so we will be on our way."

"Well, Mrs. Moi is going to be a live-in governess, so I shouldn't worry so much."

"No, Mother, you shouldn't worry. We will be fine. Father, console your wife. She is having grandparent withdrawal already."

"Don't worry, son. Your mother will be fine. Go home and enjoy your son."

Ras had equipped his luxury SUV with all of the paraphernalia designed to keep a baby safe and entertained. He took his son from his grandmother and said good-bye as Amara continued kissing the soft, round cheeks of her grandson while his grandfather and father looked on with pleasure. On the way home, the baby began to whimper a little, reminding Ras that he might be hungry. Ras tried to reassure himself and the baby by saying, "Okay, my son, your dad has you now. You are going to be just fine. Just give me a little time, little one. I am going to figure this all out. To tell you the truth, I have no idea what I am doing, but I am going to figure it all out. It's just the two of us, buddy, and I will always take good care of you." The quiet, soothing sounds of Ras' voice calmed the baby, and the whimpering was replaced with the soft sounds of sleep. Ras looked through his rearview mirror and smiled at the fact that his first lecture to his son had put him to sleep.

*Punta Cana—One Week Later*

Cassandra had been unable to settle her nerves after Ras left. Her emotions were running wild, and her mind could not rest. Sleep was sporadic. She desperately missed the man she loved, but she was certain that loving him could not rectify the omission of truth, the angry words and the hurt feelings that had erected themselves as monuments between them. She knew she needed to talk it all out with someone or some ones who could and would objectively hear her out and help her get her balance back. She was grateful that she knew a group of women who could help her through anything, her sisters. She had put in a call to Amara earlier to contact the other sisters, Afiya and Adana, in their different time zones and arrange a conference call time that was convenient for everyone. Just as she was sitting thinking about the love and loyalty that she and her sisters shared, her telephone rang, and she was comforted by the sound. She picked up the receiver and said, "Hello."

Three voices on the other end said simultaneously, "Hey, Sis. Hi, Cassandra. Hi, Sis. How are you doing?"

Cassandra almost wept again at the sound of her sisters' reassuring tones.

"Thank you for getting back to me. I really need you today. All of you bring a different perspective to the table, and I need a new view of this situation. I'm so hurt, and I'm so in love, I don't know whether I'm coming or going. I know Amara has brought everybody up to date, so help me. What do I do?"

Afiya was the first to speak. "Cassandra, what does your heart tell you?"

"I can't trust my heart. I trusted my heart with this man before, and here I sit, away from home, family and friends, in a beach house, crying my eyes out, not sleeping and not eating. No, I can't trust my heart."

Afiya continued, always the one to bring the spiritual, mystic perspective. "Always trust your heart, Cassandra. You may factor in some other things, but never discount the messages of the heart."

"Okay, my heart says run to him, grab him and never let go."

Adana, a lawyer by training and analytical by nature, interjected, "Cassandra, have you looked at the ramifications of tying your life to a man who has a child? Not just a child but a baby? I understand he wants to marry you. Would you then become the legal mother of the baby by adoption? What about your life? Becoming an instant mother with no time to prepare . . . what would happen to your business, to your life? Love is one thing, but there is always a business side, even to love. Even though we're not talking about you preserving a mega fortune like Ras', it is still your livelihood, and you've done pretty well for a little Virginia girl."

They all smiled at the thought. Cassandra answered Adana. "Sis, I've thought about all of that. If I married Ras, I would like nothing better than to adopt his son. I would want him to be mine, and I would want to operate as his mother. As far as the baby's care goes, you know Ras has the resources to make life as easy as is humanly possible. Women run businesses all the time and are still good mothers. We would just have to work that out."

It was Amara's turn. "I think the most important thing to consider is this. Who is Ras, and is he the man for you? It really doesn't matter much what he has or doesn't have if he's not the man that you know you can build a life with for the rest of your life. Personally, I think you two were made for each other, but it doesn't matter what I think. What matters is what you know."

"He lied to me, Amara."

"Did he lie, or did he take too long to find a way to tell you the truth? There is a difference."

With a bit of levity in her voice this time, Cassandra said, "Amara, you've been listening to Adana too long. Lawyers make a practice of stretching the truth, manipulating the truth and reinterpreting the truth."

Now they all laughed, with Adana adding, "So that's what you think of my practice of the law, that I'm a common perpetrator of falsehoods, a purveyor of untruths, a willful prevaricator?"

Now everyone was laughing out loud as Adana continued joking, "Oh, and so no one is coming to my defense? Okay, that's all right. I hope you never need my ability to reinterpret the truth."

As the gaiety faded, Afiya spoke. "I saw the brother in action, and he loves you, Cassandra. He wouldn't intentionally hurt you, so I think whatever he did, you need to chalk it up to being human."

"I wish it were that easy. I called him so many horrible names that when I think about them, I cringe."

Amara spoke. "Cassandra, you were angry."

"I know, but sometimes words can be so hurtful, you can't take them back."

Adana asked, "Was it that bad? What did you call him?"

Cassandra answered reluctantly in a very low voice. "I called him a rabid dog and the son of a cockroach."

Her sisters howled and screamed with laughter. Cassandra tried to contain her laughter. "He didn't think it was funny at the time," she added.

Afiya joined in. "I'll bet he doesn't think it's funny being without you, either."

Amara added, "Cassandra, you should see the baby. He is so beautiful. Knowing the way you are about little ones, you will instantly fall in love."

Unable to contain her interest, Cassandra asked, "Where did you see him?"

"Ras' mom had the Mazruis and the Selassies over on Saturday for a huge meal, and we had a chance to see the baby."

Cassandra continued pressing for information. "What's his name? Who does he look like? How is Ras handling fatherhood?"

Amara began thoughtfully. "His name is Ras Kebran. He looks like a miniature Ras. He has his father's light brown eyes, his nose, his full lips, and that stare that Ras has, the baby has it, too. It's as though they see more than they are looking at."

Cassandra said, with a half-smile, "I know that look."

Amara continued. "Ras seems to be handling fatherhood well. I'm sure he's being challenged. Keino told me that Gisela quit, so he had to hire another assistant. He hired a young man." She laughed. "I guess he was tired of the wrath of women scorned. He also has a live-in nanny, but he and that little boy are joined at the hip. I hear there have been days when he has had him in the office and even out on the construction site when there's no work going on.

Sounds like he is filling his days and his nights with his son and his work. I am sure that's not all he wants."

Adana, in a hurry as was the norm, said, "Cassandra, I hope we've been helpful. You know I've got to run. This case is driving me up a wall, but I'm in it to win it, so I'll talk to you soon. Afiya and Amara, take care of yourselves."

Everyone chimed in, "Love you, Adana."

Afiya added, "Be safe. This case has been all over the news and not in a good way."

"Don't you all worry. Like I tell Mom and Dad, I have the best protection the state of Virginia can buy. I love you. See ya soon."

She hung up, leaving the other sisters momentarily silent until the psychic Afiya spoke. "She'll be fine. We have to know and accept that, all right?"

"All right," came Amara's and Cassandra's responses in unison.

"And so, Cassandra, how are you feeling now, after this conversation?" asked Amara.

"Better. I think after a few more days, I can find my way. I do know that Ras was depending on me to finish the project for the orphans. I have to complete that if for no other reason than for the sake of the children. So in a few days I have to return to the work. The rest only God knows." The remaining sisters said their good-byes, and Cassandra once again headed for the burning rays of an unrelenting sun.

Cassandra grabbed her multicolored two-piece bathing suit and dressed slowly, reliving in her mind the multitude of emotions that surfaced when she thought of Ras. Her heart broke when she thought of losing him, but there was so much to sort through, so much to accept if they were to be together again. She really needed to clear her head, and a good swim was definitely in order.

She left her cottage and walked in the direction of the beach. The scorching sun was lasering in on every visible surface. Cassandra soaked it up. The sun energized her. It fueled her spirit. She truly needed it at that moment. As she strolled across the gleaming white sand, she could only think of Ras. As the hot sand sifted through the toes of her sandaled feet, it reminded Cassandra of Ras' searing kisses on each of her pampered toes. Everything he did was filled with sensuality and raw passion. How could she possibly give him up? In spite of his arrogance and reclusive nature, he was also a man deeply devoted to family, and he had made it clear that he truly loved her. What was she going to do? Only time would tell.

She removed her sandals. The large multicolored scarf she used as a wrap hung low on her hips. She removed the wrap and folded it neatly and placed the sandals on top of it. She walked closer to the water's edge and waded out into the ocean. It was the color of teal and sapphire with sprinkles of jade. When she was far enough in for her body to be immersed, she found her rhythm and swam as though in a race with herself to wash away remnants of Ras Selassie. She swam for her life. She swam until her arms were limp. She swam until her legs felt like weights. She swam until her lungs felt they could no longer take in air, but the remnants of Ras Selassie remained. His touch, his taste, his scent, his laughter, his scowl, his arrogance, his compassion and his love for her, they all remained etched in her heart and soul. She lifted herself from the water, barely able to walk. She felt drained of everything except Ras. She picked up her wrap and sandals from the place where they had been left and headed back to her cottage for a bath and dinner.

Once in the tub, filled with scented bubbles, she washed and soaked while listening to contemporary jazz sounds from the Bose radio, which was one of the perks of the cottage she had rented. The sounds were so sweet, she was mesmerized and lulled to sleep. She was awakened only by the cool water turning cold. She woke up feeling a slight chill and quickly got out of the tub and grabbed a towel. It was large and fluffy and was a welcome barrier to the shiver that was threatening to overtake her body.

After warming her body again, she stepped into a heated shower to wash the ocean from her Nubian knotted hair. She loosened each section and washed with a mango-scented shampoo that was fragrant to the senses and silky to the touch. She rinsed her hair, toweled it dry, applied shea butter to the superfine strands and decided to let the air naturally dry the remaining dampness. She lotioned and perfumed her body, put on an emerald green spaghetti-strapped dress and raw silk sandals of the same color, and headed out for dinner.

Near her cottage, within walking distance, one could find all of the amenities. Tonight she had no desire to sit in the cottage alone and eat. Though that was certainly an option, it wasn't an appealing one. She walked into an intimate little restaurant with open seating that served a variety of foods to suit the palates of the numerous clients it had to appease. Cassandra looked around for a table. Something private but not isolated. She laughed at how conflicted she felt about almost everything these days. She wanted company, but she wanted to be alone. She wanted Ras one minute, and the next minute she wanted to be as far away from him as was humanly possible. She conceded to herself that this was indeed a troubling time. She prayed for the strength to come through it, if not unscathed, at least not destroyed.

She saw a table for two in a corner of the room. It was private but positioned so that the entire restaurant could still be seen. She walked over to the table and made herself comfortable. She had been seated a few moments when a gentleman who appeared to be Latin, dressed in a waiter's uniform, approached her table. He smiled politely and said, "Welcome to La Estrellita." He placed a menu in front of her and continued speaking. "Our catch of the day is red snapper, and it is excellent. We pride ourselves on being able to fix any dish exactly to your liking." His accent was like music to Cassandra's ears. It reminded her once again of another accent that tantalized her ears when she heard it. Ras Selassie was embedded in her psyche. Memories of him were everywhere she turned.

The gentleman seated across the room saw Cassandra when she entered the restaurant. He was taken by her beauty, her grace and her air of total self-confidence, but he could also see a sadness in her eyes, which intrigued him. He sat staring at her, not discreetly but openly. He stared until she could feel his gaze boring into her. She looked up from her menu and looked directly into his eyes. He nodded his head in place of a verbal greeting. She acknowledged him with a tentative smile and a slight bow of her head in his direction. She continued to peruse her menu as the thought occurred to her that he seemed a bit odd.

Her waiter returned, and she ordered the red snapper grilled with rosemary and thyme. It was served with asparagus spears and a rice pilaf. As she sat enjoying her predinner Kir Royale, made with champagne, crème de cassis and a twist of lime, she was lost in a cascade of thoughts, from job-related interior designs to Adana's new case, to the fun she and Afiya had had in Addis Ababa, which of course, brought her to thoughts of Ras. She turned her head slightly, processing her many thoughts, just as the mysterious man was leaving the restaurant.

He was a giant of a man. Though he carried a cane, he walked with the gait of a dancer. He was dressed nattily in a white linen suit and a wide-brimmed panama hat. His face was one creased with time and experience. Even the deep melanin in his skin had not been able to erase the ravages of time. Almost as if he had eyes in the back of his head, he turned to see her watch him leave. He once again bowed his head; only this time he tipped his hat as he maintained his stride. Pierre Le Veaux was Haitian. He was a man of much wisdom, and he had been born with the gift of prophetic sight. He had seen into Cassandra's life and had left her a message in the form of a note, which he had asked her waiter to give to her after his departure. He did not want to be in the restaurant when she read it. He had found over the years that when alone with their own thoughts, people often came to much clearer conclusions. His job was just to spark the flames.

Cassandra thought again, *What an odd man*. She ate well. The swim had helped her to work up quite an appetite. She declined dessert and asked for the bill. When it arrived, she picked it up to determine its accuracy and found underneath it a napkin on which was printed a handwritten note, which read, *Your love waits on another continent—he is your true love. Your marriage will be blessed*. The note was unsigned, but somehow she knew it was the work of the mysterious gentleman. She sat stunned. Who was he? What did he know about her? Did he know Ras? She had to get to the bottom of the mystery note. She gestured for her waiter to return to her table and asked, a bit shaken, "Excuse me. Do you know who put this note on the tray with the bill?"

"Why, yes, *señorita*. The tall gentleman in the white suit who just left."

Now really uneasy, Cassandra asked, "Who is he? Do you know him?"

"No, *señorita*. I only saw him tonight, never before."

Cassandra paid the bill and left a generous tip and said, "Thank you very much."

She crumpled up the handwritten note, left it on the table and walked quickly back to her cottage. As she thought back over the entire scene, she became more and more nervous. She unlocked the door to her cottage, entered, bolted the door behind her and then went from room to room, turning on every light. She checked windows and doors at least twice before she finally calmed herself. To calm herself further, she knew she needed to talk to one of her sisters, and the sister for this job was Afiya. She pressed in Afiya's numbers and waited for a ring. It rang twice, three times, and just as Cassandra had decided to hang up, a very groggy Afiya answered with a low "Hello."

Cassandra, feeling guilty for not having checked the time, said, "Afiya, I'm so sorry. I should have looked at my watch."

A yawning Afiya rushed to reassure her. "No, Sis, you're OK. Normal people are still up. I just took a little nap because I have a gallery installation that is going to be an all-nighter, and you know I need my beauty rest." She laughed, fully awake now. "So what's going on in Punta Cana?"

Cassandra started slowly. "I had an experience today that only you and a few other people would understand, and I'm hoping you can help me make sense of it."

Her curiosity now piqued, Afiya said, "OK, tell me."

"Tonight at dinner an older man whom I had never seen before stared at me for the longest time, then nodded a hello. Before he left the restaurant, he left me a note saying my love waits on another continent and that my marriage would be blessed."

"Wow, that's quite a gift."

"A gift? Afiya, that was crazy."

"I don't think so, Cassandra. I think it was a gift. You know I believe we have angels, and you know I believe in prophetic sight. I believe it because I've had flashes of it myself. You know I have. I just think it was your message about Ras. You've been in a quandary, you've prayed and your answer was sent. If I were in your shoes, I would accept the message. Call it your prophetic sign."

"Afiya Terrell, you are truly a gift. I don't know if that message was, but you are."

Afiya chuckled at Cassandra's remark and said, "Thanks, Sis."

Cassandra responded, "All right my psychic hotline sister. I'm going to let you finish your nap. I think I'm ready now to get back to Addis Ababa. That man freaked me out, so I'm afraid not to go."

They both laughed at Cassandra's humorous remark and said their good-byes.

The next day Cassandra called Amara, and they arranged her flight back to Addis Ababa via a Mazrui company plane.

# Chapter 19

The Addis Ababa morning sun was beaming when Cassandra once again returned to Ethiopian soil. She felt strangely as though she were returning home. She hopped into one of the omnipresent blue-and-white taxicabs that lined the streets and told the driver to take her to the Sheraton Addis. Once she arrived at the hotel, she was welcomed like a long-lost friend. Her original suite was still unoccupied, and so she checked in, unpacked and went for a swim. As she swam, the thought occurred to her that she would never again be able to come to Addis Ababa without thoughts of Ras Selassie. For her, he was Addis Ababa. The sights, the sounds, the tastes, the smells. It was all imprinted on her soul, and it was all Ras. Gliding through the water, she remembered their first kiss. As she caressed the water stroke after stroke, she remembered the way he stroked her body in their heated exchanges of raw passion. The water washed over her just as his love did when he could hold it no longer, and it spilled and flowed, leaving her wrung out from pleasure, yet crying for more. She swam until she was near exhaustion, and then she poured herself out of the pool and headed for her suite to get ready to begin her first day back at RS Development. Though she had been gone nearly two weeks, it felt like a lifetime had passed since she had seen Ras or touched him or been held by him. Her need for him could not be measured.

Cassandra, attired in monochromatic cream-colored silk shirt and linen pants, walked into the RS Development building and was greeted by the receptionist, who lifted her hand and smiled while busily fielding incoming calls. Cassandra continued on to her temporary headquarters. Once she reached the office, unseen by others in the building, she closed the door behind her, sat behind her desk, took a deep breath and began pulling meticulously labeled files from her briefcase and from her file cabinets. She rolled up the sleeves of her cream-colored silk shirt and kicked off her taupe-colored mules and sat with bare feet. She fingered the long strand of pearls she wore around her neck with one hand as she calculated room dimensions with the other.

Hours later, after staff members had left for the day, Ras found her in a similar state when he opened the office door and saw her poring over weeks of work in various stages of completion. She was so engrossed in the work, she did not hear the door open and did not see Ras as he stood transfixed by her image. There had been times in her absence when he had come to her office just to feel her presence, to be brushed by a lingering fragrance, to move into a meditative state, to remember every passionate encounter they had ever had. The room held memories of her, of sights, sounds, touches and tastes he never wanted to forget. She felt his presence and looked up into the eyes that had in the past riveted her with worshipful stares of longing and lust and with angry moments of threatened retribution and with raw, sensual power. In a low, melodic voice dripping with need, Ras uttered "I've missed you."

With desire for him racing through her body, she replied, "I've missed you, too."

Ras walked into the room and, with kingly elegance, sat

down in a chair in front of her desk, crossed his legs, sat back and, with a calm that was far from what he was feeling, said, "No one told me you were here."

She responded almost in a whisper. "No one knew except Anya, the receptionist. It was early when I arrived. I didn't want to disturb anyone." She gestured to the stacks on her desk. "I have all of these files to complete, and so I just wanted to quietly come in and work on them."

Ras looked at her with weeks of desire visibly haunting his eyes and asked, "Are we talking about work? Is that what we want to talk about, Cassandra?"

Her look of longing matched his as she said, "No, it's not what I want to talk about, but I don't know where to begin."

Ras rose from the chair, walked around Cassandra's desk, helped her from her chair, held her hands and said, "Let me begin where I should have begun weeks ago. Cassandra, I have recently been told that I am a father." He swallowed and took a breath. "I am the single father of a six-month-old little boy who is handsome and precocious. He is a loving little character who these days fills his father's heart with joy. I am a man who has made a number of mistakes in my life, but my greatest mistake was not sharing with you immediately the fact of my son's birth. I love you, Cassandra Terrell, more than life itself. I cannot lose you, because I have come to understand that my life is not complete without you. In all of my arrogance, self-centeredness and fear, I underestimated how much my love for you, my divine woman, could mean to my life. Your absence has caused me more anguish than I have ever known."

Misty-eyed, Cassandra spoke. "I am so grateful that I have not driven away the man I love with my hot temper and my refusal to allow you to be a human being who was stumped by indecision. I hope we have both learned some important lessons about the value of our love."

Ras fashioned his tilted smile, looked deeply into Cassandra's eyes and, with humor and mischief in his voice, said, "I did learn that at least one of my parents is a cockroach, which makes me quite a repulsive insect, at least in part."

Cassandra opened her eyes wide and covered her mouth while saying, "Oh, my God, Ras, my temper just got out of control. I said so much. You know I didn't mean to disrespect your parents. I just wanted to slap you."

Still smiling, he said, "You did, my sweet."

Now her hands were removed from her face, and she was gesturing wildly. "You know what I mean. I felt betrayed. I wanted to slap you with my words. I wanted to hurt you as much as you hurt me."

Still standing, Ras moved slightly closer, looked at Cassandra intensely and said, "Come here, my sweet." He wrapped her in his arms and whispered in her ear, "I have been called worse than a lying rabid dog and son of a cockroach."

Now Cassandra was laughing out loud, and Ras joined her as he held her close to his chest. The laughter slowed, and all that was left was the beating of their hearts. Cassandra spoke with loving emotion and affection tied to every word.

"I have missed you so much, and I need you so much."

Ras held her closer and, with an equal mixture of love and lust, responded, "I have wanted so much in these last weeks to hold you, to feel you next to me."

In soft tones that caressed Ras' ears, Cassandra replied, "I have wanted so much for you to hold me. I need to be held by you. When I am in your arms, all is right with the world."

Ras softly touched her lips with his and said, "I don't ever want to be without you again. Please say that you will marry me."

With tears glistening in her eyes, she answered, "Yes, my darling, I will."

And then the kiss began as though they had never been apart. Their bodies remembered as though they were engaged in a well-choreographed dance designed for two. He took her mouth. She surrendered it. Her arms, instinctively knowing their places, wrapped themselves around his powerful neck. As he kissed her, his hands found the breasts that he hungered to fondle, and through the softness of sliding silk, her nipples were inflamed by his perfectly placed feathery touches, pulling from her erotic whimpers, which aroused him and left her knees weak and her body trembling.

Ras slowed the kiss and whispered, "I have tasted you in my sleep. I gave up my bed and moved to another room because the scent of you has seeped into the walls of my bedroom. My bed feels as though it still has the imprint of your body, and the sounds of our lovemaking hang in every corner. If you leave me again, I'll go mad."

In a fog of sensual pleasure, Cassandra responded, "I'll never leave you again. I can't. I need you like I need water to drink. I love you, Ras, I love you."

"And you, my sweet, fiery one, I will love for as long as the sun rises and sets. You are all I will ever need."

With his low, mellow voice washing over her, Ras said, "Come with me. There are two people I want you to meet."

They left the stacks of files on Cassandra's desk just as they had been when Ras found her and headed for the suburban community in which Ras and his parents lived. On the road in Ras' Bentley convertible, Cassandra once again marveled at the lush verdant countryside as it stood in stark contrast to the desolate images so often seen in the international media. The air was fragrant with the flora and fauna that littered the Addis Ababa countryside.

Soon Ras turned onto the familiar road that Cassandra knew led to his parents' home. He parked the car in the circular driveway, got out of the car, and opened Cassandra's door, and with his hand placed firmly at the center of her back, they walked to the front door. Ras used his key and unlocked the massive, intricately carved door. As he opened it, he called, "Mother." He paused. "Father." He turned to Cassandra and said, with a bit of anxiousness in his voice, "I know they are here somewhere. I left my son with those two this morning. They are taking their grandparenting more seriously than you can imagine. I don't think I've ever seen two people happier. I have to constantly remind them that he is my son." He smiled, thinking of the love little Ras Kebran was receiving from so many. Just as he finished his thought, he saw his parents walking hand in hand from the back of the house, smiling at each other. His father was the first to speak.

"Son, we heard you, but we were just putting the newest master Selassie down for a nap. He fought it all the way, but finally the dream weaver captured him, and he is resting peacefully."

He looked at the lovely young woman standing next to his son, and before he could form a question, his wife was embracing her, saying, "Oh, Cassandra, it is so good to see you again. You are as beautiful as ever. Meet my husband and Ras' father. He was traveling on business when you were last here. Cassandra Terrell, General Tafari Selassie."

Cassandra extended her hand, and Tafari Selassie grasped it with his two enormous ones and said with deep resonance, "My son and your father, two men who know you well, have spoken highly of you, and my wife has been singing your praises, so I am more than happy to meet you."

Cassandra was overcome with emotion. She was not sure what had taken place with Ras and his father, but she was grateful to God that there was peace in a part of his life where there had been so much pain. She replied, "General Selassie, I am so very pleased to meet you, and my father did very much enjoy his visit with you. He is still talking about how you two solved the world's problems."

Ras, basking in the glory of the magic of newly cemented relationships, interrupted. "Father, Mother, if you will allow us a moment, I must introduce Cassandra to a little person who will soon be her son, because she has consented to be my wife."

Amara Selassie's eyes were lined with tears as she said, "Oh, my beautiful children, I am so happy for you both." She reached out to embrace each of them in turn.

Tafari Selassie was deeply moved, and pride and joy were evident in his voice. "My son, you have always been a source of pride for your mother and for me. Tonight you have made us more proud than ever. You have taken the step to become the head of your household. That, my son, truly makes you a man of strength and character. And you, my lovely Cassandra, we welcome into the bosom of our family. As of this day a place for you has been carved into the family record, never to be removed."

He held them both tightly as he fought back his tears. Cassandra was experiencing more joy than she had ever known. She expressed her tear-filled thanks to the Selassies and thought silently about how wonderful it was going to feel to share her joy with her parents and her sisters. Interrupting her thoughts, Ras caressed her and whispered softly, "Come, my future wife. I want you to see your son."

As he and Cassandra walked away arm in arm, Tafari and Amara Selassie embraced, holding on to one another with eternal gratitude that their son had found his place and a passionate encounter had given rise to a life of love.

Ras and Cassandra walked into the room Ras' parents had furnished for their grandson. The room was bright and sunny, wallpapered and painted in yellows and blues. They had commissioned a ceiling mural that was a replica of a sky on a clear, sunny day. Cassandra and Ras walked over to the elaborately carved crib, a Selassie heirloom, and watched as master Ras Kebran Selassie slept with the peace of an angel. When Cassandra saw him, she began to cry softly, and tears of joy ran slowly down her face. Ras, seeing the tears, wrapped her in his arms and asked, "Why are you crying, my sweet?"

Cassandra wiped her eyes with the back of her hand

and whispered, "He is so beautiful. He looks like a miniature you, and I am so happy that I will be his mother. Here he is, healthy and beautiful, waiting to be loved, and I have more than enough love to give."

Ras whispered into her ear, "This, my darling, is our first son. If God and the ancestors are good, we shall give him as many brothers and sisters as we can handle."

"Yes," was Cassandra's response. They read each other's hearts and moved into each other's arms. Ras lowered his head, and with full, sensuous lips as soft as cotton and as warm as a summer breeze, he kissed the nape of Cassandra's neck, causing her to expel a soft breath. As they looked into each other's eyes, they knew their future held long nights and days of passionate encounters.

Ras spoke, evoking in Cassandra the longing and need she had come to associate with him. He held her close as he said, "You, my sweet, I want as my wife as soon as that is physically possible. How soon can you marry me?"

Attempting to convince her of the urgency of his desire, he continued to state his case while touching her face, her arms and her lips with his long, skillful fingers and leveling his seductive gaze at her, disturbing all of her senses. "I would say today, but I am sure there would be objections from friends and relatives who would want to witness the event. But I need you now as my wife. I only have one request, that we be married in Gonder. It has been called Africa's Camelot. It is a magical place, and you, my love, have brought so much magic into my life."

Cassandra, suffering from sensory overload, spoke quietly. "Ras, you make me so happy. I want us to be married soon, but realistically, I don't see how we can get everything that needs to be done finished quickly."

He interrupted her by placing one long finger on her lips. "My sweet, this is the era of modern technology, and in addition to that, we are people with a wealth of resources at our disposal. We can do the impossible."

Cassandra smiled. "I believe you can." She took a long

breath and continued. "Since you're the logistical expert, how much time do we need?"

With a straight face, Ras answered, "One week!"

"Ras!" Cassandra's voice rose almost to a shout. She looked at the still sleeping baby and lowered her voice. "Are you insane? What can be done in a week?"

Still holding her, Ras answered softly, "All right, three weeks."

"Ras," Cassandra said in an exasperated tone.

Ras stroked her back and planted possessive kisses on her neck, cheeks and earlobes while saying, "I need to have you always. I need your taste, your touch. I need to brand every inch of your body with my stamp."

As her skin smoldered with the heat of his touch, Cassandra wrapped her arms around his neck. Her desire for him overshadowed her sense of reality as she said, "Three weeks."

Ras smiled, his full, sensuous lips turned up at one corner. "Thank you, my love. I promise you, you will never regret consenting to be my wife. My love for you has no limits, and our passion for each other will only grow stronger with time. He kissed her softly and then added, "We will share the news with your parents together."

Then Ras began kissing her again. He kissed her as though he thought she would break. The kiss was so gentle, it caused her pulse to race and the center of her being to long for the pleasure of his touch. He stopped and just as gently moved her an inch away from him. They both looked at the sleeping baby, smiled and walked from the room, feeling the glow of lovers clothed in thoughts of the ecstasy that was to come.

The following day Ras called Cassandra at the Sheraton Addis and shared with her that the Selassies and the Mazruis were going to be with him when he formally requested from her father her hand in marriage. Logistically, that meant the Mazrui planes would be scheduled to fly out the following day to Virginia, taking Ras, Cassandra, Ras' parents, the baby and his governess, Keino, Amara,

Kaleb, Aman and Kamau. Cassandra's parents had been told that Ras' parents were coming to Virginia on business and had invited them to have dinner at their hotel. Cassandra was both nervous and excited. She knew that her days with Ras would be larger than life, and she felt ready for all of it. She was ready for her powerful, sometimes arrogant, extremely loving, complex husband-to-be. She was ready to be a mother to a little boy whom she already loved. Yes, she was ready to create a life with a man whose lovemaking made her world stand still.

As she was sitting lost in thought about the man who made her weak with a touch, her telephone rang again. She answered with a somewhat distracted "Hello."

She recognized her sister Amara immediately as the excited voice on the other end of the phone line gushed, "Congratulations, Sis. I've been crying tears of joy ever since I heard."

A smile permeated Cassandra's voice as she spoke with Amara. "I just found out a moment ago that the Mazruis are joining us to formally ask Dad."

"Yes, Keino just told me. You know I had to call. I also called Afiya and Adana and swore them to secrecy so that Mom and Dad will be totally in the dark. Can't you just see Mom crying now?"

"Yes, I can," Cassandra answered, still smiling. As if for the first time understanding the magnitude of what she was about to do, Cassandra shouted, "Oh my God, Amara, do you realize what I have to accomplish in three weeks?"

"Yes, I do, and I'm way ahead of you. As soon as we get off the phone, I'll call Camille. You know she's a pro. She pulled my wedding together, and she'll make time for yours."

"Thanks, Sis. Tell her we are mixing African cultures. A little African American and a little Ethiopian. She knows the drill. She did a magnificent job with your wedding."

"Yes, she did. I still have beautiful memories of the whole event. Okay, Sis, I've got to go. I need to call

Camille. Expect calls from those other two sisters of yours. Love ya!"

"Love you, too."

Cassandra hung up the telephone, sat down at the desk in her bedroom, took out the jewel-covered journal and the Mont Blanc pen Ras had given her as welcoming gifts, and began to make a list of all that needed to be done so that in three weeks' time she could become Mrs. Cassandra Selassie. When she had been writing and planning for about an hour, Afiya and Adana called together, sending her love and congratulations, and offering any help that she needed. She gave them each assignments that they were to coordinate with the wedding planner once she was on board. They laughed and joked about Cassandra being the second sister to marry, speculating as to who would be next. Adana assured them that she would never marry and that they could count her out. Cassandra and Afiya found that very amusing and told her so before they all hung up and went about their busy lives.

The next day the entourage boarded the Mazrui family planes and headed for Virginia. The flight was timed so that they arrived in the afternoon.

Ras, his parents, the baby and the governess checked into hotel suites. Keino and Amara had accommodations enough for everyone between their two Virginia homes, but Ras insisted upon using the hotel, saying that logistically it was more convenient, and so the Mazrui brothers stayed with Keino and Amara. Cassandra went to her own home, and it was a bittersweet pleasure to return knowing that she would never again come back to it as an unmarried woman.

As evening fell, the excitement rose and the tension heightened. Everyone had gathered in Ras' parents' suite, awaiting the arrival of Cassandra's parents, who were under the illusion that they were meeting old friends for dinner.

Walking down the ultramodern hallway leading to the Selassie suite, Ana Terrell said to her husband, "Wasn't it a surprise to hear from Tafari and Amara? I didn't realize we'd get to see them again so soon."

"Yes, it was a surprise. A welcome one. I hope Tafari is here long enough for me to run him around the golf course a few times." James Terrell laughed at the thought of beating Tafari Selassie. On the golf course, neither of them ever seemed to win.

By the time Ana Terrell finished laughing at her husband's competitive nature, they were standing at the door of the suite, and James Terrell was lifting a brass knocker with long, tapered fingers not unlike Ras'. He knocked twice. Tafari Selassie appeared at the door. With a bright smile and a warm welcome extended to Drs. Ana and James Terrell, Tafari Selassie called for his wife, Amara, who entered the room as effusively as she always did, greeting her guests with warmth and graciousness, trying not to give away the secret she wanted to shout from the rooftops. Instead of screaming for joy, she calmly said, "Come join us in the sitting room for light refreshments."

Ana and James followed the Selassies into a room that was not a sitting room at all but a dining room expansive enough to seat a large dinner party. When they entered, James was frozen in place and Ana immediately started to cry as they looked around the room and saw all of their daughters and the Mazrui and Selassie families. They did not know what the occasion was, but they knew it was important and festive. The room was beautifully decorated with long-stemmed white orchids, crystal glassware and gold-trimmed china place settings. Long-stemmed white candles in shimmering silver candelabra stood regally on the tables. Chairs upholstered in padded ivory raw silk and with bronze-colored ladder backs were strategically placed for seating. Amber lighting reflected off of candlelight, setting a warm, romantic mood.

Ras was the first to step forward. The words poured forth like liquid velvet as he said, "Dr. Ana Terrell, Dr. James Terrell, in old Ethiopia one of the ways a man took a bride was to send word to her family that he had chosen her. I am sending word today that I love your daughter Cassandra Anika Terrell. I want her to be my wife. I want to keep her all of the days of our lives." He took a breath. "You must know, too, that I am a man who does not bring himself alone to this marriage. I am a single father. I have an infant son, whom Cassandra has consented to help me nurture into manhood. You don't know me. You only know of me, but you know my parents and my relatives. My cousin is your son-in-law, and so I have brought them all to attest to my good character." When Ras finished, every woman in the room was teary-eyed and extremely happy.

James Terrell, deeply moved, extended his hand to Ras. Ras extended his hand. James held Ras' hand with his two and said, "Son, Ana and I are overwhelmed today. We could not be more surprised." He looked at his wife, read the tears in her eyes and the smile on her face, and said, "We would be greatly pleased to have you as a part of our family. I want to say to you the same thing I said to Keino when he asked to marry Amara. We love our daughters. Each one is a precious jewel. They have been nurtured and loved, and each one is special. Now Miss Cassandra is the feisty one. She's flamboyant and she's high maintenance, but she's no hothouse flower. She is fiercely loyal, and she will love you with all of her heart. Children are her weakness. She will make an excellent mother. Love her fiercely, son. Take care of my daughter. If you ever feel you can't or you won't, bring her home, son, bring her home."

Continuing to hold James' hand firmly, Ras looked deeply into his eyes and said, "Dr. Terrell, for your daughter, I would give my life. I will love her beyond death. My home will now become our home. She will never have to leave it, and I will do everything in my power to see that she never wants to leave it."

"Son, you have our blessing."

The room went up in applause. Ras reached for Cassandra,

and she walked into his arms for a kiss that was as chaste as they could make it with everyone's eyes on them. Ras spoke again, looking straight into Cassandra's misty eyes. "And so, Cassandra Terrell, in front of all of these people, I ask you again. Will you be my wife?"

Almost in a whisper, Cassandra answered, "Yes, my love, I will be your wife."

Ras looked at Keino, and Keino handed him a black velvet box. He opened the box and revealed a diamond-encrusted platinum ring, which he removed from the box and placed on Cassandra's finger. She gasped from the sheer beauty of it, and with tears now streaming down her cheeks, she said, "Ras, it is so beautiful."

"Not as beautiful as you are, my darling. There was nothing available that compared to your beauty, and so we will settle for this." He took his handkerchief and gently wiped away her tears.

Ras' father then stepped forward and toasted the couple. Following the toast, each Selassie and Mazrui man came forward and presented Cassandra with a precious piece of jewelry that was an heirloom or with a newly purchased piece, which would one day be an heirloom.

The meal that followed was lavish, a mixture of American and Ethiopian dishes. Ras' mother and Cassandra's mother spent most of the evening crying and saying how they could not believe that now they were going to be in-laws. From college friends to family, how far they had come. Cassandra's sisters and Ras' cousins had a joyous time speculating on how Ras and Cassandra would fare as husband and wife. Ras assured them all that he and Cassandra would have the last laugh. James and Ana Terrell marveled at how two of their daughters had found love on the same continent and in the same family.

# Chapter 20

Over the course of the weekend that followed, Ras, with the willing and eager assistance of his parents, his cousins the Mazrui brothers, and his Aunt Adina and Uncle Garsen, set about to simulate some of the festivities and rituals that would have taken place had they planned a more traditional Ethiopian wedding. The rituals that were to be reenacted, though done with Western flair, were no less deeply rooted in grand Ethiopian tradition and style.

The first event began with all of the men in Ras' immediate family going together as a group to call upon Cassandra's parents in their home to discuss the character and the worthiness of the groom-to-be. In traditional Ethiopia, the eldest men in the family would have been sent by the groom to speak on his behalf. Drs. James and Ana Terrell were prepared for the event and welcomed the men into their home, anticipating the joy, the solemnity and the powerful significance of the ancient ritual they were about to experience.

The Selassie-Mazrui contingent, dressed in traditional Ethiopian garments of sparkling white jodhpurs and tunics trimmed with bright, colorful borders, was led into the great room of the Terrell home. Chairs had been arranged in a circle in the middle of the room to facilitate the discussion and to symbolize the strength and unity of an undivided family. Once everyone was seated, General Selassie began in a voice filled with pride and anticipation.

"James and Ana, we thank you for welcoming us into your home so graciously. As you know, we are here to repeat what our fathers and our forefathers did in days of old. We are representing my son, Ras, who desires to make your daughter Cassandra his wife. This day we are here to formally ask permission for your daughter to become a member of the Selassie family."

Fully aware of the importance of the event taking place in his home, James Terrell was filled with a wave of emotion that had taken him by surprise. The pride he felt for Cassandra at that moment he could not have adequately articulated, but he could feel it wrap itself around his heart as he spoke.

"My wife and I want nothing more than for our daughter to be married well to a man for whom she has the utmost respect and love and who can return to her equal love and respect. As is your tradition, Ana and I must question Ras' worthiness to care for and protect our precious daughter. I will start by asking, who can speak to the character of Ras Selassie?"

Keino spoke, his face filled with a broad smile. His words flowed smoothly, each syllable reflecting the grace of his East African cadence. "Ras Selassie, my first cousin, is a man among men. Ras is principled, he is loyal and he would protect Cassandra with his life. Cassandra is the first woman he has loved, and he says she will be the last. As I have watched them together, I see fire and fire. They burn as brightly and as clearly as the future they are sure to have together."

Kamau spoke next. His stern exterior and clipped, cultured East African tone could not mask his respect for his cousin Ras. "Ras is a warrior. He is a man who, with courage and boldness, will fight to protect what is his. Drs. Ana and James Terrell, your daughter has chosen well."

Aman, the cardiac surgeon, spoke with his characteristic

precision. "Ras is a member of the Selassie-Mazrui family. Our lineage is worthy. It is strong. It is wholesome and well respected. Cassandra would be a beautiful addition to a family that would welcome her with open arms."

Kaleb's voice rose as he spoke while laughing. "Drs. Terrell, please say you will accept our humble pleading so that we can put Ras and Cassandra out of their mutual misery. I've seen those two. If they are not married soon, another world war might just be in the making."

As Kaleb looked around the room, smiling and turning from side to side, waiting for a response, the serious tone in the room was broken, and the gathering erupted in gales of laughter. James was the first to bring the room back to order.

"I think," he said, a smile still tracing the outline of his lips, "we have heard enough about our future son-in-law. We welcome you all into our family."

Ana Terrell added, misty-eyed, "It will be our pleasure to support Ras and Cassandra throughout their marriage, and to watch them raise little Kebran and produce and nurture more children. We look forward to joining our two families and celebrating with you on many festive occasions as we connect in the way families do."

James, looking at Ana as she spoke, relived again that pride that enfolded his heart. Congratulatory handshakes went around the room among the men as Ana left the room to alert the Ethiopian catering service she had hired to bring in the refreshments they were prepared to serve. The group of men, soon to become one family, were led into the spacious Terrell dining room to end their discussion with a feast. Ras, Cassandra and her sisters, Ras' mother, and Judge and Mrs. Garsen Mazrui had been waiting in another part of the house for the negotiations to end, at which time they were asked to join the rest of the party. Ras and Cassandra, holding hands, led the way. A feeling of excitement and joyous anticipation filled the air. The festive mood became even livelier when Kaleb saw the couple and yelled across the room, "Hey, cousin, you don't have to start World War III. Your future in-laws have given their consent."

The room went up in uproarious laughter, and Ras turned to Cassandra, wrapped her in his arms and kissed her as discreetly as he could, knowing that all eyes were on them. He stopped the kiss, and with his arm still wrapped around her waist, he turned to her parents and said, with a voice filled with gratitude, "I want to thank you again for trusting that I will love and honor your daughter. She has my heart."

Judge Mazrui added in his deep resonant voice, "Hear! Hear! Let us eat and drink to that sentiment." And they ate Ethiopian delicacies, drank *tej* and engaged in thoughtful and sometimes humorous conversation until early evening. Ras, though enjoying the preliminaries, wanted the wedding day to come soon. He already envisioned Cassandra as his wife. He longed to refer to her as Mrs. Ras Selassie. Though it was not at all unheard of for Ethiopian women to maintain their own surnames after marriage, Ras wanted nothing separating them, not even a name. He wanted to please Cassandra for the rest of his life.

She sat next to him, feeling his longing, knowing that it matched hers. Like Ras, she wanted the wedding day to come so that they could begin living their lives as a married couple. She also shuddered when she thought of all of the wedding arrangements and decisions that were yet to be made. She made a mental note to call Camille Evanti, friend and premier wedding planner, first thing the next day. She took a deep breath and smiled as a shiver of pleasure eased through her core like liquid mercury when Ras leaned over and whispered in her ear, "I want you, Cassandra. I want to feel you, I want to taste you, and I want to touch you."

She smiled, happy that the guests were so engaged in conversation, they could not read the passion she felt. She whispered back, leaving a wispy trail of cool breath in

Ras' ear, which almost sent him over the edge, as she said, "If you will promise to wait, I will promise to reward you in a way that you'll never forget."

They looked into each other's eyes, and Ras' seductive stare and crooked smile told her he was anticipating his reward.

The following day, as the Terrell, Mazrui and Selassie women got together to host a bridal shower for Cassandra, she took time out to contact her wedding planner to bring together some much needed details. That morning she had awakened automatically at 6 A.M., feeling surprisingly refreshed. At 9 A.M. she was still smiling at thoughts of the joyous gathering the night before. It was all becoming so real; she was soon to become Cassandra Selassie. She had to laugh out loud when she thought about the rocky start she and Ras had had. In the beginning, she thought that surely she was going to learn to hate him, not love him. Was she ever wrong. In Ras, she had found a kind of love she never knew existed. She loved him, she loved his son and she loved the idea of giving him as many children as their hearts and lives would hold.

Cassandra had taken a long, leisurely bath in a tub filled with her favorite jasmine and lavender scents. She stood in her kitchen, thinking of how good it had felt being in her own tub again if only for a short while. She knew she would miss the life she had known. Her loft brought her joy, but she had to remember it also held memories of its architect, Christopher Hunter, her fiancé who was killed, and though she would keep the loft for a while after her marriage, she knew the time would come when she would sell it and replace it with something that held only memories of Ras and their new family.

She took a cleansing breath and reached for the portable telephone. From a drawer near the telephone, she retrieved a silk zebra-patterned address book, which contained Camille Evanti's telephone numbers. Cassandra decided to try Camille's cellular number. She punched in the numbers and waited as the wireless carrier assured her that it was locating the desired customer. Shortly, Camille, came on the line, saying in a very practiced professional voice, "This is Camille Evanti."

"Hi, Camille. This is Cassandra."

A high-spirited Camille responded, "Cassandra. Hey, dahling, how are you? Amara called me and filled me in on the good news, so I know congratulations are definitely in order."

"Thanks, Camille. You know I'm calling on you to work a miracle."

"Sweetheart, I'm in the miracle-working business. Whatever it is, if it can be done, honey, I can either do it or I know someone who can. What are we looking at in terms of time?"

"Don't kill me, Camille, but we've only got about two and a half weeks."

Camille laughed out loud. "You Terrell sisters sure know how to make a girl stretch, don't you?"

Cassandra responded with a sheepish "Sorry."

"All I can say is he had better be worth it, Cassandra."

"Oh, he's worth every bit of the pain I'm going through now to get to the pleasure."

They both laughed at that vividly painted picture of ecstasy. Then Camille was all business once again.

"All right, Cassandra. Tell me about the setting for the wedding."

"It will be in Gonder, in a beautiful seventeenth-century church. The only decorations I want in the church are calla lilies and orchids, all white, mountains of them. The ceremony will resemble a high mass. I'd like a small orchestra hidden away in the choir loft, which is built into the rafters of the church, and a choir blending old African American spirituals with traditional Ethiopian songs. My sisters will be my bridesmaids. I'll let them choose their dresses. I know I'll be pleased with their choices."

"Sounds good. I have a magnificent announcement in

mind. It comes from a new vendor that I'm working with. It opens like a scroll, with beautiful tassels on each end. Very fitting for the church in Gonder. It is delivered in a gold box with ribbons matching the color of the tassels. I would also suggest that at this late date the invite be carried by messenger to each guest."

Cassandra responded, "I like that idea, and there will be only about one hundred guests on my list. Ras is another story. So it should not be too difficult to manage, but talk to him and work it out please."

"No problem. I'll check with Ras, and I'll forward reception ideas to you tomorrow."

"Thanks, Camille. You know you are a jewel."

"Anything for a Terrell. I just love watching the four of you. We can't all be as blessed. There is nothing like having a sister who is also your friend. That has to be the best."

"It is, and we do feel very fortunate. Take care, Camille. I'll talk to you tomorrow."

"Bye, Cassandra. Give my love to everyone."

Cassandra placed the telephone back in its cradle, stretched her arms toward the ceiling and flexed her back in a movement that was very much like a lounging cat. She took a deep breath, gently tilted her head back and started to easily roll it from side to side. Just as she had finished the last circular motion, the shrillness of her ringing telephone transported her immediately from peaceful serenity to an awareness of the mountains of details she had yet to address. Once again she picked up the telephone. As soon as she said "Hello," she could feel him through the wires.

"My beautiful Cassandra. I cannot begin to tell you how much I miss you. Last night I ran five miles before I could entertain sleep."

"I'm sorry, sweetheart. I wish there were something I could do."

"You know there is something you can do."

Ignoring Ras' suggestive statement, Cassandra, smiling to herself, asked sweetly, purposely arousing in Ras a slithering, silent sensuality that only she could arouse, "Sweetheart, how is Kebran?"

Ras, instantly shaken into reality, with a hint of his daydream lingering in the recesses of his mind, answered, "He is doing well. The two of us are becoming more attached every day. I must admit that I never thought that I would actually have the chance to see light in my child's eyes or a smile on his face, or spend days trying to decipher the meaning of a sound that I know must be important because he utters it with such expression and force."

Cassandra laughed. It gave her such pleasure to hear Ras express his joy about being a father.

"Ras, you are becoming such a wonderful father. You've taken to it so easily, and I am so proud of you. I do love you so."

"If you love me so, then you need to prove it by showing me how much you love me. How can you love me and deny me pleasure at the same time?"

"Ras Selassie, we are not going to sleep together with all of our parents watching. We know they know, but they don't have to see or know for sure until after the wedding."

"My sweet Cassandra, I am not asking that we sleep together. I want to make love to you. Sleeping together is such a strange description of making love. I don't want us to sleep. We will be wide awake, tasting, feeling, touching, torturing one another with divine pleasure. No, my darling, sleeping is the very last thing on my mind."

"Ras Selassie, you are impossible. You know precisely what I mean."

"And you know what I mean. I can be at your door in seven minutes. I've mapped it all out. We could be walking on a cloud by the time our next event takes place this evening. We would be deliriously drunk with the wine of love and lust. You, my sweet, are more satisfying than any honey wine and far more intoxicating. Let me come and love you, Cassandra. I promise you will have no regrets."

"Ras, Ras, no, no, no. Please just indulge me this time. Please. I promise we will both feel better about the whole situation."

"Speak for yourself, my sweet. I know what would make me feel better." He swallowed, took a breath and slowed his speech. "All right, my love, I give up. I don't want to add to the pressure I know you already feel."

A falsely contented Cassandra responded, "Thank you, my handsome husband-to-be."

Ras added, "Speaking of pressure, you do know that all of my resources are at your disposal. Anything that you need or want is there for the asking."

"I know, love, and I thank you. Camille Evanti, the wedding planner, will probably call you in a day or two just to go over some minor details. If you have any additions beyond what we've talked about, let her know and she'll run with it."

"No, my sweet, this is your wedding. The wedding night is mine."

With prolonged anticipation in her voice, Cassandra said absently, "I can't wait." Her free hand traced a path along her smooth, silky throat as those words of anticipated ecstasy slid sensually over her vocal cords. Ras fell into the sexually charged rhythm.

"Neither can I, and at this moment, though you will not allow me to enter the gates of heaven, which languish in the deep recesses of your soul, at least allow me to enter the walls of your resistance and just stand."

From the silence registering on the other end of the telephone line, Ras knew that his passion-filled imagery had rendered his wife-to-be speechless. He waited seconds for her breathy response.

"Ras, you are relentless. Just hurry."

A satisfied, smiling Ras, already in motion, responded

in a voice so deep and so laden with desire, it ripped like lightning through her core.

"While I am on my way, let my yearning for you match yours, and let it ravish you until you can surrender to me. Until then, my love."

Ras hurriedly closed his cellular phone, placed it in the armrest of his luxury sedan, and, with a broad smile on his face, turned the corner and parked in front of Cassandra's loft.

As Ras hung up, Cassandra held the telephone to her heart for a moment and smiled as a vivid picture of the man she loved floated through her mind. She released the phone into its holder and walked into her bedroom to dress in something other than her bathrobe in anticipation of Ras' visit. Just as she entered her bedroom, she heard her doorbell ring. Taken totally by surprise, she spoke out loud, her words filled with shock and disbelief. "No, he can't be here already. I know that can't be Ras."

She walked to the door and asked, almost laughing, "Who is it?"

Ras answered, "It is a lonely man who has come desiring to open the gates of heaven."

Cassandra smiled, shook her head and opened the door. Ras was momentarily taken aback. He knew Cassandra was beautiful, and he had seen her in varying states of dress, but at that moment, standing there in a long, silk ivory-colored robe, with bare feet and scarlet-painted toes, she seemed beyond beautiful and almost angelic as the light from the room's multileveled windows reflected the burnished highlights in her crinkled hair as it softly cascaded along her shoulders. He loved her face, and he loved it even more devoid of make-up. Her eyes were bright and clear, her skin flawless and taut across well-defined, exquisitely structured cheekbones.

She stood looking at him. He stood there in all of his masculine beauty, mesmerized by her. On this occasion, Ras was dressed in what was for him an uncharacteristically casual style. He wore a specially tailored warm-up suit in colors of brown and beige and matching chocolate brown leather running shoes. His long, lean, muscular physique, his piercingly haunting eyes filled with love and promise, and his full, sensuous lips ready to set her soul on fire sent her heart racing as he moved into the room and closed the massive teakwood door behind him.

Cassandra stood still, and just as she was about to speak, her lips, intending to offer conversation, were claimed and worshipped. Ras began a kiss so hungry and so deep, it left Cassandra trembling with pleasure and longing. As he released her lips and started a trail of heated kisses down her throat, Cassandra's senses were heightened and her breathing became erratic. In low, throaty whispers, she repeated over and over, "Ras, I love you, I love you," trailing off into sounds that took Ras deep inside her spirit. He ended the trail of kisses on her neck and ran long, tapered fingers in feathery strokes over the top of her silky robe, feeling the smoothness and the richness of the fabric; the coolness offered a stark contrast to the heat of his touch. His voice, filled with need, washed over her as he asked, "My beautiful wife-to-be, do you have any idea how just being near you soothes my soul?"

With a wistful stare of longing deep into his eyes, Cassandra answered, "I understand more clearly every time you touch me."

Ras slowly and carefully traced one of his fingers down the length of Cassandra's face while saying, "You know I had to come here today to see you and touch you in ways not possible with all eyes on us, and I must confess to being parked around the corner when I called. Just in case you gave me permission to see you, I wanted to waste no time."

Cassandra threw her head back in laughter at Ras' resourcefulness. She responded, "You are so sneaky, Ras. I swear you cannot be trusted to play fair." Before Ras could answer, Cassandra added, "I'm going to go change, and I'll fix you a light breakfast."

She headed in the direction of her bedroom, and Ras stood feeling as though the air he needed to breathe had left the room. Cassandra walked into her bedroom, unbuttoned her robe, slipped out of it and walked as bare as the day she was born into her closet to find something that left her feeling less vulnerable to Ras' touch. She smiled as she thought the only thing that could possibly be was a suit of armor, but she laughed to herself, knowing that the heat emanating from Ras would melt the metal. Just as she finished that daydream, she turned, and in the reflection of her bedroom mirror, she could see Ras Selassie leaning on the doorjamb, arms crossed, crooked smile in place, watching her. She was too startled to jump. She was frozen in place, head tilted, mouth slightly ajar and every perfect curve in place. She said quietly, "Ras, I thought you were waiting for me in the living room so that I could fix us something to eat."

In a voice that resonated with pure, unadulterated lust, Ras said, "The feast is in here, Cassandra."

With slow, steadied speech and a vivid awareness of her bare body, she said, "Ras, you were coming here just to see me. Remember?"

Ras was in the mood to love his woman with every fiber of his being. In a tone that dripped with raw passion, he answered, "You left out a word, my darling. You allowed me to come here to see you and to touch you."

Cassandra spoke now with a hint of panic in her voice. "Ras, if you touch me in this totally vulnerable state, how can either of us resist? Ras, be reasonable."

He moved slowly into the room, reminding Cassandra of an elegant, powerful entity for which she had no name. He continued speaking, while his eyes burned into her core. "My beautiful one, I am a man of immense control and tremendous discipline. I am also a man of my word. If I said I would come just to see you and to touch you, it does not matter what state you are in, with clothes or without. I am a man of my word."

An exasperated Cassandra, her body aching for his touch, tried in vain to smother the growing fire raging through her. She asked, "Ras, what on earth am I going to do with you?"

With his bold, seductive stare in place, Ras answered, "At this moment you are going to allow me to be a man of my word."

As he moved closer, Cassandra sat down on the edge of her ebony wood platform bed. The red satin down-filled comforter was soft and cool as it touched her bare bottom. She slid up to the head of the bed and rested her head on the upholstered headboard padded in a Chinese red-and-gold silk fabric. She partially covered herself with a few of the plush pillows in varying shades of red, gold and black, which were strategically placed at the head of the bed to bring beauty and comfort to the room. Ras continued to watch her, and when she was settled, he removed each piece of his clothing, leaving them both equally vulnerable.

Cassandra took a deep breath as she marveled at the magnificence of his body and the commanding presence of his arousal. He crawled into bed beside her and removed each pillow one by one, kissing each spot from which it was taken. When the pillows were no longer a barrier, he stopped and made love to her with his eyes. Unable to be without his touch one moment longer, Cassandra wrapped her arms around his neck and began a kiss of her own that left them both spiraling and spinning. Her thoughts left her when Ras' tenor whisper assured her, "You refuse me entrance to the gates of heaven, but I am going to treat you to divine pleasure in spite of your resistance."

He began a rhythmic pattern of tantalizing moves that flickered and fluttered along Cassandra's limbs, causing quakes and quivers to shatter her core. She whimpered, "Ras, this is torture."

He whispered in her ear, "No, my darling, it is anticipated pleasure. Knowing what is to come makes it all the more satisfying."

He lifted himself slightly and rolled the comforter back, sliding it under Cassandra's long, supple limbs, leaving the two of them resting on ivory-colored silk sheets, which were cool to the touch, waiting to be warmed by bodies fired with the heat of passion. She trusted him and surrendered completely as he paid homage to every inch of her body with his hands, his lips and his words of un-bridled, undulating sensuality. His mouth seared her ears, her eyes, her throat, each taut nipple, her smooth shoul-ders, her long, slender arms, each finger tipped in scarlet, her deeply hidden navel, the tops of her thighs, her knees, her long legs, each scarlet toe, and then he captured her mouth while her lips parted, emitting sounds of broken whimpers. As he tasted her thoroughly, his long, skillful hands moved along her thighs, while spirals of ecstasy cascaded from her center, causing her to arch her back in a move that brought her more pleasure. As waves of sub-lime satisfaction washed over her, she dug her nails into Ras' back, holding on to Earth as she felt it spinning off its axis. When ecstasy had turned to glorious peace, she found Ras looking at her while stroking her hair. He smiled and said, "Welcome back, my beauty."

With eyes fluttering, fighting the need to close, and with a voice barely above a whisper, Cassandra spoke. "Sweetheart, you are indeed a man of your word, and I am the grateful recipient." She smiled and closed her eyes.

Ras kissed her cheek and said softly. "My love, I am going to wash up and let myself out. When I see you again this evening, every time we look at each other, we will have this memory. Sleep well, my sweet, but don't sleep past your bridal shower. I don't want all of those women out looking for me."

As he laughed and walked away, Cassandra threw a pillow at him, snuggled back under her covers, inhaled the signature scent of Ras in the heat of passion, smiled, closed her eyes and slept.

# Chapter 21

An hour later, Cassandra woke up, still feeling the glow of being loved by Ras. Her body still tingled with the memory of his touch. She sat up in bed and stretched her arms to the ceiling, causing the silk sheet that was covering her to slide farther down her bare body. She stepped out of bed and made her way into the adjoining bathroom to bathe and get ready for the afternoon bridal shower being given by her family and friends. When she had taken a leisurely bath to the soft strings of a jazz guitar and floating memories of Ras, she applied her favorite Givenchy fragrance and stood in her walk-in closet to choose an ensemble for the day. Since there was a chill in the air, she chose to wear a black long-sleeved, scoop-necked angora sweater; a pencil straight, knee-length black wool skirt; fitted, knee-high, three-inch black Italian leather boots; a strand of flawless pearls with matching earrings, and a black cashmere coat.

The Virginia air was cold and wintry as Cassandra steered her two-seater Mercedes in the direction of Amara and Keino's Virginia residence. Mother Nature was carefully undressing the trees one by one, leaving lawns strewn with foliage in hues of brown, red, lime green, yellow gold, and rust with leaves turning to gray brown.

The naked trees seemed to shiver as the winds caressed their slender limbs. The sky was cloudless, clear blue and still. The sun shone brightly, but its heat was buried in the changes of winter. As Cassandra parked in front of the massive wrought iron gate emblazoned with the signature *M* for Mazrui, waiting to be buzzed in, she could see through the gate a number of cars parked in the circular driveway. She smiled, anticipating the friends and family she knew were awaiting her arrival. The gate opened, and she drove slowly along the circular driveway, admiring the beautifully manicured lawn edged with explosive blooms of perennials in a myriad of riotous colors. She parked her car alongside the others, stepped out of the car, closed the door, and with a light, sassy step, still basking in the glow of her passionate encounter with Ras, she walked to the front door of the house and rang the doorbell. Amara answered the door. She wanted to be the first to greet her sister. When they saw each other, they embraced as they had done many times before, with all of the love, affection and admiration they felt for one another.

Amara led Cassandra through the foyer into a great room that spoke to the wealth of its owners. There were plush sofas and chairs, thick Persian carpets and luxurious fabrics covering walls and draping windows. A blazing fire added to the warmth of the room. Dressed in a variety of exquisite outfits, the women sat in groups in various poses, engaged in conversation. When Amara and Cassandra entered the room, heads turned and smiles radiated. Amara announced, "Our bride-to-be has arrived." As Amara removed Cassandra's coat and took it to be hung in a hall closet, Cassandra moved farther into the room, smiling. Everyone began to greet her at once. The hugs, the laughter, the words of encouragement were, for Cassandra, like pouring rain on parched ground. She thought of how thankful she was to be loved so well by so many.

Just as Cassandra was basking in the glow of all of the

affection being shown her, Amara reentered the room, and Afiya spoke up in the way only she did. She clapped her hands quickly four times and said, "Ladies, ladies, may I have your attention. I've been told to get this party started, and I'm ready to do just that. OK, now this is the way we are going to start. We are going around the room, and each of us will give Cassandra a gift of wisdom for her marriage. Give her words that she can keep close to her heart, words that she can remember in good times and in the difficult times." She caused the entire room to erupt in laughter when she added, "We all know that with Cassandra and Ras, there will be some stormy times."

Cassandra, still laughing, came to her own defense. "Now, Afiya, Ras and I are never going to fight again. We have worked out all of our differences. From now on he is just going to do exactly what I say." Now the room broke up in uncontrollable laughter. Afiya brought them back to earth.

"OK, ladies, OK, enough of Cassandra's jokes. Let's give her some wisdom she can use. Mom, why don't we start with you." Afiya turned to her mother. By this time Cassandra had been placed in the seat of honor, a chair positioned in the room so that she could see everyone and everyone could see her. Ana Terrell looked at her daughter lovingly, and with a broad smile, she studied her daughter while she very gingerly stroked the arm of her magenta-colored raw silk suit. She spoke with the pride of a woman who was clear that she and her husband had reared a young woman of tremendous quality and worth.

"Sweetheart, when you were a little girl, you always wanted everything around you to be beautiful. You were meticulous to a fault. Everything had to be done to the best of your ability, and, of course, you held those high standards for everyone else around you."

At the moment those words were spoken, if anyone had noticed, they would have seen Cassandra's three sisters,

Afiya, Adana, and Amara, look at one another with know-ing smiles and nod yes in unison.

Their mother continued. "When you are married, dear heart, remember to use those God-given attributes to make your marriage a haven of beauty and perfection that you and your husband will never want to leave. Your profession was tailor-made for you, because you can make any envi-ronment not only beautiful but a place of comfort and peace. As meticulous as you are, work to perfect the com-munication in your marriage. Work to perfect the continued courtship that you and Ras should strive to maintain. Per-fect your loving so that over time you can speak volumes with a glance or a touch, and finally, work harder on your marriage than you ever have on your career."

When Ana finished, Cassandra, blinking back tears from her misty eyes, mouthed a silent "I love you, Mom. Thank you," while in the background could be heard mur-murings of "That was so beautiful" and long sighs and deep breaths amid almost inaudible applause.

Afiya spoke again. "Let's not go in order. Since Mom pulled at our heart strings, let's just speak as we feel moved to do so."

Amara Selassie, Ras' mom, started slowly and calmly, an air of serenity wrapped around her like an ethereal cloud. "Cassandra, I can not begin to tell you how grate-ful I am for the divine intervention that brought you to my son. From the time he was small, Ras always appeared to be an old soul. For many years his father and I wondered just what spirit God had blessed us with." Everyone in the room knew Ras and therefore joined his mother in good-natured laughter at his expense. Mrs. Selassie continued, "In all seriousness, my dear, let me say again, Ras' father and I are extremely grateful that you will soon be our son's wife and the mother of our grandchildren. As for words of wisdom, I can only say trust your instincts. When it comes to my son, you have the beauty that will keep him longing for you, the compassion that will make him run to you for comfort, and the intellect to read him well and match his wit so that he will forever seek your wisdom to add to his own as the two of you navigate the streams of life. His heart is in your hands, Cassandra. Handle it with care because in spite of his bravado and all of his courage, you are the one person who could break his heart beyond repair. Just love him, and you will never regret it."

Now Cassandra's face was streaming with tears. She had been so touched by her future mother-in-law's remarks because they so clearly spoke to the heart of the Ras Selassie she knew and loved. Amara Selassie rose from her seat, walked over and embraced Cassandra, who stood to return the embrace. This time the entire room applauded. Women, many with tears glistening in their eyes, were momentarily propelled into thoughts of present loves, past loves or future loves. For all, it was a very private, pensive moment.

Once everyone was again settled and a comfortable pause filled the air, Adana, with legs crossed gracefully, commanding the room like a queen holding court, spoke in a voice that was known to hold a jury's rapt attention. "Cassandra, I am your older sister, and since I've known you all of your life, what I want to say to you is this. You are a magnificent woman. Your integrity, your loyalty and your compassion cannot help but work to your advantage as you and Ras work to create a wonderfully powerful marriage. I love you, Sis."

Cassandra whispered softly, "I love you, too. If this day gets any more emotional, I won't be able to take it."

Afiya responded, "Yes, you will. We can never give or receive too much love. Who is next?"

Amara's silky reply was, "I'll take the plunge. Sister, you were there for me at a real turning point in my relationship with Keino. Your words of wisdom at that time helped me to make the most important decision of my life. I will always be grateful, and because you were able to see so clearly that day, I know that if you listen to your still, small voice when difficulties arise, you will rarely go wrong. I know you will have a great life. Speaking from personal experience, I can tell you that being married to a Mazrui or a Selassie is a once-in-a-lifetime adventure, and in this way, we will be doubly related. It doesn't get any better than that."

Amara's remarks brought more comic relief to the gathering. Afiya interjected, "Since my sisters seem to be taking their turns in order, I think I am next. I'll make this short and I hope sweet. Sis, I've watched you and Ras from the beginning, and from the moment of your first argument, I knew the two of you were hooked." The room went up in laughter as Cassandra feigned shock at Afiya's observation. Afiya continued. "You knew it, too, even if you didn't want to admit it." Afiya smiled lovingly at her sister as she finished her comments. "I want to leave you with this little piece of wisdom. I did not create it, but it spoke to me when I was searching for a piece that would remind me of you and Ras. The quote comes from James Baldwin. I don't know when or where he said it, but he is supposed to have said: 'Love does not begin and end the way we seem to think it does. Love is a battle, love is a war; love is growing up.' The two of you have battled and gone to war, you have loved and you have grown together. I wish you peace and many blessings."

As the afternoon festivities continued, other guests offered good wishes and words of wisdom. Gifts were plentiful and varied. Eating, drinking and merrymaking continued until early evening. Cassandra was grateful for the love and affection shown to her and expressed her gratitude many times.

As the bridal shower began to wind down, the Mazrui and Selassie men and other family members arrived to once again reenact a scene that might have taken place in Ethiopia. Traditionally, two weeks before the wedding, a singing fest takes place at the bride's family home. These singing parties often continued until just days before the

wedding. In the interest of time and logistical convenience, Ras scheduled this one event to take place at the
end of the bridal shower. He enlisted a four-piece band
and placed himself on keyboards, and his family very
skillfully sang and danced until the entire house was filled
with songs of Ethiopia. Afiya and Cassandra were more
than happy to get on the floor and throw themselves into
the music and were not at all surprised to see that their
parents had mastered the intricate steps, which required
the movement of shoulders and feet in a joyous rhythmic
pattern. Ras left his place at the keyboard and one of the
other musicians took over for him. He walked up behind
Cassandra, tapped her on her undulating shoulders and
said, with seduction dripping from his sensuous mouth,
"May I have the pleasure?" Cassandra answered with her
eyes. And they danced with memories of the morning
easing through their minds and hearts.

# *Chapter 22*

The day of the wedding arrived, and the most luxurious hotel in Gonder was taken over by the Selassie-Mazrui contingent. The modern Goha Hotel, with its breathtaking views of the city, became headquarters for the wedding party and its entourage. In Gonder, Africa's Camelot amid historic castles and palaces dating back to the seventeenth and eighteenth centuries, Cassandra and Ras were to be married.

As the limousines rolled through the city center on their way to the hotel, Cassandra gasped with joy as she saw a monument to Ethiopian ingenuity called the Fasil Ghebbi—the royal enclosure. In the heart of the city, it was surrounded by high stone walls and contained six castles and a complex of connecting tunnels and raised walkways. The magic and the beauty of it took her breath away and made her think of the Ethiopian queen Makeda, whom some called Sheba, who had stolen the biblical Solomon's heart. She understood why Ras had chosen Gonder.

The arrival of the wedding party electrified the city. The high-energy hustle and bustle of the hotel spilled out into the streets and became contagious. Word spread rapidly in the immediate vicinity that Ras Selassie, son of General and Mrs. Tafari Selassie, was being married in the Debre

Birhan Selassie Church. With the spreading of the news, people in the city seemed to stand a bit taller, smile a bit more broadly and rush about, with their neighbors trying to catch a glimpse of the bride and groom-to-be. For those who had relatives working in the hotel, tales were created of imaginary sightings of any number of people from the wedding party. Shops were dusted, sidewalks swept and merchandise more attractively arranged, on the off chance that the business from the wedding guests in the hotel would spill over into the local shops.

Camille Evanti, Cassandra's friend and wedding planner, hit the ground running. The wedding had been scheduled for five o'clock, and her task was to assure that all was well so that the production that Cassandra had envisioned and Camille herself had coordinated could proceed without a glitch. She had done much of what she needed to do long distance, but she brought her team with her to have eyes, ears and backup on the ground in Gonder, so that whatever happened, Cassandra would remember her wedding as her perfectly executed dream come true. The orchids and lilies that Cassandra requested had been flown in from a European source that Camille had worked with countless times. They had arrived in perfect condition. She had diagrams drawn so that the crew of professional set designers and decorators, led by her people and assisted by people employed from the Gonder citizenry, could arrange the flowers with ease in both the church and the Fasilidas Castle, where the reception was to take place.

Camille dialed Cassandra just to reassure the bride that everything was under control. Cassandra picked up on the second ring. "Hello."

Camille, as buoyant as ever, answered, "Hello, darlin'. How's the bride doing on this glorious morning?"

Cassandra answered joyously. "There ought to be a law against feeling this good!"

"No, sugah, you've got it twisted. You see, there ought to be a law against not feeling that good."

With that remark, they both burst into laughter. When Cassandra's laughter subsided, she asked, "How are things going?"

Confident, Camille answered, "If I'm here, you know it's right."

Cassandra's playful response was, "Yes, Camille, I know. I just had to ask."

Camille rushed on, punctuating her speech with gestures of her hands, an act which was second nature to her. "I called to say if your marriage is anything like the wedding, you two are in for a beautiful ride. Enjoy the journey."

"Thanks, Camille."

"See you soon."

Camille headed back to the church to see if the crew was on schedule. By her calculations every minute was accounted for. As she entered the church, she was pleased to see that the crew was on track. She had time to take a breath and marvel at the beauty of the structure in which her friend was to be wed. On the outer walls of the church were positioned twelve round towers representing the twelve apostles. The gateway stood as the thirteenth tower and represented Christ. The ceiling was decorated with a mural painting of eighty cherubic faces, a most beautiful example of Ethiopian ecclesiastical art. The walls were painted with dozens of biblical scenes. The colors were vibrant, and Camille noted that Cassandra's choice of white orchids and white calla lilies with sprigs of greenery would accent beautifully without overpowering. The elaborate, highly carved altar would be draped in snow-white tulle with golden threads woven through it. Long white and gold tapered candles and miniature lights positioned at the altar would weave a sensuality into the sacredness of the ceremony.

She left the church by chauffeured car and made a stop at the reception site. The grand ballroom of Fasilidas Castle was being transformed. As she watched the crew work, she knew that Cassandra was going to be more than

pleased. Crystal chandeliers were hung with jeweled lighting and crowned with halos of tapered white candles.
Round tables, enough to seat hundreds, were positioned intimately in a circle around the room so that they all faced
a dance floor that would be bathed in romantic amber
lighting. The tables were covered in white silk tablecloths,
with orchid and lily bouquets as centerpieces. Around the
ballroom were positioned tall, slender silver urns filled
with long-stemmed white roses, and each urn was draped
with a satin and organza ivory-colored bow. The beauty
of the décor made even more magical the history and tradition that had gone before. As she stood there, Camille
could imagine the splendid royal events that had taken
place there hundreds of years before. She smiled to think
that she had become a part of that history.


Cassandra heard a knock on the door of her hotel suite.
She knew it couldn't be Ras, because he was very much
occupied with the men of his family, preparing himself for
the big moment. She walked to the door and asked pleasantly, "Who is it?"

Three voices answered in unison, "Your sisters."

Cassandra opened the door, and there they stood beaming. Those smiles, looking so much like her own, were a
welcomed sight. "Come in, you three. I was wondering
when you were going to get here."

Adana, always quick with an answer, responded, "We
are here now. The cavalry has arrived. What do you need?"

Cassandra, still smiling, said, "All I need is to see you
three. You know Camille has everything under control. I
just can't wait to see it. It has been so hard not being able
to put my two cents in every second, but that's the joy of
working with Camille. Give her an assignment, and it's
done. No questions asked, no excuses. If she hits a snag,
you'll never know it, because she'll have it fixed before
you know it happened."

Cassandra stopped and looked at her sisters as they sat there smiling as she rambled on. "OK, so I'm rambling."

Afiya hugged her and said, "Yes, you are, but this is your day, and you can ramble until you pass out. This is your day."

They all laughed as Amara added, "Sweetheart, I know how you feel, and all I can say is focus on your day and try to catalogue every moment in your heart for safekeeping. You will cherish these moments the rest of your life. After you're married, on those days when you think you want to kill Ras, just think of this beautiful day."

When Amara finished, they all howled with laughter. They doubled over, giggling and laughing in a way they hadn't done since they were little girls, laughing away in their bedrooms at home. It was never lost on them that they were truly blessed to be able to enjoy one another as sisters and as friends.

Adana, Ms. Serious herself, straightened up first. "All right, ladies, we have hair and make-up appointments. Let's get with it."

Amara said, with feigned sarcasm, "Adana, if we didn't have you around to tell us when to go where, what would we do?"

Adana responded with a smile and equally playful sarcasm, "Well, little sister, I really don't know."

Before they knew it, they were all laughing again as they headed to the hotel salon, where Camille had arranged to have each sister's choice of hairstylist and make-up artist flown in on a Mazrui company jet.

Ras and his cousins sat in Ras' suite in another part of the hotel. Ras was listening to everyone talk to him about the joys and the perils of married life. Kamau spoke. "Ras, I know I am the last person you want advice from. The two of us tussle verbally as men the same way we tussled physically as boys." He stopped, tilted his head and looked as though for a split second he was considering a very weighty issue. "I must say I have never quite understood why you are so bullheaded and refuse to see things my way." The room erupted in laughter. Even Ras could not contain himself. Kamau continued once the laughter subsided. "In all seriousness, Ras, marriage is a beautiful thing. Though I have been married a short period of time, I highly recommend matrimony."

"Hear! Hear!" was Kaleb's sign of agreement. "If a good woman can settle me down, then my hat is off to Cassandra because I know she is a good woman, and you, my cousin, are no harder to handle than I was, so you two will do well."

Keino jumped in. "I don't have to tell you how I feel about my marriage."

They all said in unison, "No, you don't." The room once again fell into uncontrollable laughter.

Over the laughter, Aman said, "Ras, are you ready to marry your woman?"

Ras' deeply emotional answer was, "Yes, I am. I have never been more ready."

"Then let's finish our ceremonial obligations and get you to the church."

Ras, now in a very pensive mood, said, "Fellows, go ahead. I will catch up in a moment."

His cousins understood, and all left the room to give Ras his moment. He walked over to a comfortable leather chair, sat and stretched his long, lean, muscular legs in front of him. As was his habit when in a state of deep contemplation, he began massaging his temples with his left hand stretched across his forehead. His thoughts drifted to Cassandra. They had come so far; he had come so far. His love for her was deeper than anything he had ever known. He knew that she was a remarkable woman. Her beauty was beyond the physical. He was so grateful that she had accepted his son and was willing to make him hers. That fact alone made him love her even more. As he sat there knowing that in a few hours she would be his wife, he thanked God and the ancestors once again for the blessing. Just as he threw his head back and uttered a sound of deep satisfaction, he heard another knock.

With his tilted smile in place, he pushed himself up from the chair and walked to the door, thinking that it was one or all of his cousins. He yelled loudly enough to be heard through the door. "Keep your pants on, fellows. I'm coming." He opened the door and, much to his surprise, found his father standing there in military fashion, with his hands folded in front of him, smiling at his son's surprised look.

"Father, I thought you were the cousins."

"I suspected as much, my son. I know they are waiting for you to prepare for the evening's festivities, but I needed to stop by. I wanted a moment alone with you, son. So if I may . . . it looks as if my timing is perfect."

"By all means, please come in, Father."

Ras' father walked to the leather chair Ras had vacated and sat, making himself comfortable, while Ras sat on the sofa across from him. Both men crossed their legs, not realizing that they were mirroring each other. Tafari Selassie began.

"My son, I want you to know how proud I am of you this day. From the time you were born, your mother and I knew that we had been given a great gift. Your birth was long and arduous for your mother, but the end result was a miracle for us. We tried for years to give you brothers and sisters, but the divine plan was that we were only to be blessed with you."

Ras listened intently. He had not heard his father express himself quite as freely before as he was at that moment, and he had never been told that his birth was difficult or that his parents tried to have other children. As he listened, he gained an even deeper appreciation of the father he was just coming to love and understand. Tafari Selassie continued speaking as his son listened.

"You have chosen well. Cassandra is a remarkable young woman, and she comes from good stock. The way in which she has embraced your son"—he paused, with unbridled emotion —"and my grandson . . . our family will forever be in her debt. You are a courageous man, a good man, my son. A man with great vision who is clear about his life's purpose. I am so sorry, son, that I missed so much, but I am grateful that I am here now."

General Selassie stood and so did Ras, following his lead. Fighting back tears, the two men embraced, and an invisible cord ran from father to son, son to father, never to be severed again. Tafari released his son and said, "I'll leave you now, my son, to find your cousins and finish the preparations."

Ras cleared his throat, choking back emotion, and responded, "Thank you, Father, for everything. I will see you at the church."

"Yes, you will, son. I will be there filled with pride and thanksgiving."

General Selassie walked out of the door. Ras closed it behind him and walked again to the wingback chair and sat down, and for the second time in his adult life, he openly wept. He was so moved by the love his father expressed, he wept solitary tears of joy. He allowed himself a moment, went in to his bathroom, washed his face and left the suite to join his cousins.

Ana Terrell was having breakfast with Keino's mother, Adina Mazrui, and Ras' mother, Amara Selassie. The three of them could not stop reminiscing about the days of their youth in college and how fortunate they felt now that they were all going to be related because their children had found their soul mates continents away from one another.

Amara Selassie spoke. "Ana, all those years ago, who would have thought that you and James would produce the young women who would give birth to the children of my son and the son of my sister. Life is such a mysterious journey."

Ana spoke with heartfelt emotion. "It really is a mystery. Here I am in Ethiopia, getting ready to witness the marriage of my daughter to the son of my college roommate. And I must say, Amara, he is a wonderful young man."

"Thank you, Ana. Ras has his ways, but Cassandra is just the woman to harness all of that warrior energy he throws around."

All three women fell into comfortable laughter. Keino's mother, Adina, spoke. "Keino and Amara certainly seem to be doing well. I've tried to be helpful in navigating her through the Kenyan customs when I see her questioning herself. I had to do the same thing when I married Garsen. She is a quick study, and she and Keino are so desperately in love. I can't wait to see the grandchildren from those two so that I can add them to my brood."

Suddenly concerned about time, Ana Terrell said, "We'd better get up from here and go find our husbands before they find a golf course and think they can sneak a round in before the wedding." They settled the check and rose to leave the restaurant.

Camille had arranged for photographs to be taken throughout the day, including candid shots of every member of the wedding party and of as many friends and family as possible. Just as Ana, Adina and Amara were leaving breakfast, a young photographer walked up to them and said, "Excuse me, ladies. I have been assigned to get as many pictures of you three as I can, both separately and together. If you will indulge me, I would like to take a few shots now. We are memorializing this event so that the bride and groom will have lasting memories." The three women happily consented and posed in a variety of ways for the camera to capture.

* * *

Camille was now counting down the hours. The hands on her slender Piaget wristwatch were ticking silently away. Two hours until showtime. Everyone on her team was dressed in black and had a discreet gold-plated name tag in order to be readily identified if the need arose. The men wore black suits with fitted, lightweight, fashionable tees instead of the traditional shirt. The women wore black silk pantsuits with black sleeveless shells for comfort and low-heeled, open-toed black silk shoes. Camille's hair, which she changed often, was cut for the wedding in a short, no-fuss pixie style. She accentuated the angular structure of her pretty face with large, round gold earrings, which matched her watch. Camille stood six feet tall and was still as thin and as curvy as she had been when she was a runway model for some of the finest fashion houses in Europe. Her working style was a sugary, no-nonsense attitude that always got the job done. She dialed her ever present telephone and checked in with the best man.

"Keino, how's it goin', hon? Is Ras where he is supposed to be?"

"We've got him, Camille. We are on schedule and ready to ride."

"Good. See ya soon."

She punched in the numbers for the lead members of her team one by one, checking the status of the various pieces of her friend's wedding puzzle. She dialed Amara, the matron of honor. "Hey, Ms. Amara, is Cassandra on schedule?"

Amara hesitated. "Well, we're getting there. She just had a little crying jag a moment ago so that slowed us down."

Camille almost yelled, "What on earth is she crying about?"

"Slow down, Camille. They weren't sad tears. She's just happy."

"Thank God that's all it was. Look, I'll see you people

in one hour. In one hour I want everyone and everything in place."

A laughing Amara said, "Yes, Ms. Evanti."

Camille hung up and had her driver rush her to the reception site, where the cake was being assembled in the wrong place. She quietly said to herself, "That's my job, to make it right and to make it pretty. So let me at it."

One hour later everyone was in place for a final Ethiopian tradition before the actual ceremony. Traditionally, Ras and his groomsmen would have gone to Cassandra's home to take his bride-to-be by playful force from her parents' home. For the purposes of the ritual, on this occasion, a reception area in the hotel had been adorned with beautiful flowers and fabrics as a backdrop for the game that would take place. Ras, Keino, Kaleb, Aman and Kamau stormed through the doubled doors, announcing loudly, "Ras Selassie has come to take his bride." A joyous electricity filled the air. Cassandra, like many others in the room, could not stop laughing as her family, along with Amara Selassie; Adina Mazrui; and Kaleb, Aman and Kamau's wives, sang and danced in a group in front of Cassandra as they pretended to push back the group of men from the door. Amara Selassie and Adina Mazrui led the group in songs that were from their own Ethiopian tradition.

When they had pretended to thwart the advances of the groom-to-be and his men long enough, the women moved aside, and Ras and Cassandra could, for the first time, clearly see each other since the playful tug-of-war had begun. Cassandra's breath caught in her throat. She felt warm all over. She had never seen him more magnificent. She was caught in the memory of the first time she had looked into his face. He was so spectacular. There he stood with an outstretched hand, waiting for her to join him. His black tuxedo caressed the length of his body with the tenderness and the intimacy of a skilled lover. His eyes held so much love for her, her eyes misted at the thought of his passion. He stood there as she rose to meet him, thinking that she was, indeed, the most angelic figure he had ever seen.

All of the words he had ever used to describe her beauty were inadequate at that moment. She was a vision in a gown that was the creation of Ethiopian designer Amsale. It was a strapless, ivory lace, floor-length gown with a hand-beaded pearl train. Her hair was pulled back in a chignon, and one side of her head was draped with a cascade of white orchids. Her ears were hung with diamond and pearl teardrop earrings, one of the heirlooms that had belonged to Ras' father's mother. Her neck was bare, accentuating its swanlike appearance and her beautifully toned shoulders and arms. Her feet were covered in ivory-colored silk, bare-backed heels, which had been hand-beaded with pearls and diamonds, matching her earrings.

He took her hand and whispered to her as cameras were flashing, "My sweet Cassandra, you have never been more beautiful. I will always remember this moment." Her eyes misted again as they were led to the limousine in which they were to ride to the church. A trail of limos followed them, carrying the wedding party, family and friends. In keeping with tradition, the cars following honked their horns all along the procession route to announce to the community that the wedding was to take place momentarily.

When they arrived at the church, Ras placed Cassandra in her father's hands, and everyone, as per Camille's instructions, got in their places to begin the ceremony. The church was filled to capacity. The guests were beautifully dressed in everything from traditional African finery to Western chic. Cassandra's sisters, acting as her attendants, stood ready, wearing floor-length, form-fitting, strapless pale gold dresses. Each one wore a single strand of pearls and matching earrings. They each carried as a bouquet a large spray of rubrum lilies.

As Cassandra stood unseen by the waiting guests, holding on to her father's arm, he turned to her and said,

"Cassandra, your mother and I love you. You've chosen a fine young man, and you are going to make a magnificent wife and mother."

A teary-eyed Cassandra mouthed, "Thank you, Daddy," and then they heard the music begin. The orchestra seated in the balcony with the choir began an Ethiopian melody so haunting and so smooth that it made one want to weep and smile simultaneously. Ras and his groomsmen followed the elaborately robed and crowned Coptic cleric on to the altar. As the music continued to play, the bridesmaids, one by one in graceful rhythm, floated down the aisle. The melodic strains of another musical piece accompanied two gentlemen dressed as footmen as they rolled out a runner of ivory brocade woven with gold threads. As the music continued, Keino's nieces, serving as flower girls, appeared in gold taffeta dresses with hooped bottoms and gold brocade sashes. Their elaborately braided hairstyles were laced with profusions of baby's breath. The gold baskets they carried were filled with white roses, which they liberally distributed over the runner. The ring bearers, Keino's nephews, were dressed in black tuxedoes. They carried the rings tied on golden satin pillows. As the boys reached the altar, harps began to play and then violins, and when the violins gave way to trumpets, the audience was directed to stand, and Cassandra and her father began their walk down the aisle to smiles and tears of joy.

When they reached the altar, and Ras met them and took his bride's hand, James Terrell took his seat along with his wife, and everyone else was then directed to sit. Ras and Cassandra knelt at the altar on the satin cushion that had been used by Ras' parents at their wedding. They held on to each other's hands tightly as the choir sang African American spirituals and Ethiopian traditional songs, and as prayers were said and sacred texts were read in both Amharic and English. An elaborate mass was said in Geez, the classical language of Ethiopia.

In the taking of their vows, Cassandra and Ras knew without question that their lives were cemented in a bond that was never to be broken. With every word, they fell more deeply in love. With every word, Ras' commitment to cherish his family deepened. With every word, Cassandra's heart opened more fully to receive all of the love she knew was waiting for her. With every word, they both surrendered to the ecstasy of the life of love that was calling them.

When the officiant announced that Ras and Cassandra were husband and wife, the church went up in applause as Ras lovingly and longingly kissed his bride. As they exited the church and were showered with rose petals, Ras whispered to Cassandra playfully, "Now that you are Mrs. Cassandra Selassie, does that mean you'll do anything I tell you?"

Cassandra smiled and answered sweetly, "No, honey, that means you do whatever I tell you."

Ras responded, "Gladly, my darling, gladly."

The entourage was once again escorted into limousines and shuttled to the reception site. Ras and Cassandra were the last to enter the grand ballroom because they had been detained with the wedding party for the photographers and videographers to capture the occasion on film and in stills. When the two of them entered the ballroom to thunderous applause, Cassandra looked around and was frozen in place by the beauty of what Camille had designed. Her eyes filled with tears at the beauty of her vision come to life. Camille caught her tear-stained glance and smiled. At that moment Camille knew her job was done. She went back to her discreetly held walkie-talkie and continued giving orders, checking tasks and counting minutes.

Each guest was seated at a table and given a menu from which to choose from a large selection of Ethiopian, American, and European dishes. Champagne and *tej* flowed liberally. The wedding cake was a ten-layered masterpiece. It was fashioned as a tower of cakes wrapped in gold and silver foil with gold and silver ribbons. Many of the country's dignitaries came to pay their respects to the son of General Tafari Selassie and to congratulate him on his marriage.

Though Cassandra had already been given exquisite jewels from the Selassie-Mazrui family, they surprised her once again. One section of the reception palace had been decorated to hold the enormous number of items that represented her dowry for everyone to view.

The orchestra played, and the guests indulged themselves with delectable entrees, sang and danced until the small hours of the morning. At the end of the reception, in keeping with tradition, Ras and Cassandra's parents sat in a line in the middle of the grand ballroom while Ras and Cassandra together first bowed to their parents and then kissed the knees of each parent. The tears flowed from many of the witnesses as they watched the show of tenderness and respect. The traditional ritual was designed as a way for couples to thank their families for raising them and helping them reach the stage in their lives where they were deemed ready for marriage. Ras and Cassandra were also saying good-bye to their old lives and welcoming a new life and a new status in the community as a married couple.

A little before midnight, the newly married Ras and Cassandra were whisked away by a Mazrui private plane to a destination known only to Ras and the pilots. With their son safely tucked away with grandparents and governess, Ras was prepared to treat his wife to the time of her life.

# *Chapter 23*

"Ras, please, darling, just give me a hint. Where are we going? Just one tiny little hint." Cassandra had been asking over and over in as many inventive ways as she could devise to get Ras to tell her where he was taking her on their honeymoon.

His playful answer was, "No, Mrs. Selassie, I will not give you an answer to that question." With an expression of tremendous satisfaction, he added, "I will say though, I thoroughly enjoy saying Mrs. Selassie."

Feigning a pout, Cassandra's retort was, "Ras Selassie, you are so mean to me."

Moving closer to her on the beautiful mini sofa on the Mazrui luxury plane, he placed his arm around her and said, "I am so sorry, my darling. I promise as soon as we get to where we are going, I will be much nicer to you."

Now she laughed, hearing the double meaning in Ras' statement. Switching gears for a moment, Cassandra said, almost as if talking out loud to herself, "I've got to call Camille first thing tomorrow. She did such a beautiful job with the wedding. Everything was so beautiful."

Ras' light eyes, always so keenly observant, softened as he said, "She did do a magnificent job. That was quite a feat to do all of the transcontinental planning, and then to execute the plan as well as she did was quite something."

Still feeling the joy of her wedding day, Cassandra remarked, "We should do something special for her."

In a flash of humor, Ras quipped, "Aren't we paying her?"

Cassandra hit him playfully on his arm while saying, "Of course, we are, Ras. I meant something beyond just money."

"I understand, sweetheart. I was just trying to bring a little levity into the conversation."

Cassandra gave him a kiss on his full, sensuous mouth and said, "If that's a sample of your comedic sense, my husband, I don't want you to give up your day job."

He lifted her chin gently with the tip of his finger, kissed it and said lovingly, "Ha ha ha, was that supposed to be funny?"

Cassandra smiled, saying, "No, just true." She paused. "Ras, should we call home and check on Kebran? Did we leave all of the information your parents will need in case they have to reach us?"

"Don't worry, my love. We will call in the morning. By now little Master Kebran has been sprinkled with fairy dust and is fast asleep. Everyone who needs to know where we are going knows"—he tapped her on her nose with the tip of his finger—"except you."

Cassandra pretended to glare at him and said, "You are so unfair."

"Don't fret, my sweet. We are almost there."

A few moments after their lighthearted banter had ceased, Ras and Cassandra fell asleep on the plane, holding hands and dreaming of each other. Time passed, and though it felt like minutes, it had been hours, and they were being awakened by the attendant on the plane, who had been hired to serve them. Before Cassandra opened her eyes, she could hear the soft, feminine voice of the attendant saying, "Mr. and Mrs. Selassie, you have reached your destination."

She heard Ras say, "Thank you. Has the car arrived to transport us?"

"Yes, sir, it has. It is parked outside on the airstrip. All you and your wife need to do is disembark and step into the car. The driver is waiting."

Ras turned to Cassandra and said, "Your surprise awaits, my love. Let's go see it."

When they stepped from the plane onto the private landing strip, it was a bit too dark to see anything clearly. Ras was smiling from ear to ear, knowing that it would soon dawn on Cassandra where she was. Ras had given explicit instructions to the driver to take a route that would take them past landmarks that she would know instantly, and those landmarks would tell her where she was. As they rolled down the long stretch of highway in the back-seat of the chauffeured car, she turned to Ras and asked, "Sweetheart, where are we?"

He said, with as much seriousness as he could muster, "My darling wife, we are on our honeymoon." Then he laughed and silently laced his fingers through hers and said, "Soon you will see."

As the car moved farther down the road, they drove into a city of very old, quaint buildings. Cassandra said slowly, "Oh, Ras, I know we are in Europe by the architecture, but I can't see any street signs, so I don't know where."

"Just keep looking, my sweet."

Just as Ras was finished with his sentence, the car turned onto a wide boulevard. There were trees lining the streets and sidewalk cafés, and as if out of nowhere, the Arc de Triomphe appeared. Cassandra gasped aloud and, while laughing loudly, said, "Ras, we are in Paris. Oh, thank you, darling. I have been wanting to get back here for such a long time. Did you know this is one of my favorite cities?"

She leaned over and kissed her husband with all of the passion she felt for him and for the city of Paris. When she had completed the kiss, and Ras had released her reluctantly, she said, "Thank you again, my husband. How did you pull this off? I never guessed. How did you know about my love of this city?"

"I pulled it off, my sweet, because you were very busy, and I knew you would have to love Paris. A woman with your sensibilities would be a natural fit here. Paris, as a city, is all about the things that you love—design, fashion, beauty, food, art and international cultural pursuits. It fits you like a glove, my darling."

"Oh, Ras, how will I ever be able to let you know how wonderful this is?"

He leaned back, pleased with himself, and said, "We will be here for one week, my sweet, and you can show me every day how much you thank me."

He gently kissed her hand while he said, "The only reason we are not staying longer is because my wife insisted that our honeymoon only be one week. She does not want us to be apart from our son longer than that. Otherwise, I would keep you here a month, loving you into submission."

Tingling under his touch, Cassandra responded, "I think I'm going to hold you to that loving me into submission part."

As the car pulled in front of an elegant, opulent building with an old-world European façade, Ras announced, "Here we are, my sweet. Our home for a week. The Ritz, only the best for my wife."

"Why thank you, kind sir. Your wife most certainly appreciates your best."

The door of the car was opened for them, and they walked into the hotel, with Ras gently caressing and stroking his wife's back. The décor was magnificent. It was luxurious. The French call their upscale hotels palaces. The Ritz certainly lived up to that name with its Louis Quartorze furniture, original chandeliers, and marble fireplaces.

Ras walked up to the concierge and, in perfect French,

rattled off the particulars of their reservation. When he had finished his conversation and the young man behind the desk had gone to retrieve information from the computer, Ras turned to look at Cassandra. She was looking at him, with her mouth just slightly ajar. The look in her eyes was that of pride and amazement. Ras winked and kissed her gently on her forehead. Before she could speak, the young man came back, speaking very rapidly and being extremely solicitous. Cassandra spoke very little French, and all she understood from what the young man said was, "So happy to have you here, Mr. Selassie." Ras continued answering him in flawless French, saying his good-byes as he led Cassandra to the elevator.

Once they were alone in the elevator, Cassandra smiled and said, "Ras, you are full of surprises. Where did you learn to speak French? And besides the Amharic and English that I know about, what other languages roll off your tongue at will?"

"Well, my sweet, I studied French in boarding school, but I really learned to speak it because of my friend Ibra Diop. He is Senegalese, as you know, and French is one of the languages that is spoken in his country. So as young boys, we spoke to one another in a variety of languages, some legitimate, some we created."

He laughed as he thought back to those times. "As for the languages I speak, let's see . . . as you said, Amharic, English, French, Wolof, Ibra's original language, and Kikuyu, because of my cousins in Kenya. And I can get by in Arabic if I need to. Here we are. This is our floor."

Cassandra was speechless. She continued walking, thinking, *With this man, I'm in for the ride of my life.* She smiled knowing she was going to enjoy the ride. Ras unlocked the door to the suite, and it was all that either of them wanted it to be for the first night that they would spend as husband and wife.

Cassandra's voice lowered with deep emotion. "Ras, it is so beautiful."

He took her in his arms and said, with smoldering eyes, "I am happy that you like it, my sweet."

Filled with love for her husband, she answered, "Like does not describe it. It is absolutely exquisite."

Ras enfolded Cassandra more deeply in his arms and spoke softly. "Cassandra, I want this week to be perfect, and so while we are waiting for our bags to be brought up, I want you to take a look in the second bedroom and hopefully enjoy another surprise."

Wide-eyed and with a huge smile, Cassandra, who loved surprises, headed toward the room at which Ras was pointing. As she walked, he talked.

"I took the liberty of having a stylist on staff at the hotel shop at the designer fashion houses near us and bring back dresses, suits, bags, shoes, jewelry and lingerie. I gave her all of your sizes. Over the week you can try on everything and return whatever you want. Take everything back or keep it all. Your wish is my command. Go look."

Cassandra opened the door and once again her breath was taken away. The room had been arranged like a mini department store. It was a shopper's dream. A veritable paradise of beauty and harmony masquerading as high-end fabrics and designs in striking colors. She shrieked with joy, and Ras watched as an animated Cassandra ran around commenting on every piece like a kid in a candy store. He sat, legs crossed, composed and regal, watching her until she calmed down and came to sit beside him. She slid next to him on the silk upholstered love seat and wrapped her arms around his neck and began kissing his lips, ears, eyes and nose and throat. "Ras Selassie, you are the best husband a woman could have."

He responded, holding her close to him, "I do aim to please." Then he claimed her mouth while at the same time deftly tantalizing, with feathery strokes, her willing breasts through the pliant, soft fabric of her silk blouse. The kiss went to her head and seeped into her soul. He released her, looked at her seductively and reminded her in a voice filled with sensuality and intensity of something he had planned. "Remember, I said the wedding day was yours, and the wedding night was mine. This is our night, Cassandra, my love. For the first time I will make love to you as my wife, Mrs. Cassandra Selassie. Our lovemaking has been a continuous work of art. Tonight we create a masterpiece."

Cassandra became limp with the desire to do nothing but surrender to her husband. He picked her up and carried her in his arms into the master bedroom of the suite. Her arms were wrapped around his neck, and with her lips, she left a searing trail along his powerful throat. Every movement of his body electrified her. His touch heightened her senses, and in her face, he saw yearning and worship. She spoke in a tremulous whisper as she said, "Ras, I love you so. I want you so badly. I need you now."

In a hoarse whisper, he said, "Patience, my sweet. A masterpiece takes time."

When he walked to the bed, he saw that his instructions once again had been followed to the letter. The massive mahogany bed had been turned down, and the sheets were lined with rose petals. The room was lit with numerous white scented candles floating in water in crystal containers strategically placed around the room. The scent of jasmine eased through the air. Cassandra's voice was silent—only her breathing was audible as Ras placed her on the bed. Her eyes were filled with a look of sensual fire. The love she wanted to express was smothered by Ras' deep, hungry kiss. When he released her lips and began kissing each of her fingers, she whispered, "Ras, I can't take any more. Just love me, please."

"My beautiful one, tonight we create a masterpiece. Tonight I will be the sculptor, and if you will consent to being the clay, we will create a work that will shame the art of Paris."

His eyes held a masculine sexuality that riveted her to the bed. She looked at him with longing and need as he started slowly and masterfully removing each piece of her clothing. Her only act was to breathe, whimpering sighs through parted lips. His touch set her on fire. She wanted him deep inside of her, riding her to paradise, but he took his time. He was memorizing every inch of her. Once her breasts were bare, he took each taut nipple in turn and, with erotic strokes of his thumbs and heated licks of his tongue, caused her to throw her head back in painful cries of delight. As he suckled her breasts, she stroked his hair, feeling the velvety lushness of its wave pattern. She kissed his forehead, his ears and his head while caressing his powerful arms as they held her in a feverish embrace. Their love deepened as they felt the magic of the sexual potency that ran through them, connecting them with invisible ties that bound them forever. The divine art was being created. The clay was ready.

Ras reached for the warmed massage oils he had ordered. They were there. He stretched Cassandra out on the bed, gently stroking her limbs. As he positioned her bare body so that she could receive the loving ministrations of his skilled hands, she felt the crush of the soft rose petals beneath her. The pressure and the heat from her body caused the petals to emit a perfume that brought to mind a summer garden where the heat from the sun baked blooming flowers into a profusion of heady scents. The aroma eased through the air and permeated her nostrils, causing her to breathe in and sigh deeply, releasing a breath of air she did not realize she was holding.

He began to remove his clothing. He was the master. She watched him with lust in her eyes. She needed him more than she had ever needed him before. She wanted him to hurry. He was in control. Each piece of clothing came off as adeptly and as carefully as the expert peeling of a grape. As he undressed, he made love to her from the deepest place in his soul. With his words, he made her tremble with ecstasy. He told her how he wished to taste the melting sweetness of her deep honey-colored skin. He told her how he would enter the gates of heaven and become one with his angel. Cassandra's body shivered and burned as she heard the hunger and desire in his words.

Her body moved involuntarily in a sensual dance of love and promise. She continued watching as her husband came closer to her. The powerful, lean, strong legs that had in previous times entwined hers in the throes of passion moved him closer to her with the glide of a dancer and the power of a ruler. The length and breadth of him aroused in her a desire that burned and raged. She arched up, with legs slightly parted and nipples erect, to pull him to her. With need hanging on every syllable, he whispered, "Not yet, my love. There are so many ways I wish to give you pleasure."

He picked up the warm scented oil, and with the vial in hand, he slowly drizzled droplets on Cassandra's waiting body. He drizzled oil between her breasts, around each nipple, and then with his hands, he caressed, massaged and stroked with undulating rhythms that melted her core as she whimpered a mantra that was, "Ras, Ras, Ras."

His answer was, "Yes, my love, I am here, I am yours and you are mine. Give me all of you."

The oil slid down her stomach over her navel and between her thighs. His hands followed. When his fingers had played the music of the universe, his nimble tongue took their place. From a place deep in her being, Cassandra emitted sounds of rapture and maddening intoxication that left her reaching for Ras, offering herself to him wholly and fully. He lifted her bottom, stroking the smoothness as he guided her to him, easing his tip into her melting sweetness. He entered her quickly and deeply, filling her completely, giving them both what they craved. Cassandra sang his name in a melody that raged through him. Before their spirits left the earth, Ras whispered in ragged tones, "I love you. You are my woman, you are my wife, and I want all of you." He claimed her mouth, and they ravaged each other until Ras released his control and they returned to earth in a fiery blaze that put fireworks to shame.

They fell asleep, arms and legs intertwined. Through the night Ras remained deeply embedded in the seat of his wife's passion, and they rode the waves of ecstasy many times before the sun peeked over the horizon.

When Cassandra awoke the next morning, she found Ras in bed next to her, resting on one arm, stroking her hair, which had, through the night of passionate and tender love-making, found a way to cover almost the entire surface of her pillow. She opened eyes relaxed with sleep and still hazy with loving. He returned a seductive, satisfied stare. He kissed her sweetly on her lips and on her throat, and said, in a deep, husky tone that was almost a whisper, "Good morning, Mrs. Selassie. How are you this morning?"

Cassandra, feeling hung over from the ecstasy and the sheer joy of loving her husband, rolled over in bed to face more completely the object of her pleasure. She stretched lazily and said, "I am very good, Mr. Selassie. And how are you?"

Slowly moving his skilled thumb over her highly sensitive nipple, he said, "I have never been better. Yesterday I married the love of my life. A beautiful woman of African ancestry born in America. She has long, curvy legs leading to the most curvaceous bottom I have ever seen, and even though she is prone to violence and has a wicked tongue when angered, I will love her until the day I die." Cassandra smiled the contented smile of a well-loved woman.

Ras leaned over, kissed her gently and said, "Paris is awaiting us, my sweet. I have an itinerary planned, but remember, it can be changed in the twinkling of an eye. All you need do is say so. We can do all of the touristy things, the Eiffel Tower, Notre Dame, the Louvre"—he stopped, gave her a wicked grin—"or I can make love to you until the sun goes down."

With an equally devilish grin, she eased her flat palm

down the length of his taut, rippled chest as she tortured each of his nipples with her tongue. His wicked grin turned to a hiss as she continued gliding past his muscular thighs. When she wrapped her fingers around him, he released a deep moan that hung in the air as she continued to caress him. When he could no longer resist, he smothered her mouth in an urgent, heated kiss while he entered her swiftly and unceremoniously. She wrapped her long, smooth legs around his strong, powerful back, and he plunged deeper and deeper into her core, and together they traveled to a place of blissful ecstasy.

When they had both given way to the hot tide of sweet abandon, they lay in bed, covered in delicious exhaustion. Cassandra whispered sweetly in Ras' ear, "Now I'm ready to see Paris."

He threw his head back and laughed out loud. When his laughter had ended, he gently rubbed his wife's curvaceous bottom, one that he knew could have been material for many erotic dreams, and said, "You lead. I'll follow."

The two of them left the bed that had been the place for the start of their married life and took a leisurely shower together. They lovingly washed each other, discovering over and over again the pleasures they could elicit with a simple touch. After their leisurely shower, they decided to dress and venture out from the hotel to enjoy lunch in the city. Ras dressed in a gray suit with a pearl gray banded collared shirt and gray leather slip-on shoes. Cassandra wore a chocolate brown pantsuit, brown silk blouse, brown lizard heels and a matching bag. Diamond earrings and a tennis bracelet were the only accessories aside from her wedding ring. Her hair was worn in the crinkled curls that Ras adored. It was a style that was very forgiving of her husband's amorous nature.

Though they could easily have been chauffeured around town, they thought it might be fun to try every mode of transportation whenever the mood hit them. The streets were lined with people of every description. Ras and Cassandra walked, holding hands, down Place Vendôme, a lovely, bustling street filled with upscale shops and restaurants. Ras led her into an intimate little bistro. It was an elegant place designed for lovers. The lighting was diffused, and soft music was piped in through hidden speakers. The majority of the tables only sat two. The tablecloths were sparkling white, and the menu consisted of a small number of gourmet specialty items.

Ras pulled out a chair for Cassandra at one of the more secluded tables. She slid gracefully into the chair and picked up the menu as Ras was seating himself. After he was seated, Ras said to Cassandra, "Our life deserves a celebration. I think I'll order a nice bottle of wine for us."

Still glancing over the menu, Cassandra responded, "That sounds wonderful. I think I'll let you order for me, too. I can't make up my mind. Just surprise me."

Just as she finished her sentence, the waiter approached their table. Once again, Cassandra had the opportunity to listen and watch as her husband of one day ordered for the two of them in flawless French. In addition to the wine, Ras ordered *noisettes d'agneau*, small, tender lamb cutlets sautéed in butter, a mixed leaf salad, and *tarte tatin*, upside-down apple tart, for dessert.

They ate and played games lovers play when eating or talking. They fed each other, they read each other's moves and gestures, and they shared stories about their wedding day. Ras made Cassandra laugh at the antics of Keino, Kamau, Aman and Kaleb, and he made her cry with the touching story of his father. Cassandra shared the words of wisdom she was given at her bridal shower, and she teared up when she talked about the private moment with her father. Ras reminded her that in the not too distant future, they would be the parents **giving** their children loving words to live by as they started new phases of their lives.

They finished their meal and this time Ras called for a chauffeured car and they headed to the area of Paris called the Right Bank. Ras knew that Cassandra would enjoy this adventure because the Right Bank is known for the highest concentration of haute couture houses. He intended to take her to Chanel, Yves St. Laurent, Christian Dior, Pierre Cardin and Versace. If time permitted and her interest held, Armani, Hermès and Shimada could be added to the list.

When they visited the couture houses, Cassandra put on a show for Ras and pretended to be a runway model as Ras sat for his private showings. At each design house, Cassandra selected pieces that she knew would set her husband on fire. Though she enjoyed many of the things that she saw, her interest was more in tantalizing Ras than it was in purchasing outfits to have shipped home. In the end, Ras insisted that he buy two Dior gowns, a Chanel suit and a Versace dress.

They ended the evening with jazz at the Lionel Hampton Jazz Club. The music was alive and satisfying. The two of them listened and enjoyed while sharing their ideas about the evolution of jazz and competing to see who knew the most obscure tunes from obscure jazz musicians. Ras listened with admiration as Cassandra rattled off all of the little-known facts about jazz that her father had taught all of his girls from the time they could talk.

In the days that followed, Ras chartered a yacht, and they had dinner on the Seine by moonlight. They shopped at Cartier and Marché de la Porte de Vanves for gifts for family and special friends. They played tourist and visited many of the places for which Paris is known. They also visited the many places in Paris that are significant for those of African ancestry, such as the theater where Josephine Baker performed, the club where Sidney Bechet played and the church where James Baldwin was memorialized. They ate at Haynes Restaurant—the best soul food in Paris. Their stay in Paris was heady. They lived, they learned and they loved. They could not have been happier. When the time came to return to Addis Ababa, they were ready to get back to creating a family for themselves and for Kebran.

# *Chapter 24*

The Paris morning was gleaming as Ras and Cassandra sat on the plane waiting on the runway, ready to return to Addis Ababa. Ras held his bride's hand and stroked the beautifully cut diamond she wore as a symbol of their marriage. Feeling the warmth of his touch, her gaze, as if on automatic pilot, shifted instantaneously to his eyes, the light brown pools with flecks of gold. Whenever Ras looked at Cassandra, she could always see the last remnants of their previous passionate encounter. The haze of love and lust hung there as he said, "My sweet, I hope this was a trip you will always remember."

Her eyes fluttered, and she leaned her head back as she responded, "Ras, I will remember this trip when we are little old people who can barely move. I'll remember."

"Sweet one, there will never come a time when I am alive that you will not move me."

With a hint of laughter in her voice, Cassandra asked, "Husband of mine, do you always think about sex?"

His full-hearted, warm laughter washed over her as he answered, "Yes, whenever I think of you, passion is not far behind. May it always be that way, my love. You are always to be the object of my desire."

With intelligent eyes clinging to his and a soft smile on

her lips, she said, "Ras Selassie, you have never been more right."

During the remainder of the trip, they napped and enjoyed the light delicacies prepared by the flight attendant and verbally relived their Parisian adventure.

When the plane landed on Ethiopian soil, Ras released an almost inaudible breath, and a look of peace and contentment settled on his extremely handsome face. Cassandra was now familiar with the peaceful countenance Ras donned whenever he was in Ethiopia. It made her smile to herself. She was grateful for any person, place or thing that brought peace to the Ras Selassie she had come to know and to love. He said calmly, "We are home."

"Yes, my love, we are home." She asked, "Should we pick up Kebran first before going to the house? That way we'll all be together now instead of waiting."

Thinking that Cassandra's love and concern for Kebran was one of the many reasons why he loved her, he held her close, kissed the top of her head and, speaking as a loving father and husband, said, "Yes, my darling, we will pick our son up first, and then we will go to our home."

A limousine from RS Development arrived punctually to transport Ras and Cassandra to Ras' parents' home to gather up Kebran Selassie. As the chauffeured limousine rolled comfortably along the highway, Ras and Cassandra Selassie sat in serene silence, lost in their own thoughts, filled with the expectation of seeing their son. In a short while they pulled up in front of the home of Ras' parents. The chauffeur politely let them out of the car.

The front door of the residence was opened by one of the housemen, and they were escorted in to the sitting room where General and Mrs. Selassie were enjoying a quiet time together. The general was sitting with legs crossed, smoking his pipe and reading a daily newspaper. Mrs. Amara Selassie was sitting at her Queen Anne desk, poring over fabric samples, trying to make a selection for reupholstering a chair. Ras and Cassandra walked in holding hands. Ras said, "Well, hello, you two."

Cassandra stood smiling as Tafari Selassie placed his paper and pipe down on a nearby table and Amara Selassie looked up from her samples, put them aside and quickly got up to move in the direction of her son and new daughter-in-law. Both of Ras' parents embraced Cassandra and Ras and told them how happy they were to have them home safely. Amara Selassie looked at her new daughter and asked, "Cassandra, how did you find Paris?"

"It was so beautiful. I hadn't been in a number of years, and Ras made it so special. We had a great time."

"There is no better way to start a marriage than with a wonderful honeymoon. Tafari, do you remember?"

"Yes, my dear, I do remember."

With a glint of humor in his voice, Ras said, "Mother." He paused and then said, "Father, as much as we would like to take this trip with you down memory lane, we came to get Kebran. We need to pack him up and get home to get all of us settled in."

Mrs. Selassie, with artful pleading, said, "Ras, he just went down for a nap after eating. Sweetheart, don't wake him up. He is so peaceful. He has been such a good baby. We have enjoyed him so much. Just let him stay until he finishes his nap, and I promise I will bring him home the moment he wakes up."

Gently touching his mother's arm, Ras answered, "No, Mother, Kebran can finish sleeping at home. We know his grandmother loves him, but his parents do, too. You will have plenty of time with Kebran for the rest of his life. Alert his governess, Mrs. Moi, that we are taking him home."

General Selassie interjected, "Amara, you know Ras is correct. Get the baby ready."

Amara Selassie acquiesced. "I know. Come with me, Cassandra. Let's get your son ready to go home."

The two women walked away as Ras and his father

shared a chuckle at Amara Selassie's expense. The two men, more alike than they knew, walked back into the sitting room and sat, ready to enjoy friendly conversation while waiting for Kebran's essentials to be packed.

On the ride home Cassandra held Kebran in her lap, while Ras held the baby's soft little hand in his large, strong one. They listened carefully while the governess, Mrs. Moi, a petite, middle-aged widow, whose pecan-colored skin almost glowed against a halo of perfectly coifed salt-and-pepper hair, gave them a detailed description of Kebran's activities while they were gone. Ras liked and respected Mrs. Moi. She had been with Kebran since his birth, hired by his biological mother. He respected Mrs. Moi because she was able to combine complete professionalism with an uncanny nurturing ability, which made him trust her implicitly with his son. He also appreciated that she did not allow the loyalty she had felt for Kebran's mother to interfere with her respect and affection for Cassandra.

Kebran slept peacefully through the ride, the conversation, and the hustle and bustle of getting him into the house and settled into his nursery. When they arrived home, Cassandra and Ras were welcomed warmly by the house staff. Dinner had been prepared for them, and though they were not the least bit hungry, after they had settled the baby into his nursery, they were served their meal in their room.

They both got comfortable, Ras in silk emerald green pajama bottoms with an ankle-length robe to match. He left the sash untied, and so it hung open, revealing his taut, sculpted chest. He wore slip-on black leather house slippers. Cassandra lounged in an elegant floor-length red silk gown and robe with matching slip-on barebacks. Their dinner had been placed in heated chafing dishes to be eaten at their convenience. A table had been set in the center of the room, with a sparkling white tablecloth and a single rose as a centerpiece. Cassandra looked at her husband, looked around the room and thought their life together could not possibly get any better than it was.

Ras picked up one of the pieces of china that had been set out for them and slowly and carefully fixed Cassandra a plate of grilled salmon, mixed greens and rice. He smiled that his cook already knew how to prepare one of Cassandra's favorite meals. He placed the plate on the table in front of her and said playfully, bowing at the waist, "Dinner is served, my lady."

Cassandra couldn't help laughing as she said, "Thank you, kind sir."

Ras turned, fixed himself a plate, sat down opposite the woman of his dreams, and asked, "Sweetheart, what does your day look like tomorrow?"

Twirling her fork in her hand, Cassandra said, "Well, I know you are going into the office, and so I can get busy tying up some loose ends. I want to spend some time with Kebran. We need to get into our rhythm. That's going to be the fun part of my day. I need to review the recent design projects that have come through Willows. I'll do a conference call with Angela and a couple of nervous clients." She took a deep breath and said, "And then there's the idea I have in mind for adding pieces of my furniture and pieces we choose together to finish decorating our home so that it feels like our home and not your bachelor hideaway."

Her comment amused Ras. He reacted with a deep, throaty laugh. His laughter always pleased her. His relaxed moods gave her a sense of security. She continued, "There's also the matter of cataloguing wedding gifts and dowry gifts and sending thank-yous. There are so many gifts. I'm going to call in help so that every piece is acknowledged."

"Well, my sweet, I see you will not be bored."

In a tone that was now more serious, Ras said, "I need to ask your help with something that needs to be done soon."

He paused, and Cassandra asked, with a quizzical look on her face, "What is it?"

Ras began slowly. "In the tradition of my people, when children are born, they are christened, blessed in a ceremony in front of friends and family. I don't know if Zala had a christening. I did not ask. It was painful enough when I learned that his existence had been kept from me. It would have hurt even more to discover that he had been blessed without the benefit of his father and his paternal grandparents standing with him." His voice was filled with controlled emotion, as he continued. "Traditionally, he would have been christened forty days after his birth. For girls, the tradition is eighty days after birth. I would like us to plan a christening and a celebration afterward for our friends and family, and we will include Zala's parents and her sister Miriam out of respect. I know I am asking a great deal because of the planning and coordination involved, but we can also count on my parents and Aunt Adina for assistance. This really must be done as soon as possible. Can you help me, sweetheart?"

With a smile that put Ras at ease, Cassandra answered, "Of course, Ras, I will be happy to be a part of something so important to our family. Don't worry. We can do this in two weeks. We do have experience with hosting spectacular events at a moment's notice."

Ras touched Cassandra's hand and said, "Yes, we do. Thank you, my sweet."

The two finished their early dinner and went into the nursery to check on the little boy who had become so very important to each of them. Their love and attachment to him grew daily.

Mrs. Moi had been given the night off, and Ras and Cassandra took over their parenting duties naturally and easily. Ras fixed Kebran's dinner while Cassandra bathed him. After his meal and bath, Kebran and Ras played an energetic game of peekaboo while Cassandra laughed out loud at the hilarious faces Ras made, causing the baby to squeal with giggles. As Ras switched from peekaboo to gently tossing the baby in the air while singing Ethiopian nursery rhymes, Cassandra warned him playfully that Kebran's dinner was going to end up all over his wonderful silk pajamas. He assured her that he knew what he was doing until a soft burp from Kebran showered his father with warm liquid, which ran down his face and chest. Ras couldn't help but laugh, and Cassandra doubled over with laughter, unable to contain herself. She calmed herself, and with laughter still ringing in her voice, she took the baby to wash him up and settle him down, saying to Ras, "One day you will learn that mother knows best."

Still grinning, Ras answered, "I think today is the day."

He went off to shower and change. After he had freshened up, Ras walked back into the nursery to find Cassandra sitting in a rocking chair, holding Kebran close to her breast. Both of them had dozed off and were sleeping peacefully.

Ras walked over and kissed his wife gently, causing her to open her eyes and smile. He lifted Kebran from her arms, took him to his crib, placed him carefully in the soft cocoon, kissed him good night, took Cassandra's hand and led her into their bedroom, where he could express love of another kind.

# Chapter 25

*Addis Ababa*

It was a special day. Cassandra and Ras were hosting the blessing of their first son, Ras Kebran Selassie. He was being officially welcomed into the bosom of the Selassie and Mazrui families. Ras' Uncle Menelik, the Coptic priest who had performed his marriage to Cassandra as well as the marriage of Keino and Amara, this day asked God's blessings upon Ras Kebran and upon his parents and grandparents.

The official ceremony took place in the church in Addis Ababa that Ras' father's family had attended for generations. The church was filled with well-wishers. A cadre of church officials in elaborate, intricately woven, brightly colored robes and ceremonial crowns stood in a semicircular formation around the altar. The sun's rays danced magically off of the stained-glass windows of the church. The glasswork of the windows had been fashioned lovingly by famed Ethiopian artists and artisans. Large panels of glass done in amber, maroon, cherry, powder blue, emerald and hunter green, with black inlays, were embellished with saintly figures, whose faces were sable-

ebony- and raven-colored, superimposed on the multi-colored glass.

Cassandra and Ras stood at the altar. Cassandra held young Ras Kebran as Ras stood with one arm around his wife's waist and the other resting on his son's legs. Ras Kebran had been dressed in a christening robe that was created from the material of the gown his father had worn when he was blessed. Standing with Ras and Cassandra were their respective families: Cassandra's parents, Ana and James Terrell; the godparents Amara and Keino; Adana, Afiya, Kaleb, Kamau, Aman and their wives; Adina and Garsen Mazrui; Amara and Tafari Selassie; Miriam Zenawi; and Mr. and Mrs. Tamrat.

Through the ceremony the little one was uncharacteristically calm and quiet. Perhaps the throng of people that filled the sanctuary had grabbed his attention, or the circle of clerics around the altar. Or perhaps it was the innate understanding of an old soul who had come to earth once again with unfinished business and who understood clearly the importance of the events unfolding. Whatever the reason, his parents, Ras and Cassandra, were grateful for his compliance and stood beaming with pride and thanksgiving.

Though he had not been able to have his son blessed in the customary forty days after his birth, Ras was humbled by the fact that his son was being wrapped in the bosom of a loving family and community. Times like these made him more than proud of his ancestral heritage. He knew he was giving his son the gift of a tradition that would undergird him throughout life's perils and toils, its highs and lows. He looked over at his wife, Cassandra, and silently thanked his God and his ancestors again for placing her in his path. He knew without question that their life together would be blessed, and he looked forward to standing with her on many other occasions, at the christenings of as many children as their willing hearts could hold.

Cassandra looked lovingly at her husband and thought

that the mysterious meeting with the old man in Punta Cana was indeed prophetic. Her marriage had been blessed, and Ras was indeed her true love. The ceremony, in grand Ethiopian tradition, was lengthy. The mass was said with a sense of dignity and regalness that spoke to the magical and majestic lineage from which Ethiopian people had come.

When the last prayer had been prayed and the final song sung and the sacred texts read, the family and guests spilled out of the sanctuary to be escorted to a grand pavilion that had been constructed on the grounds to host the reception given to celebrate the completion of the ceremony. It was an incredibly beautiful scene. The regional flora and fauna were plentiful and riotous with color and fragrance. The canopied top of the pavilion was strung with yards and yards of multicolored pastels of pink, peach, lavender, blue and ivory. Hundreds of people were seated at tables decorated with lavender and pink silk tablecloths, and tapered candles in the same colors stood in silver candelabra. Each table's centerpiece was fragrant gardenias floating in sterling silver bowls. The chairs at each table were pewter-colored ladder backs with ivory-colored upholstered seats. The pavilion was festooned with hundreds of miniature lights and strategically placed chandeliers so that as the evening sun set, the festivities would be illuminated by the romance and beauty of elegant lighting. Traditional Ethiopian foods tantalized the palates of the guests, while Ethiopian songs and dances brought joy to their spirits.

Before sunset Ras Kebran was kissed good night by his parents and taken by his governess to be fed and put quietly to bed after a full day of celebration. His parents, content with themselves and their life together, made the rounds of the tables of their guests, thanking them for coming and listening to person after person wish them well and extend congratulations.

Ibra Diop had flown in for the ceremony, and he and Afiya were enjoying a heated discussion about the politics of the art world. Brad and Veronica had made the trek and had spent several hours taunting each other in a war of wits that for them seemed never to end.

Keino and Amara sat enjoying the entire event, proud that they were chosen to be Kebran's godparents and looking forward to the day when their children would be christened. They knew that the day was coming soon because they had learned earlier in the day that they were expecting a new member of the Mazrui clan. They were both overjoyed at the prospect of enhancing their love for one another with the birth of their child. Keino smiled, remembering the distinct possibility that they might, indeed, be blessed with twins, since his father was a twin. He wondered if Amara remembered. Smiling to himself, he made a mental note to refresh her memory later.

Ana and James Terrell were still basking in the glow of witnessing another daughter find happiness with a well-respected, dutiful man from the continent they had so revered in their home. They each wondered silently as they looked around the room where their other two daughter would find that magical spark that had drawn them together many years before this joyous day.

Amara and Tafari Selassie were grateful beyond words that their family was once again intact and had expanded with the addition of a daughter-in-law and a grandson. General Selassie looked forward to many years of enjoying with his grandson times and activities that he had missed with his son. Judge Garsen and Mrs. Adina Mazrui were always thrilled to be in the presence of friends and family. Today was no different.

Adana Terrell sat with family and friends, enjoying the food, the music and the company, while silently saying to herself that marriage, for all of its benefits, was not for her.

Two weeks after the christening ceremony, on a day glistening with the light and heat of the sun, the ribbon cutting for the community of orphans took place. The meticulously designed living spaces, which Ras had named Anika Village, using Cassandra's middle name, were a tremendous hit. The investors and the development and production teams were proud of the finished product. Cassandra was pleased that her interior designs were going to bring years of comfort and beauty to children who had been robbed of both. Over six hundred youngsters were to be housed, along with their surrogate parents.

Ras was to speak at the ribbon-cutting ceremony, after being introduced by one of the city officials with whom he was sharing the platform. He rose from his chair with a natural calm and commanded the lectern as though it were an extension of his person. He wore an ivory linen suit with a matching banded collared shirt. His shoes were tan Italian leather. Cassandra sat in the front row with Kebran in her lap, admiring her husband. She continued to be amazed at how deeply drawn she was to him. Even as he spoke, every word touched her heart and soothed her soul.

"Ladies and gentlemen, welcome to the beginning of a new life for some very deserving children. Though the ravages of war and lack have taken their toll, today we begin anew. Children whose lives have been shattered can now find restoration. These homes hopefully reflect not only architectural soundness but a peace and harmony within that can bring stillness to jarred emotions. The village has been named, in honor of my wife, Anika Village. She is a woman of immense beauty, talent and courage. The interiors of the homes are her designs, and she has brought to them all that she is."

Cassandra was visibly moved by Ras' words as he continued. "Enjoy today's preview of what will soon become a way of life for many worthy children."

He ended to tremendous applause from family, friends, and the general audience. He left the podium as those assembled began walking toward the area of the new community that was open for tours. He walked toward

Cassandra, who was waiting, holding their son. Misty-eyed, she spoke. "Ras, what you said was so beautiful, and this is such an accomplishment."

"Thank you, my sweet. You know I could not have done it without you." He looked at Kebran, who was staring into his eyes, and said, "I needed you, too, little one."

The baby giggled as if he understood what Ras had said. Ras and Cassandra shook their heads, continually amazed at the precociousness of Ras Kebran Selassie. Ras took his son from Cassandra's arms, and walking side by side, they joined the tour.

There were four different floor plans designed for Anika Village. As they walked through the models, Ras and Cassandra were pleased by the many complimentary remarks being made by visiting dignitaries and private citizens as they strolled through each model. They admired Ras' vision, which had come to life in the form of well-planned living spaces, comfortably and beautifully decorated by Cassandra.

Walking along, with the quiet dignity that was his nature, Ras expressed silent gratitude that he had been able to bring to fruition a community that would be a haven for the children who would need it. As his thought ended, his mother walked up to him and said, "Son, this is a magnificent day for you and for all of the children who will benefit. I am so proud."

Ras answered while stroking Kebran's back. "Thank you, Mother. I can say I am content with the results. This project was filled with many challenges, personally and professionally, but here it is. The vision that kept me awake nights is here in stone and mortar, ready to be inhabited by children who have had little or nothing." He paused and nodded in the affirmative before saying, "Yes, I am pleased."

His mother, with a broad smile of approval, responded, "I also came to get my grandson. I just want to hold him for a little while. Let me take him while you go over and join Cassandra. I see Mrs. Rono has her hemmed up trying to milk trade secrets from her. She came all the way from Nairobi just to be a pest." She laughed and said, "Go rescue your wife."

"Thank you, Mother, for the timely warning." He kissed Kebran on his chubby little cheek and handed him to his grandmother and headed off to give his wife a hand with the formidable Mrs. Rono. He was sure that Cassandra could handle herself, but he knew that Apiyo Rono was a woman who stuck like flypaper and sometimes needed to be snatched off in a way that would test anyone's patience and diplomatic skill. Apiyo Rono had wanted desperately for Keino to marry her daughter Makena. She wanted to be a part of the Mazrui family, and somehow she still held on to that hope, though she knew it was an impossibility. Her family was in disarray. Ali, her devoted eldest son, who had attempted to murder Keino, was serving a prison sentence as a paraplegic. Her husband, under the weight of his wife's greed and his family's folly, had become a depressed recluse, rarely leaving his home. The precious Ms. Makena was still unmarried and continued to be the star in her own special drama.

Ras walked up behind Cassandra, put his arms around her and addressed Mrs. Rono with all of the skill of a trained diplomat.

"Ah, Mrs. Rono, it was good of you to come to add your blessings to this event. Many children will thank you. Now I must deprive you of the company of my lovely wife. Her presence is needed elsewhere." With that statement, he gently turned Cassandra around to walk in the opposite direction of Mrs. Rono, who was left sputtering something that was inaudible to Ras and Cassandra as they retreated.

When they were far enough away, Cassandra whispered, "Thank you, darling. I don't usually need to be rescued, but that is one persistent woman."

Ras answered in a low tenor. "You are welcome, my

sweet. My mother was kind enough to clue me in on your predicament when she came to steal her grandson."

"It would have been OK if she had kept her conversation to design, but she really wanted to talk about Keino and Amara. I tried every way possible to say 'that is none of your business' graciously, but she just kept hammering away. That woman is relentless. Keino is married, and she still can't give it a rest. Sometimes I think that whole family needs to be confined to a mental hospital."

"Believe me, my sweet, you are not the only one who holds that opinion."

Just as they were fleeing from Apiyo Rono, they spotted Keino and Amara walking arm in arm down the pathway, headed in their direction. The four of them waved to one another, and as soon as they were close enough, Ras jokingly said to Keino, "Cousin of mine, I do believe you and your lovely wife are going to have to send engraved announcements to some people to let them know once again that you are married, you plan to stay married and that you will never be available for their daughters."

Amara and Keino looked at one another, baffled. Cassandra laughed softly at her husband's lighthearted joke. A bewildered-looking Keino asked, "Ras, what are you talking about?"

"I am talking about a delusional woman who just finished drilling my wife about you and your wife, because she fantasizes about slipping her daughter in Amara's spot."

More confused than ever, Keino asked again, "What, my cousin, are you talking about?"

Ras, taking pity on Keino and releasing him from his bewildered state, said, "I am talking about Apiyo Rono."

"Apiyo Rono. Is she here?"

"She is here in all of her glory."

Amara, now concerned, asked, "Is this woman stable?"

Ras responded, "Cassandra thinks the whole family belongs in an institution for the mentally impaired. And I must say, she is not alone in her opinion, but I believe the woman is harmless. She may be a pest and a nuisance, but she really is harmless."

Keino agreed. "She really is trying to make the best of her situation. Apiyo Rono is steeped in a tradition that says that through her children, she has failed. She seems to be in her own way trying not to succumb to that idea of herself. She keeps pressing on, no matter what. I think we should feel sorry for her."

Ras quipped, "You feel sorry for her? She raised those spoiled, self-centered, greedy, maniacal children. I didn't."

Keino's response as he laughed was, "My cousin, I am happy to see that you are still the compassionate Ras that we all know and love." Both men burst into laughter. Cassandra and Amara looked at their husbands, smiled at each other and kept walking.

At the end of the opening for Anika Village, Ras and Cassandra opened their home and their gardens for a reception. Ras wanted to thank all of his team members for their hard work beyond the call of duty, friends and family for continued support, and the staff of Tewodros, which was the nonprofit organization responsible for placing the children and their surrogate parents at Anika Village. Tewodros was a fitting name for the organization. Not only was it the name of a past Ethiopian king, but it meant "gift of God." It was an appropriate name for an organization dispensing gifts of homes to needy children.

Looking around, Ras thought once again that Cassandra had outdone herself. She had chosen red as the central color. Urns of red roses stood like guards at doorways in their home, fulfilling their obligations to look beautiful and emit heady fragrances for all who passed their way. The garden had been dressed with elongated banquet tables covered in red silk tablecloths, with gold ladder-back chairs for seating. The table runners were made from a West African Ashanti fabric that was done in tones of red and gold. The place settings were red plates resting on gold chargers. The tables were also adorned with gold candlesticks made in the shape of tree branches, which held pale gold candles. The centerpieces were lush bouquets of red roses and red ribbons.

Extra staff had been hired to make the day run smoothly and to allow all of the guests to feel extremely relaxed and pampered. Ras and Cassandra had earlier taken their son to his nursery and put him down to rest. Cassandra had changed his clothes from dress-up attire to pajamas while Ras talked to him about how much he loved him. They both kissed him and left him to be cared for by his governess while they went to entertain their guests.

The first to arrive were the Mazrui brothers and their wives. As the guests continued arriving, Cassandra, the perfect hostess, greeted them. She was talking to Kamau's wife when she looked up and looked directly into Ras' eyes. She wondered if he would ever stop making her heart leap. With just a look, she was ready to love him beyond reason. He smiled his tilted smile and threw her a kiss. She smiled and turned to finish her conversation. Bradford Donald chose that moment to walk over to his friend and say in pure Bradford Donald style, "Man, save all that Don Juan behavior for the bedroom. We don't need you out here telegraphin' your love thang."

Ras had to laugh out loud. He grabbed Brad, gave him an uncharacteristic hug, released him and said, "Brad, we did it! I need to thank you for being there at the beginning, during those really dark days. Only a friend would have hung with me."

Brad stepped back, tilted his head, squinted his eyes, stroked his chin and then said, "Man, being married has really cooled you out, because I remember when I used to have to battle that evil twin of yours almost on a daily basis. Now I even get a hug and a thank-you. Man, marriage must be some powerful stuff."

Ras answered, "It is not the marriage, it is the woman. Loving her gives me a freedom to be that I have never experienced."

They both smiled contentedly, and then Brad said jokingly, "You know how you used to talk about Keino. Well, I hate to tell you this, man, but you sound just like him."

Brad walked away laughing. Ras looked stunned for a split second and then joined Brad in a gale of laughter. Keino walked up, saying, "Cousin, are you losing your mind? Why are you standing over here laughing"—he gestured around him—"with no one else here laughing?"

"Don't worry, Keino. I'm not losing my mind. As a matter of fact, I am laughing because Brad was just here and he made a joke about you and I laughed."

"A joke about me? What is funny about me? When did I become material for Brad's stand-up comedy routine?"

"Actually, he just said that I am starting to sound like you when I speak of my wife."

"Is that a bad thing?"

Now Keino joined the laughter. The signal to dine was given, and the guests were seated. The menu consisted of something delectable for everyone, East and West African favorites, African American delicacies and European delights. The champagne and *tej* flowed. As guests enjoyed themselves with good food, good music and good conversation, it was evident that the day had been a tremendous success.

When the evening came to a close, Ras and Cassandra sat in the great room of their home with Keino, Amara, Judge Garsen and Mrs. Adina Mazrui, General and Mrs. Selassie, and Drs. Ana and James Terrell. Everyone else had gone. Adana and Afiya had had business that did not allow them to make the trip. James Terrell spoke.

"Son, one more time I must tell you that you have created a legacy here, and we are proud of you."

Ras uttered a heartfelt "Thank you."

Keino added, ""Anika Village is a testament to Ras' big heart. The one that on occasion he tries to hide."

Everyone laughed. When the laughter slowed, Keino took Amara's hand and whispered to her, "Should we tell them now?" She nodded yes. Keino cleared his throat and said, "Amara and I have an announcement to make."

Everyone stopped, and all eyes were riveted on Keino and Amara. There was a hush in the air and a tinge of excited anticipation. With a voice laced with joy and powerful emotion, Keino announced, "Amara and I are going to be parents. We are going to have a baby."

The room went up in joyous elation. The women in the room got up from their chairs and surrounded a misty-eyed Amara, giving her hugs, kisses and congratulations, asking a million questions. Judge Mazrui stated loudly, "Let us know as soon as you find out whether or not it is twins. Someone in this family must follow in my footsteps."

He laughed a hearty laugh, and so did the others in the room, even Amara, because she knew that with Keino she would gladly have quintuplets, so twins would be no problem.

When everyone had said their good-byes and out of town relatives had been safely seen to their cars for their return to the airport, to be shuttled to their various homes by Mazrui planes, Ras closed the door of his home, turned to his wife and said, "Cassandra, my love, you were magnificent tonight. Our home was made beautiful and, most importantly, welcoming, for everyone who entered."

"Thank you, darling. This was your very special day, and I wanted everything to be perfect for you."

"You succeeded, my sweet. It was indeed." Ras kissed his wife gently on the lips and said, "While you are giving your final cleanup orders down here, I think I will go up and say one last good night to Kebran."

"All right, hon, I'll be up soon."

Ras took a last look at his wife as she walked off to the kitchen. He headed quietly up the long staircase to Kebran's suite. He thought of how he had designed his home with a nursery and quarters for an au pair long before he knew of his son's existence. He had hoped for the family he now had.

He opened the door softly and walked with ease over to

the crib in which Kebran slept. His little chest rose and fell softly and peacefully. His breath was barely perceptible. Ras bent his head down closer to the baby's face to feel the wispy puffs of air, which signaled that he was breathing. Ras smiled as Kebran smiled in his sleep. He whispered, "I love you, son," and turned to go. As he turned, he smiled at Cassandra standing there peacefully watching him watch Kebran. She walked into the room, walked over to the crib, kissed her hand, laid it on Kebran's cheek and said, "Good night, sweet one."

Ras took her hand, and they left the baby's bedroom and headed for their own. As they walked through the door, Cassandra had a flash of the first time she had entered Ras' bedroom. It was a magical moment that had been the start of many magical moments.

Ras went into his dressing room to undress and put away his clothes. He came out wearing burgundy silk pajama bottoms without the top. He sat on the bed, legs stretched out in front of him, crossed at the ankles, head propped upon pillows, watching Cassandra as she undressed to get ready for bed. Her dressing room was clearly visible from where he sat. She removed her ivory-colored linen dress and ivory silk slip, hung them on the back of her dressing room door, and walked into the bedroom to retrieve a nightie from the dresser. She was wearing only her ivory-colored lace bra and panties, with bareback ivory mules. She had neglected to remove her shoes. She was talking as she walked. "Isn't it wonderful that Keino and Amara are having a baby?"

She slipped off her shoes. Ras answered, "Yes, I am very happy for them. Now my cousin will be even more of a madman than he is already when it comes to his wife." Ras chuckled softly. "I now know what that feels like."

Cassandra was now standing in front of the mirror in only her bra and panties, with bare, perfectly pedicured feet accentuated by the red toenails, which her husband adored. She was absentmindedly combing through her hair. Ras, with a soft gaze and aching body, eased off the bed and strolled in to the room where Cassandra stood. She saw his reflection in the mirror as he removed the comb gently from her hand, laid it down, wrapped his arms around her and asked, "Are you deliberately making me wait?"

Her breath caught in her throat as he kissed her ear and his thumbs slowly massaged the tops of her breasts, which were spilling over the lacy cups of her bra.

"No, I'm not deliberately making you wait," was her breathy answer. With the hands of a magician, Ras released the deep honey-colored mounds that he craved from their restraints, and with his lips, she was showered with a downpour of fiery sensations.

"Oh, Ras" poured from her mouth repeatedly as her center became liquid fire. Her hands became Ras' undoing as she stroked and caressed every inch of his face and his muscular chest. As he suckled her breasts, her hands moved lower. She pushed down his silken pajamas and moved her hands until they rested at the seat of his manhood. He threw his head back, and as an electricity from the universe sent a current through his body, he held her tightly and nestled his head between her breasts.

With waves of sweet passion throbbing through them both, Ras lifted his wife onto the extended ledge of the vanity and, with gentleness and skill, removed her lace panties. The coolness of the marble counter caressing her bottom was in direct contrast to Ras' heated kisses as he applied them to every inch of her body. Through parted lips, with eyes closed and voice barely above a whisper, Cassandra pleaded, "Ras, love me now."

Ras picked her up, walked her to the bed, and with the agility of a masterful lover, entered her, saying in a voice as smooth as velvet, "As you wish, my love."

The encounter was as passionate as all of their trips to paradise had been. They loved long into the night.

Dear Reader,

I would like to thank those of you who read my debut novel *A Foreign Affair*. Your expressed enjoyment of the characters and of Keino and Amara's romantic journey touched my heart. I hope you find Ras and Cassandra's story equally engaging and satisfying.

I welcome your comments. I can be reached by e-mail at *speakersdream@hotmail.com* or by mail at 484 Lake Park Avenue, Suite 303, Oakland, California 94610.

Peace and Blessings,

Chilufiya Safaa

# Grab These Other
# **Dafina Novels**
(trade paperback editions)

**Every Bitter Thing Sweet**
1-57566-851-3

by Roslyn Carrington
$14.00US/$19.00CAN

**When Twilight Comes**
0-7582-0009-9

by Gwynne Forster
$15.00US/$21.00CAN

**Some Sunday**
0-7582-0003-X

by Margaret Johnson-Hodge
$15.00US/$21.00CAN

**Testimony**
0-7582-0063-3

by Felicia Mason
$15.00US/$21.00CAN

**Forever**
1-57566-759-2

by Timmothy B. McCann
$15.00US/$21.00CAN

**God Don't Like Ugly**
1-57566-607-3

by Mary Monroe
$15.00US/$20.00CAN

**Gonna Lay Down My Burdens**
0-7582-0001-3

by Mary Monroe
$15.00US/$21.00CAN

**The Upper Room**
0-7582-0023-4

by Mary Monroe
$15.00US/$21.00CAN

**Soulmates Dissipate**
0-7582-0006-4

by Mary B. Morrison
$15.00US/$21.00CAN

**Got a Man**
0-7582-0240-7

by Daaimah S. Poole
$15.00US/$21.00CAN

**Casting the First Stone**
1-57566-633-2

by Kimberla Lawson Roby
$14.00US/$18.00CAN

**It's a Thin Line**
1-57566-744-4

by Kimberla Lawson Roby
$15.00US/$21.00CAN

*Available Wherever Books Are Sold!*

Visit our website at www.kensingtonbooks.com

# Grab These Other
# **Dafina Novels**
### (mass market editions)

# Grab These Other
# Thought Provoking Books